A HIGH PRICE

"Say Joe Bob," Smoke said, "before I send you to meet Jesus, tell me how much he paid you."

Dunkirk's forehead wrinkled and he cocked his head to the side. "Huh? What did you say?"

Smoke spread his hands. "I just wanted to know what you thought your life was worth. I know you don't never do nothing without being paid for it, so . . . how much did you get paid to die today?"

"Uh . . . a hundred dollars, in advance, and another five hundred after you're in the ground."

"Want to tell me who it was who bought you so cheap?"

"Naw, let's just get it on."

"Okay, back-shooter. Fill your hand."

Dunkirk grabbed at his pistol and actually had it halfway out of his holster when a piece of molten lead in a .44 caliber slammed into his chest and knocked him off his boots. He lay there in the dirt, eyes blinking, legs quivering, still trying to clear leather.

Smoke walked over and squatted next to him, casting his shadow over the dying man's face to shield it from the sun. "Tell me Joe Bob, did that gunhawk pay you enough for this?"

"Jensen," he croaked, his voice filled with pain.

"Yeah."

"You know he's comin' for you . . ."

"Yeah, Joe Bob, I know." But he was talking to a man staring the long stare into nothing.

BOOK YOUR PLACE ON OUR WEBSITE AND MAKE THE READING CONNECTION!

We've created a customized website just for our very special readers, where you can get the inside scoop on everything that's going on with Zebra, Pinnacle and Kensington books.

When you come online, you'll have the exciting opportunity to:

- View covers of upcoming books

- Read sample chapters

- Learn about our future publishing schedule (listed by publication month *and author*)

- Find out when your favorite authors will be visiting a city near you

- Search for and order backlist books from our online catalog

- Check out author bios and background information

- Send e-mail to your favorite authors

- Meet the Kensington staff online

- Join us in weekly chats with authors, readers and other guests

- Get writing guidelines

- AND MUCH MORE!

**Visit our website at
http://www.kensingtonbooks.com**

VENGEANCE OF THE MOUNTAIN MAN

William W. Johnstone

PINNACLE BOOKS
Kensington Publishing Corp.

http://www.kensingtonbooks.com

PINNACLE BOOKS are published by

Kensington Publishing Corp.
850 Third Avenue
New York, NY 10022

All Kensington Titles, Imprints, and Distributed Lines are available at special quantity discounts for bulk purchases for sales promotions, premiums, fund-raising, and educational or institutional use. Special book excerpts or customized printings can also be created to fit specific needs. For details, write or phone the office of the Kensington special sales manager: Kensington Publishing Corp., 850 Third Avenue, New York, NY 10022, attn: Special Sales Department, Phone: 1-800-221-2647.

Pinnacle and the P logo Reg. U.S. Pat. & TM Off.

First Printing: July 1997
10 9 8 7 6 5 4 3

Printed in the United States of America

Chapter One

Smoke Jensen swung the big double-bladed ax in a high arc, muscles bulging in his arms as the ax split a log neatly in two. The pieces fell onto a pile of wood that reached to Smoke's knees. Shirtless, his skin bronzed by bright sunlight of the High Lonesome, he was sweating freely though the air was cool and dry.

"Smoke, you think you oughta leave the heavy cuttin' to us young'uns?" a boyish voice called from behind him.

He stood up straight, stretching back muscles knotted from the unaccustomed chopping, and looked over his shoulder. Cal and Pearlie were standing next to a buckboard they had been loading with wood.

Smoke shook his head and grinned, thinking of the different ways they had come to work for him. Calvin Woods, going on sixteen years old now, had been just fourteen two years ago when Smoke and Sally had taken him in as a hired hand. It was during the spring branding, and Sally was on her way back from Big Rock to the Sugarloaf. The buckboard was piled high with supplies, because branding hundreds of calves makes for hungry punchers.

As Sally slowed the team to make a bend in the trail, a rail-thin young man stepped from the bushes at the side of the road with a pistol in his hand.

"Hold it right there, Miss."

Applying the brake with her right foot, Sally slipped her hand under a pile of gingham cloth on the seat. She grasped the handle of her short-barrelled Colt .44 and eared back the hammer, letting the sound of the horses hooves and the squealing of the brake pad on the wheel mask the sound. "What can I do for you, young man?" she asked, her voice firm and without fear. She knew she could draw and drill the young highwayman before he could raise his pistol to fire.

"Well, uh, you can throw some of those beans and a cut of that fat-back over here, and maybe a portion of that Arbuckle's coffee, too."

Sally's eyebrows raised. "Don't you want my money?"

The boy frowned and shook his head. "Why, no ma'am. I ain't no thief, I'm just hungry."

"And if I don't give you my food, are you going to shoot me with that big Navy Colt?"

He hesitated a moment, then grinned ruefully. "No ma'am, I guess not." He twirled the pistol around his finger and slipped it into his belt, turned, and began to walk down the road toward Big Rock.

Sally watched the youngster amble off, noting his tattered shirt, dirty pants with holes in the knees and torn pockets, and boots that looked as if they had been salvaged from a garbage dump. "Young man," she called, "come back here, please."

He turned, a smirk on his face, spreading his hands, "Look lady, you don't have to worry. I don't even have any bullets." With a lightning-fast move he drew the gun from his pants, aimed away from Sally, and pulled the trigger. There was a click but no explosion as the hammer fell on an empty cylinder.

Sally smiled. "Oh, I'm not worried." In a movement every bit as fast as his, she whipped her .44 out and fired, clipping a pine cone from a branch, causing it to fall and bounce off his head.

The boy's knees buckled and he ducked, saying, "Jimminy Christmas!"

Mimicking him, Sally twirled her Colt and stuck it in the waistband of her britches. "What's your name, boy?"

The boy blushed and looked down at his feet, "Calvin, ma'am, Calvin Woods."

She leaned forward, elbows on knees, and stared into the boy's eyes. "Calvin, no one has to go hungry in this country— not if they're willing to work."

He looked up at her through narrowed eyes, as if he found life a little different than she described it.

"If you're willing to put in an honest day's work, I'll see that you get an honest day's pay, and all the food you can eat."

Calvin stood a little straighter, shoulders back and head held high. "Ma'am, I've got to be straight with you. I ain't no experienced cowhand. I come from a hard-scrabble farm and we only had us one milk cow and a couple of goats and chickens, and lots of dirt that weren't worth nothing for growin' things. Ma and Pa and me never had nothin', but we never begged and we never stooped to takin' handouts."

Sally thought, *I like this boy. Proud, and not willing to take charity if he can help it.* "Calvin, if you're willing to work, and don't mind getting your hands dirty and your muscles sore, I've got some hands that'll have you punching beeves like you were born to it in no time at all."

A smile lit up his face, making him seem even younger than his years. "Even if I don't have no saddle, nor a horse to put it on?"

She laughed out loud. "Yes. We've got plenty of ponies and saddles." She glanced down at his raggedy boots. "We can probably even round up some boots and spurs that'll fit you."

He walked over and jumped in the back of the buckboard. "Ma'am, I don't know who you are, but you just hired you the hardest workin' hand you've ever seen."

Back at the Sugarloaf, she sent him in to Cookie and told him to eat his fill. When Smoke and the other punchers rode into the cabin yard at the end of the day, she introduced Calvin around. As Cal was shaking hands with the men, Smoke looked over at her and winked. He knew she could never resist a stray dog or cat, and her heart was as large as the Big Lonesome itself.

Smoke walked up to Cal and cleared his throat. "Son, I hear you drew down on my wife."

Cal gulped, "Yessir, Mr. Jensen. I did." He squared his shoulders and looked Smoke in the eye, not flinching though he was obviously frightened of the tall man with the incredibly wide shoulders standing before him.

Smoke smiled and clapped the boy on the back. "Just wanted you to know you stared death in the eye, boy. Not many men are still walking upright who ever pulled a gun on Sally. She's a better shot than any man I've ever seen except me, and sometimes I wonder about me."

The boy laughed with relief as Smoke turned and called out, "Pearlie, get your lazy butt over here."

A tall, lanky cowboy ambled over to Smoke and Cal, munching on a biscuit stuffed with roast beef. His face was lined with wrinkles and tanned a dark brown from hours under the sun, but his eyes were sky-blue and twinkled with good-natured humor.

"Yessir, boss," he mumbled around a mouthful of food.

Smoke put his hand on Pearlie's shoulder. "Cal, this here chow-hound is Pearlie. He eats more'n any two hands, and he's never been known to do a lick of work he could get out of, but he knows beeves and horses as well as any puncher I have. I want you to follow him around and let him teach you what you need to know."

Cal nodded, "Yes sir, Mr. Smoke."

"Now let me see that iron you have in your pants."

Cal pulled out the ancient Navy Colt and handed it to Smoke. When Smoke opened the loading gate, the rusted cylinder fell to the ground, causing Pearlie and Smoke to laugh and Cal's face to flame red. "This is the piece you pulled on Sally?"

The boy nodded, looking at the ground.

Pearlie shook his head. "Cal, you're one lucky pup. Hell, if'n you'd tried to fire that thing, it'd have blown your hand clean off."

Smoke inclined his head toward the bunk house. "Pearlie,

take Cal over to the tack house and get him fixed up with what he needs, including a gun belt and a Colt that won't fall apart the first time he pulls it. You might also help pick him out a shavetail to ride. I'll expect him to start carning his keep tomorrow.''

''Yes sir, Smoke.'' Pearlie put his arm around Cal's shoulders and led him off toward the bunkhouse. ''Now the first thing you gotta learn, Cal, is how to get on Cookie's good side. A puncher rides on his belly, and it 'pears to mc that you need some fattenin' up 'fore you can begin to punch cows.''

Pearlie had come to work for Smoke in as roundabout a way as Cal had. He was hiring his gun out to Tilden Franklin in Fontana when Franklin went crazy and tried to take over Sugarloaf, Smoke and Sally's spread. After Franklin's men raped and killed a young girl in the fracas, Pearlie sided with Smoke and the aging gunfighters he had called in to help put an end to Franklin's reign of terror. *(Trail of the Mountain Man)*

Pearlie, was now honorary foreman of Smoke's ranch.

Smoke stopped with his ax in mid-swing and narrowed his dark eyes at Pearlie, who was grinning from ear to ear. ''Pearlie, I suspect you've been neglecting your teaching chores with young Calvin here,'' he drawled.

Pearlie's grin faded a bit. ''How's that Smoke? The boy can ride like an Injun, herd beeves like he was born to it, and can damn near shoot as good as me.''

Smoke used a beefy forearm to sleeve sweat off his forehead. ''Well, 'pears the boy's a mite short on respect for his elders.'' Dropping the ax and moving almost faster than the eye could follow, Smoke took two steps and grabbed Cal by the pants, lifting him and throwing him over his shoulder like a sack of potatoes.

As Cal kicked and fought, and Pearlie laughed, Smoke loped down the side of the hill toward a mountain stream twisting through the valley. Since it was the second week in September, and snow was already falling on mountain peaks surrounding Sugarloaf, the water was only a few degrees above freezing.

When he stood on the creek bank, Smoke took a deep breath through his nose. "Whew, this boy is ripe, Pearlie. How long since he's had a bath?"

"No-o-o-o," wailed Cal, kicking all the more to get free. "I'm sorry, Smoke. I's jest teasing 'bout you bein' old and all."

"Why Smoke," laughed Pearlie, "I'm almost sure it hadn't been hardly two weeks since Cal bathed last. He's not due for at least another week."

"Wrong," snorted Smoke. He bent over quickly, straightened and flipped Cal ass-over-heels into the frigid water. As Cal came up gulping and yelling and flapping his arms, Smoke said, "Preacher always said a man shouldn't bathe more'n twice a year, otherwise he'd get sick and die." Smoke put his hands on his hips and smiled at the dripping boy as he scrambled out of the stream, shivering and shaking. "Course, that only applies to mountain men, not whelps like Cal here." He cocked his head at Pearlie and pointed a finger at Cal. "In the future, I expect him to have a bath at least every week."

Pearlie looked aghast. "Even in the winter?"

"Especially in the winter. Maybe it'll teach him to respect his elders. Right Cal?"

"Ye-ye-ye-yes sir!" Cal answered through chattering teeth.

Smoke ambled back uphill where he picked up his shirt and slipped it on. "Now, this old man is tired from all this hard work, so I'm gonna take me a little nap under that pine tree over yonder while you young bucks cut up the rest of those logs." He looked at storm clouds hanging like dark cotton over the mountain peaks around them. "It's gonna be an early winter, and that means we're gonna need lots of wood."

He handed the ax to Cal. "Here, young un'. Maybe chopping those logs'll warm you up a bit." He winked at Pearlie as he walked over to where his horse was ground-hitched. He dipped into his saddlebags and withdrew a handful of donuts, or bearsign as mountain men called them, and chewed as he lay back against the tree. "If you hurry, maybe there'll be a few of these bearsign left when you get done." He took a huge mouthful and mumbled loud enough for the two men to hear, "and, then again, maybe there won't be none left afterall."

Pearlie looked at Cal. "Come on boy, I've been waiting all mornin' for a taste of Sally's bearsign. Start swingin' that ax like you mean it."

The sound of a gunshot brought Smoke instantly awake and alert. Years in the mountains with the first mountain man, Preacher, had taught Smoke many things. Two of the most important were how to sleep with one ear open, and never to be without one of his big Colt .44's nearby. The gun was in his hand with the hammer drawn back before echoes from the shot had died.

"Sh-h-h Horse," he whispered, not wanting the big Appaloosa to nicker and give away his position. He buckled his gun belt on, holstered his .44, and slipped a sawed-off ten gauge American Arms shotgun out of his saddle scabbard. Glancing at the sun, he figured he had been asleep about two hours. Cal and Pearlie were nowhere in sight.

Raising his nose, Smoke sniffed the breeze. The faint smell of gunpowder came from upwind. He turned and began to trot through the dense undergrowth of the mountain woods, making not a sound.

Smoke peered around a pine tree and saw Cal bending over Pearlie, trying to staunch the blood running down his left arm. Four men on horseback were arrayed in front of them, one still holding a smoking pistol in his right hand. "Okay, now I'm not gonna ask you boys again. Where is Smoke Jensen's spread? We know it's up in these hills somewheres."

Cal looked up, and if looks could kill, the men would have been blown out of their saddles. "You didn't have to shoot him. We're not even armed."

"You going to talk, boy? Or do you want the same as your friend there?" The man pointed the gun at Cal, scowling in anger.

Cal squared his shoulders and faced the man full on, fists

balled at his sides. "Get off that horse, mister, and I'll show you who's a boy!"

The man's scowl turned to a grin. His lips pulled back from crooked teeth as he cocked the hammer on his weapon. "Say good-bye, banty rooster."

Smoke stepped into the clearing and fired one barrel of the shotgun, blowing the man's hand and forearm off up to his elbow, to the accompaniment of a deafening roar.

The men's horses reared and shied as the big gun boomed, while the riders clawed at their guns. Smoke flipped Cal one of his Colts with his left hand as he drew the other with his right.

Cal cocked, aimed, and fired the .44 almost simultaneously with Smoke. Smoke's bullet hit one rider in the middle of his chest, blowing a fist-sized hole clear through to his back. Cal's shot took the top of another man's head off down to the ears. The remaining gunman dropped his weapon and held his hands high, sweating and cursing as his horse whirled and stomped and crow-hopped in fear.

Smoke nodded at Cal, indicating he should keep the man covered, then he walked over to Pearlie. He bent down and examined the wound, which had stopped bleeding. "You okay, cowboy?"

Pearlie smiled a lopsided grin. "Yeah, boss. No problem." He reached in his back pocket and pulled out a plug of Bull Durham, biting off a large chunk. "I'll just wet me some of this here tabaccy and stuff it in the hole. That'll take care of it until I can get Doc Spalding to look at it."

Smoke nodded. He remembered Preacher had used tobacco in one form or another to treat almost all of the many injuries he endured living in the mountains. And Preacher had to be in his eighties, if he was still alive, that is.

With Pearlie's wound seen to, Smoke turned his attention to the man Cal held at bay. He walked over to stand before him. "Get off that horse, scum."

The man dismounted, casting an eye toward his friend writhing on the ground trying to stop the bleeding from his stump.

"Ain't ya gonna hep Larry? He's might near bled to death over there."

Smoke walked over to the moaning man, stood over him, and casually spat in his face as he took his last breath and died, open eyes staring at eternity. With eyes that had turned ice-gray, Smoke turned to look at the only one of the men still alive. "What's your name, skunk-breath."

"George. George Hampton."

"Who are you, and what're you doin' here looking for me?"

"Why, uh, we was lookin' fer Smoke Jensen."

Smoke sighed, shaking his head. "I *am* Smoke Jensen, you fool. Now you found me, what do you want?"

Hampton's eyes shifted rapidly back and forth from Cal to Smoke. "You can't hardly be Smoke Jensen. You're too danged young. Jensen's been out here in the mountains killing people for nigh on ten, fifteen years."

"I started young." He drew his .44 and eared the hammer back, the sear notches making a loud click. "And I'm not used to asking questions more than once."

Hampton held up his hands. "Uh, look Mr. Jensen, it was all Larry's idea. He said some gunhawk gave him two hundred dollars to come up here and kill you." He started speaking faster at the look on Smoke's face. "He said he'd share it with we'uns if we'd back his play."

Smoke raised his pistol. "What was this gunhawk's name?"

Hampton shook his head. "I don't know. Larry never told us."

Smoke looked at Hampton over the sights of his .44. "You sold your life cheap, mister."

Cal cried out, "Smoke! No!"

Smoke lowered his gun, sighing. "Cal's right. I've gone this long without ever killing an unarmed man. No need to change now, even though you sorely need it." He stopped talking, a funny expression on his face. He sniffed a couple of times, then looked at Hampton through narrowed eyes. "That smell coming from you, mister?"

Hampton's face flared red and he looked down. "Uh, yessir.

My bowels kinda let loose when you cocked that big pistol of yours.''

Pearlie let out a guffaw. "Hell, Smoke. You don't want to kill this 'un. Let him go and if he's any kind of man he'll die of shame 'fore the day's over.''

Smoke holstered his gun and turned to walk away. Cal nodded at Hampton. "Drop your gun belt and rifle and get out of here while the gettin's good.''

As Hampton stepped in his saddle and took off looking for a hole, Pearlie called out, "And you can tell your kids you once looked over the barrel of a gun at Smoke Jensen and lived to tell about it. Damn few men can say that!''

Smoke flipped open the loading gate of his .44 and began to punch out his empties as he spoke to Pearlie. "I'll bet you think that little scratch on your arm is going to keep you from loading up all this wood Cal cut, don't you?''

Pearlie looked back through wide eyes, then grabbed his arm and moaned, loud and long.

Smoke continued reloading his gun without looking at Pearlie. "Course, if you're hurtin' that bad, I don't guess you'd want any of those bearsign I've got left.''

The moaning stopped and Pearlie jumped to his feet and started back toward Smoke's horse. "I'll just go and get some java started while you and Cal finish loading up. I'll wait for you at camp.''

"Leave a few for me, you polecat!" Cal yelled to the rapidly disappearing man.

Chapter Two

On their way back to his cabin, with Cal driving the buckboard and Pearlie in the back cussing every rock and bump in the trail, Smoke reflected on how many men he had carried home with enemies' lead in them. Quite a few, he thought. Horse, Smoke's Palouse, had been sired by old Seven, a gift to Smoke from the Nez Perce who started the breed. He knew the way home without prompting, leaving Smoke to his thoughts about his early days in the mountains.

Young Kirby Jensen had come to the mountains with his father while barely in his teens. The pair teamed up with a mountain man, who some call the first mountain man, named Preacher. For some reason, unknown even to Preacher, the loner took to the boy and began to teach him the ways of the mountains: how to live when others would die, how to be a man of your word, and how to fear no other living creature. On the first day they met, Preacher gave the boy a name that would become legend in the West over the years, Smoke.

Preacher was with Smoke when he killed his first man during an Indian attack, and he took the boy in when his dying father left him in Preacher's care. *(The Last Mountain Man)*

While still a teenager, Smoke left Preacher's tutelage and

set out on his own to marry and raise a family in the wilderness he learned to call home. Marauders raped and killed his wife and baby son while Smoke was away. He tracked them down and killed them to a man, then he rode into an Idaho town owned by the men who had sent the killers and wiped it and those that lived there off the face of the earth. *(Return of the Mountain Man)*

Smoke had been married to Sally, a former school teacher, for years and was happier than he thought any man had a right to be. Their ranch in the valley called Sugarloaf was just beginning to become famous as a source of fine-bred Palouse horses and beef that grew fat and juicy on the sweet grass of mountain meadows.

As Horse neared the cabin, he nickered, glad to be home. Sally came running out of the door, an anxious expression on her face at the sight of Pearlie lying in the wagon, a blood-soaked bandage around his left arm.

Her face softened as she reached into the wagon and brushed the bearsign crumbs off his face. "Well, I can see your wound hasn't hurt your appetite any. Are you okay, Pearlie?"

"Yes, ma'am. It's just a scratch. I'll be back at work in no time."

Smoke swung his leg over the saddlehorn and slid to the ground, giving Sally a hug that lifted her off her feet. "Pearlie's lucky, Sally. That bushwhacker was using one of those new .44/.40 pistols, otherwise that slug would've taken his arm off clean."

Cal looked up, eyebrows raised. "What's a .44/.40, Smoke?"

"It's a .40 caliber barrel and works on a .44 caliber frame. Gives less of a kick and is more accurate for amateurs, but has lots less stopping power." He nodded his head toward the valley where the other hands were with the beeves. "Cal, would you ride down to the herd and send one of the boys to Big Rock to see if Doc Spalding can come up here and take a look at Pearlie's arm?"

Before Cal could answer, Pearlie said, "Oh boss, you don't have to do that. I'll heal just fine without any old doctor messing with it."

Cal chuckled. "He's just afraid the doc'll give him some stitches, Smoke. I'll get someone to go fetch him right now."

Sally put her hand on Pearlie's shoulder. "It'll heal a lot faster if Doctor Spalding closes the wound."

Pearlie shook his head. "Well, I'm not in any real hurry, Miss Sally, and I'm not real partial to needles."

"Well," she said with a wink at her husband, "I've got some fresh hot apple pie cooling in the kitchen. If you're not in too much pain, perhaps you can have a piece while we're waiting for the doctor to get here."

"Yes ma'am, I mean, no ma'am . . . oh, you know what I mean."

As tough as mountain folks needed to be to survive, Sally thought, the men were like little kids when it came to sweets from the oven. Miners and farmers had been known to endure a day's ride for bearsign, and pies cooling on the window sill would make cowboys forget their branding and spur their mounts home.

That night, after Doc Spalding had tended to Pearlie's arm and been treated to Sally's home cooking and an after dinner whiskey and cigar for his trouble, Smoke and Sally strolled through the moonlight, arm in arm.

"Smoke, who do you think that man meant when he said a gunhawk had paid them to kill you?"

He shrugged. "I don't know. I've been in this country for a lot of years and made a lot of enemies." He looked out over their valley, shimmering in the moonlight, and sighed. "It could be any one of a dozen or more, I suppose."

Sally took his face in her hands and pulled it close for a gentle kiss. "You ride with your guns loose, Smoke Jensen. Sugarloaf wouldn't be the same without you."

He grinned. "You mean you'd miss me?"

She took him by the sleeve and pulled him toward their cabin. "Follow me and I'll show you."

The next morning, over scrambled eggs, bacon, and coffee, Smoke told Sally he was going in to Big Rock to discuss the disposition of the bushwhackers' bodies with Sheriff Monte Carson.

She arched her eyebrows. "You mean you left those men lying on the ground up in the north woods?"

He blew on his coffee, then sipped cautiously. "Yep."

"Smoke, those men deserve a Christian burial."

"Well Sally, they weren't acting like Christians when they came up on our mountain to kill me."

"But—"

He placed his hand over hers on the table. "But nothing, dear. I know you're a forgiving lady, one not taken with revenge and such, but in this country, a man deserves only what he can carve out of the mountain, nothing else. Those men up there made the decision to ride the owlhoot trail, to live or die by their guns. Well, they died. That's the long and the short of it. I don't owe those men nothing but what I gave them, an ounce of lead in a .44 caliber."

Smoke knew Sally was no fool. She realized when Smoke put his foot down it was time to keep her opinions to herself. In the way of women since time immemorial, she would bide her time, come at him from a different direction, and, more often than not, get her way in the end without him even realizing it. Such was marriage, even in the High Lonesome and even among the singular breed called the mountain men.

As he sauntered outside and climbed on Horse, she handed him a package of jerked beef, biscuits, and a couple of apples. He laughed, "You never forget my trail food, do you?"

She smiled, a mischievous smile. "Got to keep your strength up." She walked up to his horse and put her hand on Smoke's thigh. "I don't want you too tired when you get home. There's lots of work to be done around the cabin."

He laughed out loud, making her blush a fiery red. "I was about to say I'd stay the night in Big Rock, but now I think I'll come home if I have to ride the entire way after dark."

He whirled the big Palouse around and took off down the trail toward town, waving his hat at Sally as he rounded the curve in the road.

Chapter Three

Smoke was halfway to Big Rock when Horse began to act up. First the horse snorted, pricked his ears, and looked back toward Smoke with eyes wide. Smoke had been lost in thought about who might be gunning for him, letting Horse find his own way to town. He came fully awake and alert when the animal began to nicker softly.

Leaning forward in the saddle, he patted Horse's neck and whispered, "Thanks, old friend. I hear you." Mountain-bred ponies were better than guard dogs when it came to sensing danger. Smoke shook his head, thinking Preacher would be disgusted with him. If there was one thing the old mountain man stressed, it was the mountains were a dangerous world, not to be taken lightly. Riding around with your head in the clouds, especially when you knew someone was trying to nail your hide to the wall, was downright stupid, if not suicidal.

Smoke slipped the hammer thongs from his Colts, then put his hand on the butt of the Henry rifle in the scabbard next to his saddle and shook it a little to make sure it was loose and ready to be pulled.

He tugged gently on the reins to slow Horse from a trot to

a walk and settled back in the saddle, hands hanging next to his pistols.

Even with his precautions, he was surprised when a man jumped out of the brush into the middle of the trail in front of him. It was George Hampton, and he was pointing a Colt Navy pistol at Smoke.

"Get down off that horse, you bastard."

Smoke spread his hands wide and swung his leg over the cantle and dropped, cat-like, to the ground. "Hampton, I thought you'd be halfway home by now."

"I ain't gonna go home 'til I've put a bullet between the eyes of the famous Smoke Jensen."

Smoke glanced at the revolver Hampton was holding, smiled, and shook his head. "Hampton, I really don't want to kill you. Why don't you just put that gun down and head on home?" He spread his hands wider, stepping closer to him. "And just where is your home anyway? You never got around to telling me yesterday."

Hampton licked his lips, the gun trembling a little in his hand. "Just keep your distance, Jensen. I'll admit I ain't no expert with this six-gun like you are, but I can't hardly miss at this distance."

Smoke kept his hands in front of him. "Okay, okay, don't get nervous. I'll stay back, but it seems to me a man oughtta know just why he's bein' killed."

Hampton nodded. "Well, you're right. I can see the justice in that, 'cept I don't rightly know. Larry, the man you kilt yesterday, he made me and the other boys the offer down on the Rio Bravo in Texas. Seems that gunhawk met him in a saloon in Laredo and told him he wanted you dead in the worst way . . . somethin' about how you had humiliated him awhile back and he wanted you in the ground because of it."

Smoke's eyes narrowed and turned slate gray. "So you and the other boys decided to pick up some easy money on the owlhoot trail, huh?"

Sweat was beading on Hampton's forehead in spite of the cool mountain air. "Naw, it wasn't like that. We're just cowboys, not gunslicks. There's an outbreak of Mexican fever in the cattle down Texas way and there ain't much work for wranglers, leastways not unless you're hooked up with one of the big spreads.'' He shook his head, gun barrel dropping a little. ''Hell, it was this or learn to eat dirt.''

Smoke relaxed, his muscles loosening. ''I'll tell you what, Hampton. There's always work for an honest cowboy in the high country. If you're willing to give an honest day's labor, you'll get an honest day's pay.''

The pistol came back up and Hampton scowled. ''You're just sayin' that cause I got the drop on you.''

Smoke smiled, then quick as a rattlesnake's strike, reached out and grabbed Hampton's gun while drawing his own Colt .44 and sticking the barrel under Hampton's nose. ''No George, you're wrong. You never had the drop on me.'' He nodded at Hampton's pistol. ''That there is a Colt Navy model, a single action revolver. You have to cock the hammer 'fore it'll shoot, and I can draw and fire twice before you can cock that pistol.''

Hampton's shoulders slumped and he let go of his gun and raised his hands. ''Okay Jensen, it's your play.''

Smoke holstered his Colt and handed the other one back to Hampton. ''I told you George, you got two choices. You can get on that pony there and head on back to Texas, or I can give you a note and send you up to one of the spreads hereabouts and you can start working and feeling like a man again. It's all up to you.''

Hampton looked down at his worn and shabby boots and britches, then back to Smoke. ''That's no choice, Mr. Jensen. You give me that note and I promise I'll not make you sorry you trusted me.''

Smoke walked to Horse and took a scrap of paper and pencil stub out of his saddlebags. After a moment, he handed the paper to Hampton. ''Take this note to the next place you see up to the north of mine. It belongs to the North's. They can always use an extra hand, and Johnny pays fair wages.''

Hampton held out his hand. ''I don't know how to thank you, Mr. Jensen, but . . . thanks.''

Smoke grinned, knowing Hampton was a friend for life. In the rough-hewn country of the West, favors, or slights, were not soon forgotten. Help a man who's down on his luck, and he's honor-bound to repay you, even at the cost of his life, if it comes to that.

Smoke rode into Big Rock, Colorado, the town he had helped build, and began to relax again. If there was any place he felt safe, other than the Sugarloaf, it was here. Though it was growing faster than he liked, Smoke knew just about everyone in town and counted all of them as friends. In spite of his reputation as one of the most feared shootists in the country, the citizens of Big Rock knew Smoke personally for what he was, a good neighbor who would never let a friend down and a man any would be proud to ride the river with.

As Smoke nodded to the men and tipped his hat to the ladies he passed, he saw Sheriff Monte Carson in front of the jail. He was sitting in a chair tilted back on its hind legs with his back against the wall and his hat down over his face, snoring loudly.

Smoke smiled at the sight of the sheriff sleeping peacefully. He and Monte Carson had become very good friends over the past few years. Carson had once been a well-known gunfighter, though he had never rode the owlhoot trail.

A local rancher with plans to take over the county had hired Carson to be the sheriff of Fontana, a town just down the road from Smoke's Sugarloaf spread. Carson went along with the man's plans for a while, 'til he couldn't stomach the rapings and killings any longer. He put his foot down and let it be known that Fontana was going to be run in a law-abiding manner from then on.

The rancher, Tilden Franklin, sent a bunch of riders in to teach the upstart sheriff a lesson. The men killed Carson's two deputies and seriously wounded him, taking over the town. In retaliation, Smoke founded the town of Big Rock, and he and his band of aging gunfighters cleaned house in Fontana.

When the fracas was over, Smoke offered the job of sheriff of Big Rock to Monte Carson. He married a grass-widow and settled into the job like he was born to it. Neither Smoke nor the citizens of Big Rock ever had cause to regret his taking the job.

Being careful not to make a sound, Smoke eased down off Horse and took one of the apples Sally had given him from his saddlebag. He walked over to stand in front of Carson and pitched the apple into his lap.

Carson snorted, flipped his chair forward, and drew his pistol with his right hand while pushing his hat back with his left, all in one quick movement.

As his pistol cleared leather, Smoke reached out and grabbed the barrel in his left hand, saying, "Hold on there, Hoss."

A sheepish Monte Carson grinned. "Oh, it's you, Smoke."

Smoke released the weapon and hooked another chair over with the toe of his boot. He straddled the chair backward, leaning his arms on the back of the chair and his chin on his arms. "Pretty fast draw for an old fart like you, Monte. Been practicing?"

"An old fart, am I?" Carson glared at Smoke through narrowed eyes. "Best I remember, I'm only a couple of years older than you, and you're—"

"Too old to remember all my birthdays, that's for sure." Smoke interrupted. "Matter of fact, I'm old enough to remember when a fella used to be offered some coffee or a drink when he came to visit the big city, but I guess times have changed."

Carson shook his head. "Smoke Jensen acting like company, now that's a laugh. The coffee pot's in the same place it's always been, and this here jail ain't no restaurant and this here sheriff ain't no waiter. You want some, you're welcome to it."

With that statement, Carson leaned his chair back and pulled his hat down over his eyes.

Smoke laughed and got up to pour himself a cup of coffee. As he was pouring the evil-looking brew, he heard Carson say, "And pour me a cup while you're at it. These legs are so old I don't know if they'll carry me in there to get my own."

Smoke carried both cups out on the boardwalk and handed one to Carson. "Monte, I know cowboys like their coffee strong and all, but," he looked down at the liquid in his cup that had the color and consistency of axle grease in winter, "don't you think this bellywash is just a touch past due for thinning?"

Carson smiled as he blew on the coffee to cool it and drank a mouthful. He smacked his lips and said, "Ahhh. That's good. It's like an old trail cook once told me. The secret to makin' good coffee is that it don't take near as much water as you think it do."

Laughing, Smoke set his cup down and pulled his tobacco pouch out. As was the Western way, he offered it first to Carson, who declined and began to fix his pipe. Smoke sprinkled tobacco on the paper, tamped both ends with his fingers, and rolled the cigarette into a tube. As he licked the paper, he glanced up at Carson. "Heard anything interesting lately, Monte?"

They had been friends long enough for Carson to catch the change in Smoke's tone and he looked up from his pipe with raised eyebrows. "No, why? Something going on I ought to know about?"

Smoke scratched a match into flame with his thumbnail, lit his cigarette, and handed the match to Carson. "Well, something strange happened the other day up on the Sugarloaf. Four men came gunning for me and shot up Pearlie a little bit."

Carson narrowed his eyes. "Oh? Well, men gunning for Smoke Jensen, now there's a novel thought. Did you bother to bury 'em or do I have to send someone from town to go and cart the carcasses back down here to boot hill?"

Smoke shook his head, "Now there's no need to be sarcastic, Monte. These men were different from the usual type that are just after making a name for themselves. Cal and I let the hammer down on three of them, but I let one of the men live. He said a gunhawk down Texas way, on the Rio Grande, hired them to kill me to pay me back for something I did to him awhile back."

"Oh, well then. That narrows the field of men who want to kill you down from a thousand to maybe only a hundred or so."

"Yeah, those were my thoughts, too." Smoke flipped his butt out into the dusty street and drank the last of his coffee.

"Well, guess I'll amble on over to the saloon and see if there's been any newcomers to town that might have heard something."

Carson looked up from under his hat-brim. "You want some company?"

Smoke put on an innocent expression. "Naw, you know me. I'm a peaceable rancher, not looking for any trouble, just going to have a sociable drink at the neighborhood dog hole."

"Yeah, and I'm my aunt Bertha. Smoke, you know if things get out of hand, you've always got help right here." He patted his pistol. "I may be old and half civilized, but I haven't forgotten how to use this pea-shooter if the need ever arises."

Smoke put his hand on Carson's shoulder. "Thanks Monte, but you know out here a man saddles his own horse and kills his own snakes."

Just then a small boy of about seven years old ran up to Smoke and Carson. "Sheriff Carson, there's a feller down at the saloon who's plumb alkalied. He's dressed up like a sore toe and tellin' everyone he's gonna kill Smoke Jensen."

"Oh shit. Thanks, Jerome. You run along home now and get off the street, and get your friends off the street, too." He turned to Smoke. "I don't guess you'd ride on out of town and let me handle this, would you?"

Smoke gave a smile that didn't go to his eyes. "Monte, that sounds like one of those snakes we were just talking about."

Carson drew his pistol and opened the loading gate to check his loads. "Well, if you've only got five beans in the wheel, you'd better load up six and six; no telling if he's got friends to back his play or if he's alone."

Smoke loaded his Colt, spun the cylinder for luck, then holstered the big gun. "You got my back, Monte?"

Carson grinned like a schoolboy about to bust some noses out in the yard. "Don't I always?"

They walked down the center of the street, women-folk and children scattering at the serious expressions on their faces and at their purposeful strides. In the mysterious way of Western towns, faster than any telegraph, word spread that there was going to be trouble, meaning gunplay, and that Smoke Jensen was involved. The streets and boardwalks emptied, and the townspeople gathered behind windows and doors to watch some other poor fool try his hand against Smoke Jensen.

Smoke pushed through the batwings of the saloon and immediately stepped to the side, giving his eyes a moment to adjust to the dusky light of the place. Through the cigar smoke and beer smell, he could see a young tough leaning on the bar, waving his hands in drunken hyperbole, talking loud and being whiskey-brave.

"Yeah, tha's right. I'm gonna kill me a Smoke Jensen, tha's for sure. Soon's that yellow sonofabuck gits here, he's a dead man."

Smoke took in the stranger's garb with a glance. Shiny black leather vest over a boiled-white shirt, string tie, and a double-rig holster of fancy tooled leather with rawhide strings hanging from the belt. Two brand-new Colt Peacemaker .45's were in the holsters, conspicuous notches cut in both handles so new that fresh wood showed at the bottom of the cuts.

Smoke and Carson looked at each other and laughed. Smoke whispered, "He's so booze-blind he couldn't hit the ground with his hat in three tries."

Carson grinned and sat down at a table while Smoke walked to the bar and stood next to the man doing all the talking. When the man looked up at him, Smoke grinned a huge grin and said, "Hi there, Pilgrim. Can I buy you a drink?"

The man swayed as if he might fall, before nodding and saying, "Sure, then someday you kin tell your kids you bought a drink for the man that kilt Smoke Jensen."

Smoke's eyes opened wide and he let his mouth drop open. "You mean you're going to go up against the famous shootist Smoke Jensen?"

"Yep. Gonna kill him, too."

"Well let me shake your hand, pardner." After they shook hands, Smoke opened his shirt and showed the man an old bulletwound scar. "See this here scar? That's where Smoke Jensen shot me through the arm."

The man narrowed his eyes. "You mean you faced Jensen in a gunfight and he didn't kill ya?"

Smoke shook his head. "Wasn't no need. Hell, I didn't even clear leather 'fore he shot me and my partner both."

"Ya mean there was two of you and he got you both?"

"Yep. The bastard gut-shot my partner and winged me without even breaking a sweat. Left us both on the trail to die. Took my partner three days to die, and he died hard, let me tell you."

The man leaned his head back and tried to focus on Smoke. "You a gunfighter?"

"Naw, I'm just a rancher and cowhand. I'm much too slow on the draw to be a gunfighter. Hell, half the men in town can outdraw me. Here, I'll show you." Smoke stepped away from the man and in the blink of an eye his Colt was drawn, cocked, and pointing at the man's face. "See, I couldn't touch Smoke Jensen. The only reason we tried was his back was turned and we thought we had the drop on him."

Frowning, the man asked, "You mean his back was to you and he still beat you to the draw?"

"Sure." Smoke leaned close to the man and whispered, "Jensen said he heard our guns leaving our holsters and knew he had to draw."

"Jesus!" the man whispered back. "That's mighty fast."

"Yeah, my partner and I thought so, too. But I've been practicing since then. I think maybe I can surprise him if I use my left hand." No sooner had Smoke finished his sentence than his lefthand gun appeared in the man's face, the draw so quick it was just a blur. "Course," Smoke continued as he holstered his pistol, "since you're obviously a gunman, you're probably not too impressed with my draw."

Smoke put an anxious expression on his face. "Say, do you think maybe you could show me how fast a real gunslinger is? Maybe even give me some pointers?"

Sweat beaded the man's forehead and he turned back to his whiskey, drinking it down in one quick draught. "No, I think you'd better leave gunfighting to us experts." He pulled his hat down and threw two bits on the bar. "Well, it don't look like Smoke Jensen is gonna come to town today, so I guess I'll just mosey on down the road a ways."

Smoke put a hand on the man's shoulder. "Hey, I could get one of the guys here in town to ride out to his ranch and bring him in, if you want."

"No, no, not today. I think I'll just let him live another day and come back some other time." With that, the sweating man bolted from the saloon to the raucous laughter of the other patrons, got on his horse, and got out of town in a hurry.

Carson walked to the bar and clapped Smoke on the back. "Smoke, it's a shame old Erastus Beadle wasn't here to see that show you put on. He'd have you in one of his dime novels going up against Deadwood Dick, sure as shootin'."

Smoke grinned. "Yeah, and maybe I'd win the fair hand of Hurricane Nell, if'n she didn't shoot me first."

From a dark corner of the saloon came the sound of someone clapping their hands very slowly, then a gravelly voice growled, "Yeah, that was some show, Jensen. You sure impressed that tinhorn. Too bad he didn't have the sand to go against you anyway, since I think you're all blow and no do."

Smoke looked at Carson and sighed, before turning and facing the man in the corner. He narrowed his eyes as he recognized Joe Bob Dunkirk, a man who had made his name in the Lincoln County wars a few years back. He hired his gun to the highest bidder and wasn't above back-shooting to earn his money.

"Well, Monte, look who's here. Old Joe Bob himself." Smoke took a sip of his whiskey with his left hand, unhooking the hammer-thong of his Colt with the right. "Guess I'm lucky you were sitting there next to the door or I'd probably have been back-shot, like the others he's killed."

Dunkirk jumped to his feet, knocking his chair over and pointing his finger at Smoke. "Shut up, you bastard! I don't need to back-shoot you, I can kill you face to face."

Smoke smiled a slow, contemptuous smile. "That's not the way I hear it, Joe Bob. I hear unless a man's blind in one eye and can't see out of the other, you tend to wait until he's facing the other way 'fore you gun him down."

Dunkirk's hand quivered as he held it out from his side, while Smoke continued to sip his whiskey, seemingly unconcerned.

Carson held out his left hand and the bartender placed a Greener sawed-off double-barrelled 12 gauge shotgun in it. Carson pulled both hammers back with a loud click and said, "Okay, Joe Bob, you want to commit suicide, it's okay with me. But you're gonna do it outside so the bartender don't have to spend all day cleaning your guts off the floor."

Dunkirk flicked his eyes over at Carson. "What do you mean, commit suicide? I'm gonna kill Mr. Smoke Jensen here."

Carson sighed loudly. "Like I said, Joe Bob, it's your funeral." He waved the barrel of the shotgun and both Joe Bob and Smoke walked out onto the street. As they faced off, Carson called, "Speaking of funerals, Joe Bob, what do you want carved on your cross after Smoke curls you up—other than *here lies a man who died of a case of the slow?*"

"Shut up Carson, or you'll be next!"

"Say Joe Bob," Smoke said, "before I send you to meet Jesus, tell me how much he paid you."

Dunkirk's forehead wrinkled and he cocked his head to the side. "Huh? What did you say?"

Smoke spread his hands. "I just wanted to know what you thought your life was worth. I know you don't never do nothing without being paid for it, so . . . how much did you get paid to die today?"

"Uh . . . a hundred dollars, in advance, and another five hundred after you're in the ground."

"Want to tell me who it was who bought you so cheap?"

"Naw, let's just get it on."

"Okay, back-shooter. Fill your hand."

Dunkirk grabbed at his pistol and actually had it halfway out of his holster when a piece of molten lead in a .44 caliber slammed into his chest and knocked him off his boots. He lay there in the dirt, eyes blinking, legs quivering, still trying to clear leather.

Smoke walked over and squatted next to him, casting his shadow over the dying man's face to shield it from the sun. "Tell me Joe Bob, did that gunhawk pay you enough for this?"

"Jensen," he croaked, his voice filled with pain.

"Yeah."

"You know he's comin' for you . . ."

"Yeah, Joe Bob, I know." But he was talking to a man staring the long stare into nothing.

"Monte," Smoke said softly, "give whatever money he's got left of the hundred to the preacher's wife for her fund for widows and orphans. She can always use a donation."

"Sure Smoke, and I'll keep my eyes open for any more trash like this that blows into town. What are you gonna do?"

Smoke shrugged as he punched out his casings and reloaded. "Guess I'll go back up to Sugarloaf and wait. Not much else I can do."

As Smoke stepped in his saddle, a man came running up to him waving a piece of paper in the air. "Mr. Jensen, this telegram just came over the wire for your wife, Miss Sally. The telegraph operator asked me to give it to you."

Smoke reached down and took the paper from his hand. "Thanks, Mr. Hanson. I'll see that she gets it."

Hanson's brow furrowed. "Sure hope it's not bad news."

Smoke smirked. "You ever know anybody to telegraph *good* news?"

Chapter Four

The Silver Spur Saloon in Laredo, Texas was over half full even though it was only ten o'clock in the morning. Since the outbreak of Mexican Fever in local cattle herds two months before, a great many area cowhands had been out of work. Those who hadn't left town were spending what little money they had getting and staying drunk.

The border punchers, rowdy and wild to begin with, were now surly, quarrelsome, and downright mean. Fights were a daily occurrence in town, and the doctor was kept busy sewing up knife wounds and trying to plug bullet holes as best he could.

In a dim corner of the Silver Spur, a poker game was in progress that had been going on for three days straight. One man, sitting with his back to the wall, had a bandanna over his head, draping down to cover his ears and tied in the back, over which he wore his hat. If any of the other players thought this strange attire for a cowhand, they took one look at his eyes and didn't mention it.

The man was lean to the point of emaciation, with a scraggly moustache, yellowing, tobacco-stained teeth, and haunted eyes that continually swept the room as if for danger. Every time the batwings would swing open, his hand would slip under the table to wrap around the handle of a belly-gun he kept in his waistband.

The man won a hand with two pair, beating a pair of aces and a king-high hand. As he raked in his winnings, one of the two Mexican *vaqueros* sitting at the table said, "Tha's pretty good playin', Mr. Morgan. You winnin' most of our moneys."

Lester Morgan's eyes flicked from his winnings to the man across the table who spoke. He growled, "I win because you don't play poker any better than you speak English."

When the Mexican's eyes narrowed, his friend put a hand on his shoulder, "Easy, *amigo,* we got plenty time to win it back."

As Morgan leaned back and put a cigar in his mouth, the batwings swung open and a dust-covered cowboy ambled in. He stood just inside the door, letting his eyes adjust to the light, sleeving sweat off his forehead with his arm. When Morgan lit his cigar, the flaming of the match illuminated his face, drawing the man's attention to it.

The stranger took off his hat and dusted some of the trail dirt off his clothes with it, and set it back on his head. He slipped the hammer thong off his pistol, worn low and tied down, then walked over to stand in front of the table in the corner.

At his approach, Morgan's hand slipped out of sight. The newcomer nodded at him, "How'r ya doin' Sundance?"

Morgan's eyes slitted and shifted quickly around the room to see if anyone else was listening. He took the cigar out of his mouth with his left hand and blew smoke at the ceiling. "You must be mistaken, mister. My name's Lester Morgan."

"No, I'm not mistaken. I followed you here from Del Rio. You was calling yourself Sundance there—at least you was when you gunned down my kid brother by shootin' him in the back."

"I never—"

Before Morgan could finish, the stranger reached across the table and jerked the hat and bandanna off his head, revealing a missing left ear. He grinned. "Maybe you should change your name to the One Ear Kid instead of Sundance."

Other men at the table began to pull their chairs back. One of them said, "Sundance? Isn't that the name of the man who shot that old gunfighter, Luke Nations, just before Smoke Jensen shot his ear off?"

The gunman standing at the table laughed. "Yeah, it is, only the bastard shot Nations in the back, too. Seems the only way this snake can make a reputation is to back-shoot someone." He squared his shoulders and flexed the fingers of his right hand. "Well, Mr. One-Ear, I ain't gonna turn my back on you, so if you ain't completely yeller clear through, let's get it on."

Morgan smiled, just before he fired his short-barreled .44 Smith and Wesson belly-gun up through the table. The shot blew a hole in the tabletop, then traveled upward and hit the gunman under his chin, shattering it and taking the top of his skull off. He was dead before he hit the ground. Money, cards, and pieces of brain were scattered all over the floor.

Morgan took a deep drag on his cigar, and with smoke trailing out of his nostrils, yelled, "Bartender, clean this mess up and bring us another table. This one seems to have a hole in it."

While two cowboys were dragging the dead man's body out and the bartender was spreading sawdust on the pool of blood on the floor, the other men in the poker game quietly gathered up their money and began to leave.

Morgan spread his hands. "Hey boys, what's the matter? My money not good enough for you?"

One of the players stopped and said, "If we'd known you was Sundance, we'd never have sat at the table with you to begin with." He pulled a pocketwatch out of his vest and snapped it open. He glanced at the time before looking up at Morgan, "The sheriff's due back from the county seat at sundown. I'd make myself scarce 'fore then if I was you." He snapped the watch closed and walked over to the bar with the other players, turning his back on Morgan and ignoring him.

Goddammit, thought Morgan, run out of another town, thanks to that bastard Smoke Jensen and the way he marked me for life.

He scrapped his winnings into his hat and left the saloon with as much dignity as he could muster.

Not having anywhere else to go, he mounted and walked his horse over the wooden bridge across the Rio Grande into Mexico and pulled up at the first saloon he could find, *El Caballero Cantina,* where he swung down.

The clientele here was a mixed bag of Mexican *vaqueros,* professional and semi-professional outlaws, both Mexican and American, and cowboys so down on their luck they couldn't afford to drink on the American side.

Sundance sat alone in a corner, his back to the wall as usual, and began to observe his fellow drinkers. He was formulating a plan to get even with Smoke Jensen, but he needed just the right sort of men: men who were born with the bark on; men who were as hard as the sun-baked caliche of the Sonoran desert; men who would kill for a dollar and give you change. Evidently, the others he had sent to kill Jensen had not been up to the task. Time to get some men who were used to earning their keep with their guns. The Mexicans had a word for them: *Buscaderos.* Tough, pistol-toting gunslicks who lived only to kill. If it was the last thing he ever did, he would make Jensen pay for ruining his life.

By midnight he had made his selection. First, he picked a Mexican who went by the name *El Gato,* the cat. To a Mexican, the only cat worth mentioning is the puma, or mountain lion. El Gato lived up to his name. He was big for a Mexican, over six feet tall. With wide shoulders and massive arms, and a belly to match, he looked like he weighed over three hundred pounds. He had a drooping moustache and smelled like he didn't believe in bath water. He drank his tequila straight, laughing at the *gringos* who had to cut it with salt and lime juice. In the last hour alone he had knocked two men out cold who didn't laugh with him at one of his jokes. His English was tolerable, and he wore two pistols and acted like he knew how to use them.

The next man Sundance picked was an American who answered to the name Toothpick. He was thin and wiry, all gristle and muscle without an ounce of fat on his body. He wore a thick, hand-tooled belt with a pistol on the left side with the butt forward, and a knife scabbard on the right. At first Sundance thought he got his name either because he was never without a toothpick between his lips, even when he smoked or drank, or on account of his thinness. Then, about an hour before midnight, one of the Mexican peons in the bar spilled his beer on Toothpick's boots. In the blink of an eye, Toothpick pulled a long, narrow-bladed knife out of the scabbard on his belt and sliced the man's moustache off. When El Gato complimented him on the knife, Toothpick said, "Yeah, this is my Arkansas Toothpick. I never go anywhere without it." As he looked at the knife, his hands unconsciously caressed it, as if it were a woman, and his eyes glittered with madness. He was just the sort of man Sundance was looking for.

The third man Sundance chose that night was quieter. He stood at the bar without drawing attention to himself, just watching the other patrons through narrow, suspicious eyes. He was stockily built, more square than long, and had hugely muscled arms more suited to a blacksmith than a cowboy. Sundance recognized him from a Wanted poster he had seen in Laredo. His name was Lightning Jack Warner. He rode at one time with Quantrill's Raiders, until his savagery and ruthlessness made him unwelcome even among that bloodthirsty crowd. He was called Lightning not because he was fast with a gun, but because he was originally from Alabama, and had an inordinate fondness and need for moonshine whiskey, or white lightning. He was mean as a snake when sober, and even worse when drunk. Sundance remembered hearing that he was nearsighted and therefore used a Greener ten-gauge shotgun as his weapon of choice. It was never out of his reach, and could be seen leaning against the bar next to him.

When the Regulator clock on the saloon wall struck midnight, Sundance made his move. He sauntered over to the bar and invited El Gato, Toothpick, and Lightning Jack to have a drink with him at his table. They were suspicious at first, until he said, "Give me five minutes of your time and you get a free drink. What have you got to lose?"

When the men were seated around his table in the rear corner of the saloon, Sundance got a bottle of tequila and a handful of limes from the bartender. While Toothpick sliced the limes with his slender knife, Sundance filled everyone's glass. Lightning Jack took a deep draught, coughed once, then whispered, "Smooth. Bitter, but smooth," in a rasping voice.

El Gato laughed and clapped the Southerner on the back. "I like this *gringo*. He knows how to drink the fruit of the cactus . . . quick and deep, like a man should take a woman."

Toothpick sipped his drink, made a face, and quickly sucked on a lime. He blew through his mouth once to cool it, then looked at Sundance with a furrowed brow. "Okay, Sundance, or whatever you call yourself. We're here, and we've had our drinks. Now what?"

Sundance took a cigar from his pocket and struck a match on his spur. As he held it under the end of the stogie, puffing it to life, he peered over the flame at the men who sat around the table looking at him expectantly.

"First, let me tell you about me." He drew deeply on the cigar and let the smoke trail out of his nostrils as he spoke, eyes unfocused and almost dreamy as he recalled his past. "A few years ago, I was just a kid, dreaming of becoming a famous gunfighter. I bought me some fancy clothes and a couple of pearl-handled Peacemaker Colts, and went on the prod to make my reputation. I hired out my gun to a rancher named Tilden Franklin, who planned to take over his town. Things were goin' pretty good until this bastard named Smoke Jensen got a bunch of old broken-down gunslicks to back his play against Franklin."

At the mention of Smoke's name, Toothpick's eyes narrowed and Lightning Jack snorted, a half-smile on his face. El Gato just sat there, staring into his tequila.

Sundance continued, as if talking to himself, his mind in the past. "During the final shootout, I happened to get the drop on one of Jensen's old friends, a man named Luke Nations . . ."

They all heard the shot and whirled around. Luke Nations lay crumpled on the boardwalk, a large hole in the center of his back.

Sundance stepped out of a building, a pistol in his hand. He looked up and grinned.

"I did it!" he hollered. "Me. Sundance. I kilt Luke Nations!"

"You goddamned back-shootin' asshole!" Charlie Starr said, lifting his pistol.

"No!" Smoke's voice stopped him. "Don't, Charlie." Smoke walked over to Sundance, one hand holding his bleeding side. He backhanded the dandy, knocking him sprawling. Sundance landed on his butt in the street. His mouth was busted, blood leaking from one corner. He looked up at Smoke, raw fear in his wide eyes.

"You gonna kill me, ain't you?" he hissed.

The smile on Smoke's face was not pleasant. "What's your name, low-life?"

"Les . . . Sundance. That's me, Sundance!"

"Well, Sundance!" Smoke put enough dirt on the name to make it very ugly. "You wanna live, do you?"

"Yeah!"

"And you wanna be known as a top gunhand, right, Sundance?"

"Yeah!"

Smoke kicked Sundance in the mouth. The young man rolled on the ground, moaning.

"What's your last name, craphead?"

"M . . . Morgan!"

"All right, Les Sundance Morgan. I'll let you live. And Les, I'm going to have your name spread all over the West. Les Sundance Morgan. The man with one ear. He's the man who killed the famed gunfighter Luke Nations."

"But," his face wrinkled in puzzlement. "I got both ears!"

Before his words could fade from sound, Smoke had drawn and fired, the bullet clipping off Sundance's left ear. The action forever branded him.

Sundance rolled in the dirt, crying and hollering.

"Top gun, huh, bushwhacker?" Smoke said. "Right, that's you, Sundance." He looked toward Johnny North. "Get some whiskey and fix his ear, will you, Johnny?"

Sundance really started hollering when the raw booze hit where his ear had been. He passed out from the pain. Johnny took that time to bandage the ugly wound.

Then Smoke kicked him awake. Sundance lay on the blood and whiskey-soaked ground, looking up at Smoke.

"What you do this to me for?" he croaked.

"So everybody, no matter where you go, can know who you are, punk. The man who killed Luke Nations. Now, you listen to me, you son of a bitch! You want to know how it feels to be a top gun? Well, just look around you, ask anybody."

Sundance's eyes found Charlie Starr. "You're Charlie Starr. You're more famous than Luke Nations. But I'm gonna be famous too, ain't I?"

Charlie slowly rolled a cigarette and stuck it between Sundance's lips. He held the match while Sundance puffed. Charlie straightened up and smiled sadly.

"How is it, you ask? Oh, well, it's a real grand time being a well-known gunfighter. You can't sit with your back to no empty space, always to a wall. Lots of back-shooters out there. You don't never make your fire, cook, and then sleep in the same spot. You always move before you bed down, 'cause somebody is always lookin' to gun you down . . . for a reputation.

"You ain't never gonna marry, kid. 'Cause if you do, it won't last. You got to stay on the move, all the time. 'Cause you're the man who kilt Luke Nations, dogscrap. And there's gonna be a thousand other piles of dogscrap just like you lookin' for you.

"You drift, boy. You drift all the time, and you might near always ride alone, lessen you can find a pard that you know you can trust not to shoot you when you're in your blankets.

"And a lot of towns won't want you, back-shooter. The marshal and the townspeople will meet you with rifles and shotguns and point you the way out. 'Cause they don't want no gunfighter in their town.

"And after a time, if you live, you'll do damn near anything so's people won't know who you are. But they always seem

to find out. Then you'll change your name agin. And agin. Just
lookin' for a little peace and quiet.

"But you ain't never gonna find it.

"You might git good enough to live for a long time, mister
Sundance Morgan. I hope you do. I hope you ride ten thousand
lonely miles, you back-shootin' bastard. Ten thousand miles
of lookin' over your back. Ten thousand towns that you'll ride
in and out of in the dead of night. Eatin' your meals just at
closin' time . . . if you can find a eatin' place that'll serve you.

"A million hours that you'll wish you could somehow change
your life . . . but you cain't. You cain't change, 'cause *they*
won't let you.

"Only job you'll be able to find is one with the gun, if you're
good enough. 'Cause you're the man who kilt Luke Nations.
You got your rep, boy. You wanted it so damned bad, you got
'er." He glanced at Johnny North.

Johnny said, "I had me a good woman one time. We married
and I hung up my guns, sonny. Some goddamned bounty hunters
shot into my cabin one night. Killed my wife. I'd never broke
no law until then. But I tracked them so-called lawmen down
and hung 'em, one by one. I was on the owlhoot trail for years
after that. I had both the law and the reputation hunters after
me. Sounds like a real fine life, don't it? I hope you enjoy it."

Smoke kicked Sundance to his feet. "Get your horse and
ride, you pile of crap! 'Fore one of us here takes a notion to
brace the man who killed Luke Nations."

Crying, Sundance stumbled from the street and found his
horse in back of the building that once housed a gun shop.

"It ain't like that!" the gunfighters, the gambler, the
ranchers, and the minister heard Sundance yell as he rode
off. "It ain't none at all like what you say it was. I'll have
women a-throwin' themselves at me. I'll have money and
I'll have . . ."

His horse's hooves drummed out the rest.

"What a story this will make," Haywood Arden, the newspaperman said, his eyes wide as he looked at the bullet-pocked
buildings and empty shell casings on the ground.

"Yeah," Smoke said wearily. "You be sure and write it, Haywood. And be sure you spell one name right."

"Who is that?" the newspaperman asked.

"Lester Morgan, known as Sundance."

"What'd he do?" Haywood was writing on a tablet as fast as he could write.

Smoke described Sundance, ending with, "And he ain't got but one ear. That'll make him easy to spot."

"But what did this Lester Sundance Morgan *do?*"

"Why . . . he's the gunfighter who killed Luke Nations." *(Trail of the Mountain Man)*

Lightning Jack interrupted Sundance's reverie. "Luke Nations? I heard that old man was a mean sonofabitch and about as fast on the draw as anybody."

Sundance studied the glowing end of his cigar. "Well, he weren't fast enough. Anyway, after I dusted him, Smoke Jensen stuck his nose in and drew down on me when I wasn't ready. He wounded me, then shot off my ear."

El Gato looked up from his tequila and stared at the lump of scar tissue on Sundance's head. "He shot off your ear, man? *Santa Maria!* Why he do such a thing?"

"He said it was to teach me a lesson. He wanted to mark me so that all the other young guns who were on the prod to make a reputation would come after me, hoping to make their name by killing the man who shot Luke Nations."

El Gato's lips curled in an evil smile. "Ah. I see."

Sundance paused to refill their glasses with tequila, then went on. "Well, it happened just like he said. For the last few years I haven't been able to take a breath without some gun-happy *hombre* trying to kill me. I've been on the owlhoot trail ridin' low, and haven't been able to spend more'n two nights in a row in any town since then."

Lightning Jack chugged his drink down without a blink. "This is all real interestin', Sundance, but what the hell does it have to do with us?"

Sundance stabbed his cigar out on the table, face turning

red. "Just this. Since I have to live as an outlaw anyway, I decided to make it pay. I've robbed lots of banks, stages, and pilgrims in the years I've been on the trail. I can't go into town and live it up, so I still have most of the money I've stolen. I plan to use every cent of that money to get even with Smoke Jensen."

Toothpick's eyebrows raised. "Just how much money are we talkin' about Sundance?"

"Twenty thousand and change."

"So just what is your proposal?"

Sundance took a swallow of tequila and leaned his head back and squeezed a lime into his mouth. After a deep breath, he croaked, "I want to put together a gang of men to go up into the Colorado mountains and put Jensen in the ground. I figure it'll take between thirty and forty men to get the job done."

Toothpick shook his head. "Twenty thousand isn't a lot of money to go around among that many hands."

Sundance grinned. "The twenty's just seed money to get us started. With all the cattle around here sick with Tick Fever, most of the big spreads haven't been buying any beef. They're fat with cash and have let most of their punchers go since there's not any work to be done. I figure with a gang of the right sort of men, we could hit a few spreads here and there and anything else that interested us between Texas and Colorado. By the time we get to Jensen's ranch, we'd probably have twenty thousand for every member of our group."

Lightning Jack whistled. "That's a mighty ambitious plan, but that much activity would bring down a lot of heat on us. Every lawman in Texas would be after us."

Sundance shrugged. "So what? If we keep on the move, hit and run, they'll never catch up to us. By the time they know where we are, we won't be there anymore."

Just as he finished speaking, the batwings flew open and a group of ten men walked in, laughing and talking. Their leader was a short Mexican with a huge potbelly. He was unshaven, had a large black moustache, and was wearing crossed cartridge belts on his chest and a double-holster rig around his ample waist. He had a long purple scar running down his face from his left eyebrow to the corner of his mouth. The men with him were covered with trail dust and looked as tough as horseshoe nails.

El Gato cursed under his breath and pulled his hat down to shadow his face. Sundance leaned over and asked him, ''What's the matter? Who's that?''

He whispered, ''That's Benito Valdez, the meanest *hombre* in Mexico, and he swore to kill me the next time he saw me.''

Sundance shrugged and leaned back in his chair. ''Don't worry, El Gato, you're with me now.'' He reached under the table and loosened his pistol in its holster, leaving his hand wrapped around the butt.

Valdez took the drink the bartender poured him and turned, leaning back with his elbows on the bar. After a moment, he saw El Gato and called, ''Hey, *amigos,* look who's here. It is El Gato.'' As his men turned and stared, Valdez growled, ''How're you doin' pussy cat? You remember what I said I was going to do if I saw you again?'' He let his hand drop to his pistol.

Before he could do anything, Sundance gave a big yawn. He flipped a handful of change on the floor at Valdez's feet. ''Hey lardbutt. How about bringing my friends and me another bottle of tequila. We've about finished this one off.''

Valdez's eyes slitted and he glared hate. ''What means lard-butt?''

Sundance grinned. ''It means your ass is so fat that I bet you have to tie two horses together to ride anywhere. Now are you going to bring me my drink or am I going to have to kick your fat ass outta here?''

Valdez screamed, ''Filthy *gringo,*'' and grabbed for his gun.

Sundance kicked his chair over sideways and rolled once on the floor, coming up in a crouch, both hands filled with iron. Before Valdez's pistol cleared his holster, Sundance opened fire.

Twin holes blossomed in Valdez's chest, the bullets punching through his body and out his back to star the mirror over the bar. Valdez was knocked off his heels, bounced once against the bar, and fell to the floor.

His men drew and began to fire just as El Gato, Toothpick, and Lightning Jack opened up on them. The big Greener in Lightning Jack's hands boomed twice, spitting death and cutting two of the Mexicans almost in half and showering the others with blood and guts.

One of the Mexicans' bullets gouged a shallow furrow along Toothpick's cheek before the thin man's Navy model Colt blew his face into a bloody pulp.

El Gato screamed, *"Chinga tu madre!"* as he fired with both hands, pumping the pistols as if that would make the bullets go faster. Two more of the *bandidos* whirled and fell to the floor, to die among the bloody entrails and bodies there.

Sundance fired at the last of Valdez's men left standing, blowing a hole in his heart at the same time Toothpick's knife twirled through the air and entered the man's open, screaming mouth, to pierce his neck and embed itself in his spine. He dropped like a stone, dead from two mortal wounds.

The survivors walked through the fog of heavy smoke and cordite to the pile of bodies next to the bar. Sundance used his boot to roll Valdez over onto his back, where he lay convulsing and kicking, his big Mexican spurs gouging tracks in the wooden floor that soon filled with blood.

Toothpick bent over and jerked his knife free from his victim's mouth and wiped it on the man's bloody shirt. Eyes dreamy and unfocused, he brought his beloved Arkansas Toothpick up and kissed the blade, licking the last drops of blood off, murmuring something to the instrument the others couldn't hear.

El Gato stood over the bodies, smoking pistols still in his hands, greasy hair hanging down, and sweat making rivulets in the dirt on his face. "Well, *companeros,* we fixed those men's wagons pretty damn *bueno,* eh?"

Sundance holstered his Colt. He looked around the room, which was now empty except for his men. "Well, we'd better burn the breeze outta here." He looked into each of their faces. "We did good tonight. We make a pretty good team, *compadres.* Gather all the men you think are tough enough for what I outlined earlier, and we'll meet on the American side of the Rio tomorrow at noon. There's a grove of cottonwood trees about ten miles north of Laredo. I'll make camp there and wait for you and your men.

They shook hands and swaggered out of the saloon to their mounts without looking back.

Chapter Five

Sunset comes early in the high lonesome, and the sun was disappearing over the edge of the western peaks when Smoke spurred his mount toward home. Though he wondered what was in the telegram that came for Sally, he didn't look. He figured he would find out soon enough.

Smoke could almost taste the crispness and tang of early fall on the night air, and the sky was cloudless and clear, making the stars as brilliant as diamonds scattered on black velvet. He leaned back against the cantle, letting Horse have his rein, as he watched the stars and dreamed dreams of wilderness lands unsullied by people. His reverie led him to think of Preacher, wondering momentarily if the old grizzly was still alive and sitting around a small fire in the up-high enjoying the feel and smell of the mountain air as he was.

He thought the first shot he heard was thunder, until it was repeated several times in quick succession. He leaned forward in the saddle and used his spurs. "Come on, Horse," he cried, "that's coming from home!"

The deep booming of an express shotgun was answered by the higher pitch of some .44's and the slightly deeper cough of a Henry rifle. As he came closer to the conflagration, Smoke first slowed Horse to a trot, then a walk.

Just before he came within sight of his cabin, Smoke slipped off Horse and tied him in some brush beside the path. He shucked his Winchester from its saddle boot and eared back the hammer. He ducked and weaved through the forest of high-mountain pines and underbrush, until he came to a small brook, gurgling in the darkness.

Kneeling, he reached down and spooned a handful of mud into his palm, smearing it over his face and neck and the brass of his rifle to minimize the glare in the starlight. With his dirt-covered face and dun-colored buckskins, he was all but invisible in the night. His mountain man training kept him from making the slightest sound as he scurried up the ridge overlooking his compound.

From this vantage point, he watched as gunfire exploded in several windows of the cabin, to be answered by at least four other guns in the woods surrounding it. He could make out two bodies lying motionless in the yard by the hitching post in front of the bunkhouse, and another sprawled spread-eagled partway up the ridge to the south of the cabin. So, he thought, at least two of ours and one of theirs down.

He grinned a death grin, time to even up the odds and bring religion to the scum attacking his home. Leaning his head back, he opened his mouth and let out a great, screaming cry of a mountain lion on the hunt. While the yell echoed and reverberated throughout the small valley, the shooting stopped for a moment. From inside the cabin, the wailing, undulating cry of a she-wolf calling her mate emanated, lifting a great weight from Smoke's shoulders. His beloved Sally was alive and now she knew he was nearby.

Smoke crouched and began to move through the forest as silently as a wraith. He seemed to know instinctively where to place his feet so as not to make a sound. Even without being able to see where his target was, he found his way to the spot by following the ripe smell of unwashed flesh, mingled with beer and tobacco odor and the sharp scent of turnips the man had eaten for supper.

Within less than five minutes, Smoke was standing directly behind a figure kneeling beside a fallen tree. The man was firing a Henry rifle at flashes of gunfire from the cabin windows. The gunman never knew what struck him until seconds after Smoke's huge Bowie knife sliced through his trachea and carotid arteries.

The bushwhacker turned, blood spurting from the gaping hole in his neck, and Smoke reversed the knife and swung backhanded with all his strength, severing the head from its neck. The body stood there for a moment, as though uncertain what to do next, then crumpled as if boneless. Smoke picked up the head by its hair and trotted toward his next appointment.

Jesus Garza, called *Borachon* by friends and enemies alike because he was seldom seen completely sober, pulled back from his position on the hillock overlooking the rear of the cabin. Both his pistols were empty and he needed to reload. He also needed another swallow of the tequila he always kept handy.

Squatting, with his back to a tree to prevent being hit by a lucky shot, he tilted his bottle up toward the stars and gulped until there was nothing left but air. He belched loudly and returned to his position, when something hit him in the back. Whirling, both pistols cocked and ready to fire, he looked down at his feet. Lying there among the pine cones and needles, staring up at him with unblinking, dead eyes, was the head of his *compadre,* Jorge Bustamonte.

"Aiyee-e-e! *Madre de Dios,* aiyee-e-e," he screamed, firing both pistols into the darkness while backing up as fast as he could.

As he backed into the clearing, still firing, the angry grunt and growl of a grizzly bear came at him out of the night. He turned and ran as fast as his boots would carry him toward the cabin, forgetting in his terror what waited for him there. The last thing Garza saw was the flame blossoming out of a Greener ten gauge shotgun as it blew him into hell.

A voice from the woods on the other side of the cabin called out, "Jorge. Are you there, boy?"

Smoke picked up Jorge's head and spent a few moments

preparing his next surprise as he trotted toward the sound of the voice. He found the man's horse reined to a tree and placed his surprise on the saddle horn, then stole quietly over behind a nearby bush.

Jerry Mason was worried. He had just seen Jesus Garza blown almost in two by that big shotgun in the cabin, and now Jorge Bustamonte wasn't answering his yells. That meant there was only himself and old Pig-eye Petersen against God-only-knew how many in the cabin. It had seemed like easy money when that gunslick down in Texas offered the four out-of-work cowhands three months' wages to come up here and kill some old mountain man, but it sure as hell wasn't working out like they thought.

"Damnation," he whispered to himself. "I think I'll just head on over to Petersen and see if he's ready to skedaddle on outta here." With that, Mason holstered his pistols and walked to his horse. He untied the reins from the tree branch, put his left foot in the stirrup, and reached for the saddle horn.

"What the . . . ?" he murmured as he felt something hairy and sticky under his hands. He pulled the object off his saddle horn and held it up where he could see it. The air left his lungs in a loud whoosh and he bent over and vomited all over his boots.

Gulping and swallowing bile, he threw the severed head of his friend, Jorge, back into the woods. He leaped up on his horse and spurred the animal into a run.

Smoke stepped out of the bushes he was hiding in as Mason galloped past and swung his Winchester rifle in a horizontal arc, catching Mason full in the face and catapulting him backwards off his mount. Smoke stood over the moaning man and kicked him once in the side of the head, turning out his lights temporarily.

He wiped blood and pieces of teeth off the stock of the Winchester and went after the lone remaining gunman. No stealth this time, he walked directly toward the man, not bothering to mask his noise.

Petersen stepped back from the tree he had been firing around and began to reload his Colt Peacemaker .45. He looked up when he heard someone coming through the underbrush toward him from where Mason had been stationed.

"Hey Jerry," he whispered loudly, "you gettin' tired of shootin' those fish in that barrel down there?"

His eyes narrowed when there was no answer. He cocked the Peacemaker and pointed it toward the sounds. "Jerry, that you, boy?"

Light blossomed and exploded in the darkness and the bullet from Smoke's rifle smashed against Petersen's gun-hand, knocking his pistol spinning away. He screamed and bent over, holding his broken hand and moaning. When he looked up, one of the biggest men he had ever seen was standing before him, grinning a grin with no mirth in it.

Smoke backhanded him across the face with his fist, smashing his nose and loosening his teeth. As the man spun away from him, Smoke propped his rifle against a tree and pulled his big Bowie knife from its scabbard. "You wanted to fight, skunk-breath. Well, here's your chance. Pull that frog-sticker I see there in your belt and let's dance."

Petersen straightened up, squared his shoulders, and said, "No, I don't want to fight. I give up."

Smoke's grin widened. "No, I don't think you understand. You weren't given a choice, just like those two boys lying dead down there in front of my cabin weren't given a choice. You are going to die, mister. The only question is, are you going to die like the coward you are, gutless and unarmed, or are you at least going to die like a man, with a weapon in your hand." Smoke shrugged. "It's up to you."

Petersen's lips tightened into a thin line and he drew his knife lefthanded. "I can't hardly use my good hand."

"Not to worry. I never take advantage of a coward." Smoke shifted his weapon to his left hand. As they circled each other in the darkness, weaving their knives before them, Smoke asked, "Where you from, fatso?"

Petersen sucked in his gut, trying to hide his substantial paunch. "I'm from Texas, and that's where I'm goin' back to soon's I gut your ass." He feinted left, then moved quickly to his right, swinging his left arm in a round-house swing at Smoke's stomach.

Smoke didn't even move back. As Petersen's knife sliced through his buckskins, barely scraping the skin, Smoke flicked his arm straight out and sliced off Petersen's right ear. The fat man gave a high-pitched yell and put his ruined right hand up to staunch the flow of blood, staring at Smoke with fear-brightened eyes.

Smoke continued to move in a slow circle, talking as if in a normal conversation. "You know what I hate, fat-butt? I mean, what really makes me want to throw up?"

Petersen narrowed his eyes, but didn't answer as he shuffled sideways, looking for an opening. "I hate back-shooters, ambushers, and bushwhackers almost more than anything," Smoke continued, flicking his left hand out again so fast that Petersen didn't even see it, just felt the sting as his left ear was left hanging by a thread. With an agonized growl, he reached up and tore the ear loose, looking at it for a moment before he threw it to the ground. Blood was streaming down both sides of his face, giving him an unearthly look in the starlight. "I'm not gonna stand here and let you cut me up, mister."

Smoke smiled, a little. "Oh? Well just what are you gonna do about it, snake-scum?

"I'm gonna kill you right now." With a terrible, insane yell, Petersen rushed straight at Smoke, his arm extended in what he hoped was a killing thrust.

Smoke brushed the attack aside with his forearm, and as Petersen came up against him, he calmly buried his knife to the hilt in his opponent's right eye. Petersen uttered a strangled scream which quickly turned into a gurgle, then a death rattle as he collapsed to the ground.

Smoke left him where he fell and retraced his steps to where Mason lay unconscious. He took the rope off his saddle, looped it under the sleeping man's arms and back to the saddle horn, and led his horse down toward the camp.

"To the cabin," he yelled.

"Smoke, is that you?"

"Yeah, Sally, it's me. Hold your fire, I'm coming in with a prisoner."

Sally, Cookie, Pearlie, Cal, and the remaining men from the bunkhouse gathered in the cabin yard to meet him. When he walked up, Sally was bending over the two hands lying on the ground. One was dead, the other seriously wounded. She straightened and waved over one of the men standing in front of the bunkhouse.

She put her hand on the cowboy's shoulder, "Sam, would you take one of the horses and ride into Big Rock and see if you can get Doctor Spalding out here. Tell him we have one dead and Woodrow has a bullet in the shoulder and one through his chest." She looked over at the man Smoke had dragged into the camp yard, noticing his ruined face. "Also tell him Smoke has worked a little on one of the attackers in his usual manner, so he may need to do some reconstruction of a face." Hesitating for a moment, she smiled and shook her head. "I know it's no use, but I'd better ask. Smoke," she called, "did you happen to leave any up in the woods who might need Doctor Spalding's attention?"

He pursed his lips, "Not unless he's considerably more skilled than I remember. You might send word to the undertaker to get busy cuttin' some wood, cause he's gonna have some business shortly."

While Smoke was talking to Sally, Cal and Pearlie untied his prisoner and dragged him over to the front porch, propping him up against the hitching post. The men gathered around him with angry, sullen faces. Hank Collier, Woodrow's saddlemate and best friend, eared back the hammer on his pistol and aimed it at Mason's face.

Smoke put his hand on the gun, gently pushing it toward the ground. "Not just yet, if you don't mind, Hank." He looked over his shoulder at the man lying there. "I've got some questions for this pile of cowcrap, then you men can take care of business."

Hank's eyes never left Mason. "Yes sir, Mr. Smoke. But if Woodrow dies 'cause of this man, don't try to stop what's gonna happen next."

Smoke slowly shook his head. "Wouldn't think of it, Hank."

Pearlie walked out of the cabin with a pitcher of water and threw it on Mason's face and smiled as the man coughed, strangled, and sat up gasping for breath.

Smoke squatted directly in front of Mason, elbows on knees, and asked in a kind, quiet tone. "What's your name, mister?"

Mason looked over Smoke's shoulder at the crowd of men gathered with angry, set faces and eyes that looked at him as if he were already dead. "Uh . . . Mason, Jerry Mason."

"Where you from, cowboy?"

Mason's eyes narrowed suspiciously. "I'm . . . that is, we . . . my friends and I are all from Texas."

Smoke smiled. "That wouldn't be down Laredo way, would it?"

Mason shook his head. "No. We worked near there, on a little shirt-tail spread down to Del Rio."

"Well Jerry, I'm kind'a wondering why a bunch of sorry-assed dumb ole' boys from Texas come all the way up here and decide to shoot up my home in the middle of the night."

Mason's gaze lowered and he mumbled. "I don't know either, mister. I just rode with them others and took orders from the big guy, Petersen. Maybe you could ask him?"

Smoke shook his head. He pulled his knife and reached down and wiped some of the blood and tissue off the blade onto Mason's pants. "I'm afraid Petersen ain't gonna be talkin' again real soon, not without no tongue anyway."

Mason's face twisted in terror as Smoke said this, then he screamed in fright when Smoke dropped Bustamonte's severed head into his lap. "I believe this belonged to one of your other friends, and I don't think he's in the mood to talk, either."

Mason sat there, staring into the glazed, lifeless eyes of his friend.

Smoke said, "Tell us what happened. Who hired y'all to come up here and attack us?"

Mason sleeved snot and tears off his face with the back of an arm. "Will ya let me go if'n I tell ya?"

"I'm afraid not, Jerry. You've killed at least one of our friends, and maybe another if the doc can't fix him up. In this country, murder is a hangin' offense.'' He reached out and flipped the head off Mason's lap with the point of his knife. ''But, hangin' is preferable to some other ways of dyin', if you get my meanin'.''

Mason moaned, closed his eyes, and hung his head. ''Okay, okay. Some man came up to us in a saloon and asked if we was lookin' for work. We said sure, so he said he'd give us three months' pay to come up here to the high country and put a bullet in Smoke Jensen. Said there was dirt between 'em.''

''What was this man's name?''

He looked up into Smoke's eyes. ''I don't know, and that's the honest truth, 'cept there's one thing funny 'bout him.''

''What's that?''

''He ain't got but one ear. Said his right'un had been shot off.''

Smoke's brow furrowed. ''Was he a shootist?''

''I dunno.'' Mason shook his head. ''Wore a fancy double-rig though, and looked like he knew how to use it.''

Smoke patted him on the shoulder. ''Okay, boy, thank's for bein' honest with me.''

''You gonna hang me now?'' His eyes were streaming tears.

''I don't know. That's up to the boys here. After all, it was them that you ambushed and one of them that you killed.'' Smoke stood and dusted his hands on his pants, as if to rid them of the stain of having touched the killer.

''Smoke,'' Sally said, ''I think we ought to wait for Sheriff Carson and let him take this boy into town for a trial.''

Smoke looked at her a moment. ''How's Woodrow?'' he asked quietly.

She lowered her eyelids. ''He's pretty bad. He was hit hard, but he's young and strong and fightin' back. If he lives until Doc Spalding gets here, I think he'll make it.''

Smoke cut his eyes over to Hank Collier. ''Sally, I'm gonna leave it up to the men what to do. If they want to be merciful and let Monte have him, okay. If they want to form a string party and decorate a cottonwood tree with his carcass, that's okay, too.''

''But . . .''

He put his arm around her shoulder and began to lead her into the cabin. "I know it's hard dear, but this is a hard country, and those men made their choice to come up here and kill people for money." He opened the door for her and followed her in.

Hank went over to stand before Mason. "Men, we have a choice here. Do we take this bandit into town to hang, or do we do it here and save the town the trouble?"

"Let 'im stretch hemp!"

"Make 'im do a midair dance!"

"Let him do a Texas cakewalk!"

Hank shook his head, sympathy in his eyes. "Sorry, Hoss. Looks like you go to meet Jesus tonight."

Mason wiped his eyes and nose again and got to his feet. "Okay. I'm not gonna cry about it. Let's do it."

The men put him on a horse and rode into the woods. Pearlie and Cal went into the cabin to sit with Woodrow until the doc came.

Chapter Six

Doctor Cotton Spalding had Pearlie hold a cloth with chloroform on it while he put some deep stitches in the wounds to Woodrow's chest and arm. It wasn't long before Pearlie's face was the color of chalk and he was swallowing rapidly to keep from fainting at the sight of the doctor's needles at work.

Sally was helping by handing Spalding his instruments as he needed them. She looked up when Pearlie started to sway, with sweat beading his forehead. "Pearlie, hand me that cloth and go sit in the other room until you feel better."

"Yes ma'am." He wasted no time doing just as she suggested, pausing in the kitchen to grab a couple of biscuits and a cut of beef left over from supper. He walked out the door onto the porch to find Smoke sitting there, cigar in hand, looking over the Sugarloaf range.

Smoke glanced up to see Pearlie standing in the doorway. "Light and set, Pearlie. Is the doc through in there?"

"No sir, but might near. He says Woody's gonna be okay if'n he don't get suppuration."

Smoke nodded, blowing cigar smoke toward the stars. "Pearlie, what did you make of Mason's description of the man who paid them to come up here?"

Pearlie thought on it for a moment, then shrugged. "Could be most anybody, I reckon." He stuffed the biscuit-surrounded beef into his mouth. " 'Cept somethin' about that one ear business is kinda familiar."

Smoke offered him a cigar. "No thanks, I'll just roll me a blanket of my own." He pulled a cloth bag of tobacco out of his pocket and began to build a cigarette. "What do you make of it, Smoke?"

"I only remember one *hombre* who fits that description who has cause to hate me enough to pay someone to kill me, and who's coward enough to be afraid to do it himself."

"Who's that?"

"Lester Morgan."

Pearlie thought for a moment, then snapped his fingers. "You mean that dandy who went around acting like some big gunhawk? The one that shot Luke Nations in the back?"

Smoke shrugged. "You recollect any other man with one ear who's crossed our paths in the last few years?"

"Naw, I don't. But I heard old Lester Morgan had gone to Mexico, tryin' to outrun his reputation."

"So had I, Pearlie. But when you think on it, Texas isn't that far from Mexico, is it?"

Just then, Doctor Spalding and Sally walked out onto the porch. Smoke jumped up. "How's Woody, Doc?"

"I think he's going to be all right, Smoke. I've asked Sally to let him rest in the cabin tonight, then send him in to Big Rock on a buckboard tomorrow. I'll have to probe for the bullet in his chest, and I want him to get a little stronger before I put him through that."

Sally asked, "Can we fix you some supper, Cotton, or would you like coffee or a drink?"

He shook his head. "No thanks, one of the town ladies is in labor and I need to get back down there." He smiled. "Can't have these women learning they can have those babies without me; wouldn't be good for business."

"I'll bring old Woody to town first thang in the mornin', Doc," said Pearlie.

"Okay, thanks Pearlie. Goodnight all." He tipped his hat,

climbed into his buggy, and settled back to grab a quick nap as his horse found its way back to Big Rock.

Pearlie waved goodnight to Smoke and Sally and sauntered toward the bunkhouse, cigarette dangling from his lips.

Smoke put his arm around Sally and she laid her head on his shoulder. "Tired?"

"Yes. We'd just finished feeding the hands supper when those men opened fire on us." She sighed. "It's been pretty much non-stop since then."

"Is Woody taken care of?"

"Yes, he's sleeping soundly. Doctor Spalding gave him some laudanum."

He gently steered her through the door and toward their bedroom. "You get in bed, I'll get us a glass of wine, and we'll relax a little before trying to go to sleep."

She caressed his cheek with her palm, then walked tiredly toward their room as he turned to look for the wine glasses.

When he entered the bedroom, Sally was propped up in bed wearing one of her silk nightshirts. He could see the outline of her breasts through the thin material and had to concentrate to keep from spilling their wine.

They touched glasses and he said, "To us." She answered with a smile and repeated the toast, "To us, dear."

After taking a sip of the dark-red burgundy, Smoke handed her the telegram he had been given in town. She pursed her lips, looked at him once, then drank the rest of her wine in one swallow as if to fortify herself against whatever news was in the message.

Tears formed in her eyes as she read, and Smoke put his hand on her thigh, squeezing lightly to let her know he was there for her. "My father's had a stroke," she whispered, voice cracking.

Smoke refilled her glass and said, "Is it bad?"

She shook her head. "My brother says not, but he has some weakness in his right arm and leg, and the left side of his face droops a little." Her eyes found his. "They ask if I can come and be there with him while he heals."

Smoke nodded without speaking. Sally clenched her jaw and

blinked away her tears. "I'll send an answer with Pearlie in the morning, telling them to give my love to Dad, but that I won't be able to join them."

Surprised, Smoke asked, "Why not? I could take you over to the railhead and you'd be there in less than a week."

She looked at him with a defiant expression. "Why? Because someone is after my man, trying to kill him. I'm damned if I'm going to let anyone hurt you, Smoke. We've worked too long and too hard to build a good life here in the mountains, and nobody is going to take that away from us. Not without a hell of a fight, they're not."

Smoke took her in his arms and hugged her tight, loving her more at that moment than he ever had. "You're right, darling. Someone is trying to kill me, or have me killed. I think it's that young gunfighter, Lester Sundance Morgan, that I treed and marked a few years back."

She leaned back and looked him in the eye. "All the more reason for me to stay where I belong, right here by your side."

He shook his head. "No, dear. I think it'd be better if you were somewhere else for a while."

Sally opened her mouth to speak, an angry expression on her face. He put a finger to her lips. "Hang on and listen to me for a minute. With you here, I'm not free to move around and do what I need to do to prepare for when this skunk gets tired of sending second-raters up here to be killed. Sooner or later he's going to come and try to do the job himself, and since I know he's a devout coward, he won't be coming alone."

"But Smoke, sweetheart, I want to help you when that time comes."

"No, sweetheart. I don't want a war here in our valley. Too many of our friends might get hurt. I plan to set up some hands as guards to keep any sizable force away from our home here, and I'm going to go to the high lonesome, where they'll have to come and get me on my terms and in my country."

She searched his face, trying to decide if he was just saying this to give her a way out so she could go to her family. After a moment, she shrugged. "Okay, Smoke Jensen. I'll go and take care of my Dad, and leave you here to take care of whoever is behind tonight's attack.'' She took his face in her hands, ''But you hear me and hear me well. You ride with your guns loose and your temper short and you stay off the ridge-line, because if you let anybody kill you, I'll never forgive you.''

He laughed and kissed her softly on the lips. ''You hear me, Sally Jensen. You get your father well in a hurry, 'cause every minute without you is like a month to me.''

Sally smiled a familiar smile. She pulled the nightshirt over her head and sat there, looking at Smoke with heavy eyelids and chest heaving. ''How come you're not undressed yet? Don't you know it's time for bed?''

Smoke blew the lamp out and began to rip off his bloody, torn shirt. ''Yes ma'am, I do. Do you want some more wine?''

From the darkness came her answer. ''No. Just you.''

The next morning, as Pearlie loaded Woodrow on the buckboard, Smoke gave him a telegram to send to Sally's family in New Hampshire telling them she would be there within two weeks or so, depending on the weather and the state of the railroad tracks.

After Pearlie left, with Hank riding in the back with the wounded man, Smoke called the hands together. ''Men, Sally's in the cabin packing now, and in a little while, I'm going to take her over to where she can catch a train back East to see her folks. After I leave, I want you all to keep a skeleton crew on the horse and cattle herds—just enough men to keep them safe and protected. I want the rest of you scattered along the various trails that anyone could use to get to Sugarloaf.''

One of the men asked, ''You expectin' more trouble, Mr. Smoke?''

''Yeah. Some low-life gunslick I took down a few years back is out to pay me back. I figure he'll have to have plenty of help before he gets the courage to come up here and face me, so I want you men to cover all the places on the trails where one or two men can keep a large party from passing. Most of you know this country about as well as I do, and there are plenty of passes and tight spots where you can bottle up those flat-landers so they can't get up here to do any mischief.''

Another asked, ''What are you gonna be doin', boss?''

''I'm gonna let it be known around the territory that I've gone up into the high country for a while to visit some of my ole mountain man friends. That way, hopefully, all the action will be away from here and you all will be safe.''

''To hell with bein' safe,'' the man who had spoken said, ''you need any help boss, all you gotta do is ask.''

''I know, Billy, but if I can get those scum to come after me in the up-high, they're the ones who'll be needin' help. Thanks for your loyalty and your help. Now, I'd better get in the cabin and help Sally pack or I won't have to worry about it, she'll kill me.''

The men laughed as they broke into small groups to decide who was going to which pass and who would be minding the herd.

Smoke went into the cabin and found Sally filling a steamer trunk, tears running down her face. ''Sweetheart, what's the matter?''

She looked at him with red-rimmed eyes. ''I don't like to be away from you. You always seem to get into trouble when I'm gone.''

He smiled and put his arms around her as she continued, ''Of course, you also always seem to get into mischief when I'm here.'' She leaned her head back and kissed him on the lips. ''It's a good thing I love you so much, Smoke, 'cause you sure need a lot of taking care of.''

''But worth it, right?''

''Oh yes,'' she said, remembering the night before.

When she was finished packing, and Smoke had loaded her trunk and small valise onto the buckboard, she motioned him into their bedroom. As he entered, she began unbuttoning her shirt. ''Smoke, there's one thing you forgot.''

He raised his eyebrows. ''Oh?''

She stripped her shirt off and began to undo her britches. ''Yes. You haven't told me good-bye yet.''

Smoke was astounded. Surely she couldn't intend for them

to do it in the daytime, with all the hands roaming around. Naked, she pulled the curtains and looked back over her shoulder at Smoke as she slid under the covers and into their bed. "Am I going to have to start without you?" she asked, smiling a lazy half-smile.

"Oh no, not on your life." he answered huskily, shucking boots and pants as fast as he could.

As they approached Big Rock in the buckboard, Smoke asked Sally, "Have you got your short-barrelled .44 handy?"

Before he could turn his eyes back to the road, she had it in her hand, grinning at him. "Why, are you expecting more trouble this morning?"

He shook his head, proud of her readiness. "Well, like I told you, one of the first and strongest lessons Preacher taught me was that if you always expect trouble, it never surprises you when it comes, as it usually does sooner or later in this country."

Sally smiled as she put the .44 away in her handbag. "You think about Preacher often, don't you?"

"Every day." He shook his head as he spoke. "You know, it's funny, but even as civilized as we've become here, with towns and railroads and people all over the place, not a day goes by that I don't use one of the lessons that Preacher taught me about survival in a wilderness."

Sally snorted. "Hmph, perhaps we're not as civilized as you think we are, Smoke. Most of the people out here are just one generation away from the frontier folks like Preacher who settled this country in the first place."

He smiled. "Yeah, and some are less than one generation up from the animals that preceded the mountain men."

"Oh, so now you're insulting the grizzlies and wolves, huh?"

They laughed together as the buckboard pulled into the main street of Big Rock. Townspeople of all ages waved and shouted hello. Smoke pulled the wagon up in front of the Emporium, so Sally could stock up on some female essentials she said she needed for the train trip.

He left her to her shopping and ambled down the street to

the saloon owned by Louis Longmont, his gambler friend of many years. There Louis plied his trade, which he called teaching amateurs the laws of chance.

Louis was a lean, hawk-faced man, with strong, slender, clean hands and long fingers, nails carefully manicured. He had jet-black hair and a black pencil-thin moustache. He was, as usual, dressed in a black suit, with white shirt and dark ascot—something he'd picked up on a trip to England some years back. He wore low-heeled boots, and a pistol hung in tied-down leather on his right side. It was not for show, for Louis was snake-quick with a short gun and was a feared, deadly gunhand when pushed.

Louis was not an evil man. He had never hired his gun out for money. And while he could make a deck of cards do almost anything, he did not cheat at poker. He did not have to cheat. He was possessed of a phenomenal memory, could tell you the odds of filling any type of poker hand, and was one of the first to use the new method of card counting.

He was just past forty years of age. He had come to the West with his parents as a very small boy, arriving from Louisiana. His parents had died in a shanty-town fire, leaving the boy to cope as best he could.

He had coped quite well, plying his innate intelligence and willingness to take a chance into a fortune. He owned a large ranch up in Wyoming Territory, several businesses in San Francisco, and a hefty chunk of a railroad.

Though it was a mystery to many why Longmont stayed with the hard life he had chosen, Smoke thought he understood. Once Louis had said to him, "Smoke, I would miss my life every bit as much as you would miss the dry-mouthed moment before the draw, the challenge of facing and besting those miscreants who would kill you or others, and the so-called loneliness of the owlhoot trail."

Sometimes Louis joked that he would like to draw against Smoke someday, just to see who was faster. Smoke allowed as how it would be close, but that he would win. "You see, Louis, you're just too civilized," he had told him on many occasions. "Your mind is distracted by visions of operas, fine foods and wines, and the odds of your winning the match. Also, your fatal flaw is that you can almost always see the good in the lowest creatures God ever made, and you refuse to believe that anyone is pure evil and without hope of redemption.''

When Louis laughed at this description of himself, Smoke would continue. ''On the other hand, when some snake-scum draws down on *me* and wants to dance, the only thing I have on my mind is teaching him that when you dance, someone has to pay the band. My mind is clear and focused on only one problem, how to put that stump-sucker across his horse toes down.''

Louis looked up from his breakfast table and smiled as Smoke entered his saloon. ''Smoke, my old friend, have a seat and let Andre fix you something to chase the pangs of hunger away.''

Smoke flipped his hat onto a rack next to the door and sat at Louis's table, narrowing his eyes at what was before him on his plate. ''Good morning, Louis.'' He pointed at the eggs covered with what appeared to be curdled buttermilk. ''Just what is that you are fixing to eat?''

''It is called eggs Benedict, and it is truly *magnifique*,'' said Louis, kissing his fingertips in the French fashion.

Smoke pursed his lips, then shook his head. ''I don't think so, Louis. If your fancy French chef, Andre, can remember how to make some bacon and plain old hen eggs and fried taters, I'd 'preciate it.''

''Oh Smoke,'' Louis looked disappointed. ''At least try these eggs Benedict. They are to die for!''

''I'd just as soon live, if you don't mind. Just have him pour a little sweet cream in with the eggs and scramble 'em up. That'll do me just fine.''

''Okay then, how about some *cafe au lait?*''

''If that's coffee, I'll have about a gallon.''

Louis's eyebrows raised. ''Late night last night?''

Andre appeared with a large silver service coffee pot and a china cup and saucer which he placed in front of Smoke. ''Good morning, Mr. Smoke, sir. May I serve you some eggs Benedict?''

Louis relayed Smoke's order, and Andre went away with a pained look on his face.

Smoke took a drink of his coffee, making sure his little finger was out and that Louis saw it. Then he pulled his makin's out and said, "You mind?"

Louis waved a dismissive hand, "No, of course not. What is morning coffee without tobacco?"

After Smoke had his cigarette going and had taken another sip of coffee, he said, "Had a little excitement up at Sugarloaf last night."

"Oh?"

"Yeah. Seems four bushwhackers thought they was good enough to take on Sally and the hands. Had 'em pinned down for a while until I showed up."

Around a mouthful of food, Louis said, "All dead, I presume?"

Smoke looked startled. "Of course, what'd you expect?"

"Nothing less, my friend. Are you aware of the reasoning behind the cowardly attack?"

Smoke filled him in on what he had heard and who he suspected was behind the various attacks on him recently, and of his plan to send Sally to New Hampshire to see her folks.

"And I'd like you to spread the word to the patrons of your establishment that I've gone to the high country for a visit with some old mountain man friends up there."

"Certainly, Smoke, but wouldn't you like another pair of Colts to help you when Sundance finally comes for you? Knowing his character, or complete lack thereof, as we both do, I'm certain he's going to come with lots of company."

Smoke shook his head and put out the cigarette as Andre served his breakfast. "No thanks, Louis. I 'preciate the offer, but the more men he brings up into my country, the worse off he'll be. Easier to sow confusion and doubt when there's a crowd."

Louis put down his knife and fork and pulled a huge, black cigar out of his vest pocket. He lit it and blew a large, blue cloud of cigar smoke at the ceiling. "Yes, I understand your strategy. Still, someone to watch your back might not be inappropriate.''

Smoke grinned. ''Things must be awfully slow around here. You sound bored to me, Louis.''

''Well, now that you mention it, there has been a notable lack of excitement in Big Rock lately. I'm afraid that word has gotten out that this is Smoke Jensen's town and the rowdier element bypasses us for more suitable entertainment.'' He took another pull on the stogie, ''Hell, I may have to move to a livelier town before dry-rot sets in. I haven't drawn my gun in anger in several months. I'm afraid I'm getting out of practice.''

Before Smoke could answer, there came the sound of a gunshot from the direction of the Emporium, and Smoke and Louis bolted out the door together.

Sally was standing in front of the store, holding her short-barrelled .44 in front of her. One sleeve of her shirt was torn, a man lay doubled over the hitching post, blood dripping from a hole between his eyes and out of the enormous gap in the back of his head, and four other men were standing arrayed around her, hands near their guns.

Smoke, Louis, and Sheriff Monte Carson, carrying a sawed-off shotgun, arrived at the same time. Smoke went to stand beside Sally, fire in his eyes. ''What happened, Sally?''

She inclined her head toward the dead man. ''This . . . fellow,'' she spat with distaste, ''saw me carrying some packages out of the Emporium and thought if he offered to help, that gave him other rights, too.''

One of the saddlebums pointed his finger at Sally and shouted, ''She kilt our friend. He wasn't doin' nothin', jest bein' friendly, that's all.''

The man next to him joined in. ''Yeah, now she's gonna get a whuppin'.''

Smoke's smile didn't include his eyes. ''Oh? And just which one of you thinks he's man enough to do it?''

The biggest one of the four, a man well over six and a half feet tall and weighing two hundred and fifty pounds, hitched his thumb in his belt and stepped forward. ''I figure I'm man enough. I see you're wearing a mighty fancy shootin' rig, but I'm wondering jist how good you are with your fists?''

Smoke looked at Sally. ''Did any of these men bother you?''

She shook her head. ''No, but the tall one there was encouraging the other one to show me what a real man is like. As if he knew!'' She looked at the big man and spat in his face.

He sleeved the saliva off and backhanded Sally, almost knocking her down. He raised his hands when suddenly he was looking down the barrels of Smoke's and Louis's Colts and Monte's shotgun with both hammers eared back. ''Hey wait a minute,'' he cried. ''She started it.''

Smoke holstered his pistol and put his hand on top of Louis's gun, pushing it down. ''Hold on, Louis, Monte. Killing this big, brave man who hits women is too fast and too painless for him. Let me show him what happens to men who abuse women in this country.''

He took his gun belt off and handed it to Louis, first removing his padded, black gloves and putting them on. He stepped into the street and waved the man toward him.

The big fellow spit in his hands and rubbed them together. ''What rules you want to fight by?'' he asked.

Smoke raised his eyebrows. ''Rules? I promise to quit hitting you after you're dead. That's the only rule I fight by.''

The man grinned, showing yellow, rotten teeth. ''Good. My kinda fight.'' He showed no finesse, just put his hands up and walked toward Smoke, evidently counting on his size to overpower the shorter man. He hadn't noted the size of Smoke's biceps, as big around as most men's necks, or his forearms, steel-hard from years of labor in the mountain woods.

When he was within arm's reach, he took a big round-house swing that would have taken Smoke's head off if it had connected. Instead, Smoke ducked under the blow and swung a straight right punch with all of his weight behind it into the cowboy's exposed right kidney.

Everyone present could hear the snap of the lower two ribs on that side, even over the man's grunt of pain. As he doubled over, Smoke stepped in close and clipped him behind the right ear with a left cross, spinning the giant around with his back to Smoke.

When he straightened up and turned around, he was holding a knife he had pulled from his boot. Blood was running down the right side of his face from his ear, and he was canted over to the side, cradling his broken ribs with his arm. He extended his knife hand and rushed at Smoke, screaming incoherently.

Smoke leaned to the side as he rushed past and planted the toe of his boot in the man's ample paunch, burying it all the way to the spurs. The man bent over, heaving his breakfast onto the street. Smoke grabbed a handful of hair in one hand and his chin in the other, and twisted. The bully's neck broke with a loud snap like dry wood and he fell dead on his face in the dirt.

Smoke looked at the cowboy's friends. "Only a man with a death wish brings a knife to a fist fight. Now you gents have two choices. You can apologize to the lady and ride out of town, or I can put my guns on and you can spend eternity eating dirt in boot hill over there."

with downcast eyes, the cowboys all told Sally they were sorry before they mounted their horses and began to ride down the street. Smoke went over to the horse trough and splashed water on his face. He turned to get his pistols from Louis and was startled to see Louis draw his Colt in a blur and fire right over Smoke's head.

He whirled. One of the cowboys had turned his horse around and was riding back toward Smoke with a pistol in his hand. He was blown out of the saddle by Louis's shot. The snap shot had taken the man in the throat and almost decapitated him. The other two wasted no time in high-tailing it out of town.

Smoke turned to Louis with upraised eyebrows. "I thought you were out of practice, old friend."

Louis frowned. "I am. I was aiming between his eyes."

Smoke put his arm around his shoulders. "No problem, he was just taller than you remembered, that's all."

Smoke helped Sally up into the buckboard and they rode out of Big Rock with a wave.

Louis said to Monte Carson, "Monte, would you care to join me for a drink?"

Monte sleeved the sweat off his forehead and shouldered his shotgun. "Sure would, Louis. All this excitement has given me a powerful dry I need to wet."

Louis looked after the couple leaving town. "Sheriff, you ever seen anyone with hands as fast as Smoke's?"

Monte winked. "Nope. He's faster than a hound dog goin' after a bone, all right. Main difference is, though, that ole mountain dog is all bite and no bark!"

Chapter Seven

Sundance stood on a small knoll near the grove of cotton-woods he had designated as a meeting place for his lieutenants and their men. They arrived an hour before and were now drinking coffee by the gallon, most of them trying without much success to sober up and get rid of their hangovers.

El Gato brought twelve men with him, all *pistoleros,* with no Anglos among them. He was most proud of Carlito Suarez, a man he called *Perro Muerte,* the hound of death. Suarez, according to El Gato, had killed so many men he could not keep track of them on his fingers and toes. He carried two pistols, each facing butt forward, and the usual crossed bando-liers holding spare cartridges, and had an ancient '73 Winches-ter slung over his shoulder that looked as if it had seen better days. He was said to be able to knock the eye out of an eagle in flight with the rifle. We'll see, thought Sundance, with some skepticism. The remainder of El Gato's men were the usual assortment of scruffy looking Mexican *bandido* types. Heavy moustaches that drooped low, uncut, scraggly hair and beards, and a smell of onions and unwashed flesh that made Sundance's nose curl when they came upwind of him.

Toothpick brought ten men with him. They were a mixed

bunch, mostly Anglos with a few Mexicans thrown in. They were all hard cases, and Sundance recognized several faces from Wanted posters he had seen around towns in south Texas. One-Eye Jordan, wearing a patch over his left eye, was wanted for robbery, rape, and murder in at least four towns that Sundance knew of. He wore only one gun, but was reputed to be as quick as a rattlesnake with it, and just as likely as the dreaded serpent to strike without provocation. It was said he lost his eye in a fight, gouged out by his opponent's thumb. Jordan, according to local legend, had bitten the man's thumb off and swallowed it before killing him.

Another of Toothpick's gang was Curly Bill Cartwright. This angelic-faced kid was no more than eighteen years old, and looked only fourteen. He was, however, a stone-cold killer whose pretty face was inhabited by eyes as dead as dirt, and the same color. He was reputed to kill without mercy and could use a knife as well as a pistol.

One of his Mexicans was called Chiva, which Sundance didn't understand. The word *chiva* was like *cabron,* one of the worst insults you could give a Mexican. He later learned it meant not only cuckold, but also scurrilous outlaw, or thoroughly bad *hombre.* Chiva was all of that. He had a scar from ear to ear, and was said to have choked to death with his bare hands the man who gave it to him, after the gent had cut his throat. He never smiled and rarely talked, just sat constantly worrying his knife blade on an old whetstone. Sundance could see why he and Toothpick had teamed up together.

Lightning Jack Warner brought fourteen men, all Anglos and all sporting distinctly Southern accents. Several still wore parts of Confederate Army uniforms and smelled as if they hadn't bathed or washed their clothes since the end of the war. These men eyed the Mexicans nervously and acted as if they would rather fight them than make some money. One of his men, simply called Bull, was one of the biggest, widest men Sundance had ever seen. He made even El Gato seem small. He rode a horse that must have been seventeen hands and it looked like a pony between his legs. In spite of his size, he had a high, almost girlish voice with a bit of a lisp. God help the man, or men, who mentioned it, however. His hands were so big it was hard for him to handle a six-gun; his fingers wouldn't fit in the trigger guard. He carried a pair of twelve gauge shotguns cut down to fourteen inches long. He wore a homemade rig for his converted shotguns with two holsters fitted to a belt like scabbards for pistols. It was said that he was as fast with his scatterguns as most men with Colts. He made his own loads for the shells out of wire, glass, and cut off heads of horseshoe nails. His effective range was only about twenty yards, but it was a rare man who could hit the side of a barn with a Colt at a greater distance. His friends bragged that anything Bull shot at he hit, and anything Bull hit, he killed. He was known to have been wounded eleven times, three in one battle, and had never gone down from his injuries. Either too mean, or too stupid to die, thought Sundance.

Sundance stood on his knoll and whistled shrilly to get the gunmen's attention. Several, those with hangovers of larger than average proportions, winced and held their heads, or just lay on the ground with their eyes shut. *"Compadres* and partners. I don't know what the men who brought you here told you, but if you ride with me, you'll either become rich, or you'll die."

A few of the men stopped cleaning their guns or drinking their coffee and looked up with puzzled expressions.

Sundance paced as he spoke, waving his arms with excitement. "Together, we can form the most feared gang the West has ever seen. We can rob and pillage and steal anything we want. We can go wherever we want, and no town, no marshal, no sheriff can stand against us. For every man we lose in battle, we'll have two more who want to join the Sundance Morgan gang. We'll move fast and strike hard. No one will be safe and nobody will know where we're going to hit next."

One of the Southerners stood and shouted, "Okay, now we know how we'll die. Just how will we get rich?"

Sundance laughed. "A man after my own heart. We'll split the proceeds of every job equally among us. Even though I will plan the jobs and our raids. I will take no more than anyone else. We are all equals where money is concerned." He paused, and walked a few steps in silence before turning back to the group. "On this there can be no disagreement, however. I'll be the boss and I'll call the shots—where we go, who we hit, and when we leave camp. Are there any questions about that?"

One of the *pistoleros* who had come into camp with El Gato came to his feet. He had an Army Colt in his hand and was idly spinning the cylinder. "I got a question. Why should we, *los pistoleros,* take orders from *un gabacho?*"

Sundance smiled and cocked his head. "Excuse me," he said with sarcasm, "but what does *gabacho* mean?"

The Mexican grinned insolently. "Is not so nice word for *gringo,* my friend."

Without hesitation, Sundance drew and fired in an instant, his bullet taking the man in the forehead and blowing brains and blood all over his friends behind him. The gunman stood there for a moment with a surprised look on what was left of his face, before he toppled into the dust.

Sundance aimed his Colt in the air. "What do you call a dead Mexican?" he shouted. When no one moved, he yelled, "The same thing you call a dead American. A corpse!" He shook his head and spread his arms to include all of the men gathered under the cottonwood trees. "We are all *compadres* here, we are all *companeros,* we are all partners. There is no race or religion in this gang. We will fight together, whore together, and live or die together." His expression turned fierce. "Anyone who can't live with that can leave now, or be killed later. It's your choice."

Most of the group cheered and waved their bandannas in the air or fired off their pistols. A few of Lightning Jack's Southerners got on their mounts and rode off silently, and a couple of Mexicans took their horses and went toward the Rio Bravo just beyond the trees. Overall, Sundance thought, he now had a gang of better than thirty of the meanest, lowest, and most deadly men in the state of Texas riding with him.

He aimed his pistol at a grove of trees nearby. "Over there, I've got two cases of tequila and two cases of whiskey. What say we have a few drinks to settle our partnership and help cut the trail dust?"

A great shout of joy erupted and the men all scrambled to get a bottle, get some shade, and get alkalied.

It was almost sundown by the time Smoke and Sally made it to a small station on the Rocky Mountain Line railroad tracks that served as the closest point to Sugarloaf where they could board an east-bound train. The station consisted of a small, one-room cabin and loading platform, with a pole to hang a lantern on to signal the engineer to stop.

Smoke lit the lantern, hung it on the pole, and settled back to await the train's arrival. He built a cigarette and poured himself and Sally a small dollop of whiskey to cut the ever-present dust.

Sally took his cigarette between her fingers and pulled a drag, then took a small sip of liquor. As she exhaled, she looked at him. "I'm going to miss you, Smoke," she said huskily.

He took her hand. "I'm going to miss you, too, honey." He smiled, "but I'll tell you this, the boys are going to miss you almost as much. Cookie just doesn't know his way around a kitchen nearly as well as you do. They'll all probably lose weight while you're gone."

She leaned away from him and gave a mock frown. "Oh, so it's just my cooking you're going to miss, huh?"

He placed a huge callused palm against her cheek and gently pulled her face to his. Kissing her lightly, he said, "Now, you know that's not true. I value your cleaning and washing just as much as your cooking. I won't hardly have any clean clothes by the time you get back."

Without warning, her eyes flashed and she punched him in the stomach. "You keep talking like that, and I may just decide not to return to my old mountain man at all, Smoke Jensen!"

They both laughed and hugged each other tightly. The remaining time until the train arrived was spent saying those things that a man and woman who are deeply in love say to one another when they are about to be separated for a lengthy time.

Finally, as the sun was sinking below the mountains to the

west, a locomotive chugged toward the tiny station and pulled to a stop amid squealing wheels, belching clouds of steam. Smoke loaded Sally's luggage into the baggage car, then helped her up the steps and to a seat in the passenger section. A final kiss, a quick caress of her face, and he was gone.

In typical mountain man fashion, Smoke didn't watch the train as it took his beloved far away. He put her and that tender part of his life out of his mind and concentrated on the task before him: luring Sundance into the mountains and dealing with him in his usual manner—as harshly as he knew how.

He drove the buckboard toward peaks to the north. After driving roughly ten miles, he unhitched and ground-reined the two horses, made a small cold-camp, and ate his supper of jerked beef, cold biscuits, and a small sip of whiskey to wash it down. He rolled one cigarette while lying on his back gazing at the stars, then he dropped off to sleep. He wanted to get an early start at dawn.

Smoke figured he was at seven thousand feet when he decided the buckboard had carried him far enough. He unharnessed his team and pulled the buckboard off the trail into the brush. He donned his buckskins, moccasins, and leggings, fixed his pack of supplies on one of the horses, and put his saddle on the other. Now he was ready for the final portion of his journey, to get to the up-high where the old cougars, his mountain man friends, camped and lived most of their lives.

As the sun peaked over the mountains and began to burn off the early-morning fog, Pearlie yawned, stretched, and scratched. Padding over to the stove in the center of the bunkhouse, he started a fire to get some coffee heating.

He stropped his razor and began to scrape at the stubble on his face, gasping as he splashed the near-freezing water over his cheeks. Holy Jesus, he thought, the summers are short in this high country.

While combing his unruly hair, he noticed in the mirror that

Cal's bed was empty. "Hmmm, ain't like that boy to be first outta his bunk," he mumbled. It was no secret among the hands that Cal liked to sleep almost as much as Pearlie liked to eat. He pulled on his boots and jeans and shirt and hurried out into the chilly fall air.

Cal was just putting his boot in his stirrup when Pearlie came out of the bunkhouse.

"Whoa there, Cal. Just back on outta that saddle and tell me what you figger you're doin'."

Cal blushed a dark crimson. "Well, uh, I'm goin' for a ride."

"I can see that, boy, I ain't blind. Where are ya' aimin' on ridin' to, and why are ya' takin' off a'fore breakfast?"

"I'm just going to go up into the hills around the ranch, to, uh, look around a bit."

Pearlie walked to Cal's horse, a small buckskin Palouse with blood-red spots on its rump. He ran his hand over the .22 rifle in the saddle boot and over a bedroll and full saddlebags behind the cantle. "Uh-huh. And I'm gonna go on a diet, too!" Pearlie shook his head. "What's goin' on, young'un?" He put his finger in front of Cal's face and wiggled it. "And don't you try and feed your uncle Pearlie any bull-splat, neither."

Cal's face got a determined look on it and he hitched his pants up and pulled his hat down. "I'm plannin' on ridin' up in the mountains and helpin' Smoke out when those *bandidos* come up after him."

"You figger that pea-shooter," Pearlie said, pointing to Cal's .22 rifle, "and that little .36 caliber Navy Colt you're sportin' is gonna help the big man?"

Smoke's first pistol had been a Navy Model Colt .36 caliber, and when Cal came to work for him, Smoke unpacked his old gun and gave it to Cal, figuring a smaller caliber would be easier on the young boy's arm.

Smoke had been right, for Cal became a dead shot with the handgun, though Pearlie and some of the other hands teased him that it was so small it would only irritate and anger whoever he shot. Cal had replied that any gun good enough for Smoke was good enough for him—and besides, the folks Smoke had shot with it surely died as dead as those he shot with his .44's.

Cal's blush deepened and spread to include his ears. "You're damn right, Pearlie. Maybe I don't carry the biggest artillery in the territory, but I can damn sure hit what I aim at, and that's what counts in a gunfight."

Pearlie grinned, raising his eyebrows. "Oh, and how do you know what counts in a gunfight?"

Cal raised his chin and assumed a haughty look. " 'Cause that's what Smoke tole me counts."

"Well, it don't matter none no-how, 'cause I can't let you go. Smoke said we was to hang here at the ranch and make sure the beeves and horses are all right."

"Well, it does matter, and I'm damn sure goin'."

Pearlie glared at the boy. "No you're not, not as long as you work for this spread, and not as long as I'm ramrod."

"Then I quit, 'cause I don't intend for Smoke to fight a gang of hardcases all by hisself."

Pearlie rolled his eyes and gritted his teeth until his jaws ached. What was he going to do, he thought. Smoke would flay him alive if he let Cal go up into those mountains alone, especially with a madman like Sundance Morgan on the prowl. "Okay, okay, just wait a minute and let me think."

He went into the bunkhouse and poured himself a cup of coffee to get his juices going, and built himself a cigarette. He sat on the small bunkhouse porch and smoked and drank his coffee while trying to figure out what Smoke would want him to do, short of hogtying the kid to keep him out of trouble.

Finally, he thought of a way to handle the situation that just might let him keep his job, and his hide. "Okay, Cal. Here's the deal. I'm gonna get you a rifle that'll do more than just piss those polecats off, then we're gonna get supplied up plenty good, an' we're both gonna go up in the high country and look for Smoke." He held up his palm to halt Cal's ear-to-ear grin. "Hold on there. Unless I miss my guess, when we find Smoke, he's gonna kick your butt all over them mountains and send us right back down here, but I'm gonna give you a chance to talk him into lettin' us lend him a hand."

"Great, then let's shag the trail. We're burnin' daylight."

"Whoa there, bronco. First, I gotta eat, then I gotta get my horse saddled and get Cookie to fix us up with some vittles for the trail, then we gotta get you a man's gun for that saddle boot.''

He rubbed his chin in thought. "I figure we got an old Winchester '73 around here. It shoots .44's so you'll have to carry double ammunition since you cain't use those .36's your little pea-shooter needs."

"That's okay. You go get Cookie to get your breakfast, an' I'll pack your horse and get the rifle and extra ammunition outta the tack room, and we'll be ready to get gone as soon as you finish stuffin' your face."

Pearlie shook his head and mumbled something about angels rushing in as he walked over toward the main cabin to get Cookie started on breakfast and their provisions.

Chapter Eight

Sundance lay on his belly in the moonlight on a small bluff overlooking a Mexican *hacienda*. He and his lieutenants, Toothpick, El Gato, and Lightning Jack, had decided to strike one of the rich Mexican ranches near the border for their first target. Sundance explained this was important for two reasons. First, the American authorities were notoriously lax in prosecuting crimes that occurred in Mexico. And, second, he wanted to test his gang in an area where there was likely to be only token resistance.

El Gato told Sundance that he knew of just such a place. A distant cousin of his, Enrique Hernandez, owned a fine spread a few miles from Laredo. Since the outbreak of fever in the cattle of the region, Hernandez had let most of his *vaqueros* go in order to conserve his cash until such time as healthy beeves could be bought to replenish his herd.

Sundance asked, "Why would you want us to hit one of your relatives, El Gato?"

El Gato's eyes burned with hatred. "The filthy *bastardo*." He spit on the ground at Sundance's feet. "He turned his back when El Gato asked for help. *Federales* wanted to hang El

Gato, so I asked Senor Hernandez to hide me. He refused. Called me, how you say in English, garbage!''

"Is he wealthy?''

"That *cabron* has more money than *El Presidente de Mexico.*'' El Gato frowned. "And he does not even give moneys to church.''

Toothpick grinned around a *cigarillo* dangling from his mouth. "And you, my friend. Do you give to the church?''

El Gato's lips curled in an evil smirk. "Me? I am but a poor *peon.* God made church to help *peons.*'' He shrugged. "When I come to *El casa de Dios,* is to take moneys from poor box. Is what is for.''

Sundance interrupted. "But what about Hernandez? I don't want to rob his place and end up with a handful of paper *pesos.*''

"*No, el Patron* does not deal in paper moneys. He keeps *oro* at his *hacienda* because that is what is required by *Americano* cattle buyers and sellers.''

Lightning Jack grunted. "Gold? Well, like I always said, it's easier to liberate gold from a man's poke than it is to dig it outta the ground. Let's go for it.''

It was almost midnight as the moon reached its zenith over the northern Mexican desert. The sky was clear and the moonlight reflecting off the sand made the night as bright as day. Sundance lay on the parched caliche of the bluff, which was still warm from the scorching daylight sun even though the air was chilly. He was peering through his binoculars at Hernandez's ranch below. "I don't see no lights nor any activity. He doesn't 'pear to have any guards out.''

El Gato snarled. "The old man thinks he safe because is far from town.''

Sundance got to his feet, brushing dirt off his pants and elbows. "Okay, this is it, then. El Gato, take your men to the bunkhouse and have them ready to bust in on my signal. Lightning Jack and the rest of the men will surround the house in case any of the family wants to make a stand there.''

"What are you gonna be doin', boss?" asked Lightning Jack.

Sundance's teeth glowed in the moonlight. "Me? Why, Toothpick and me're goin' into the house and see if Senor Hernandez won't agree to make a donation to the Sundance Morgan gang."

"And if'n he don't?"

Toothpick pulled his knife from its scabbard and licked the blade, causing it to shine and reflect the moon. "Then me and Baby here will have a talk with him."

After his men were positioned, Sundance and Toothpick walked their horses up to the front of the *hacienda* and dismounted, Sundance draping a coil of rope over his shoulders. They tried the door, but it wouldn't open. Toothpick inserted his blade into the doorjam and gently lifted, raising a wooden bar blocking their way.

Easing into the house, they began to search it room by room, aided by the moonlight streaming through windows. They found three young males, looking like they ranged in age from twelve to eighteen, and two females of about thirteen and sixteen sleeping soundly in their beds. Taking several pistols from the bedrooms, they continued their search until they came to the master bedroom.

Hernandez and his wife were asleep, covered only by a light sheet, curtains billowing in the gentle night breeze. Hernandez appeared to be in his early fifties, while his wife looked to be no more than forty. Toothpick used the point of his knife to gently pull the sheet down, revealing a full-figured woman clad only in a sheer nightshirt. He licked his lips and grinned at Sundance, raising his eyebrows.

Sundance put the barrel of his Colt against Hernandez's temple and thumbed back the hammer. The loud click brought the man instantly awake, his hand reaching under his pillow. Sundance drew back and rapped him sharply in the face with the gun, breaking his nose with a cracking noise and awakening his wife.

She opened her mouth, but gasped and swallowed her scream when Toothpick stuck the point of his blade against her throat, drawing a small drop of blood which rolled slowly down her neck. The crimson liquid appeared black against her pale skin in the moonlight.

Hernandez's eyes rolled frantically, as Sundance removed a large-bore *pistola* from underneath his pillow, his shattered nose streaming blood all over his chest. "What do you *gringos* want?" he asked urgently in English.

"First of all, we're not *gringos,* we're outlaws, and we want your gold."

He shook his head, wincing at the pain it caused. "I have no gold. You must be mistaken."

"Oh?" Sundance asked politely. "Then, I guess we'll just be on our way."

Toothpick glanced across the bed at him, a puzzled expression on his face.

"Of course," Sundance continued in the same quiet tone, "if there's no gold for my *compadres,* they're probably gonna be very angry." He let the terrified rancher see his eyes shift to his wife. "I may have to let them amuse themselves some other way, just to keep them in line."

"Bastardos! My *vaqueros* will cut you to pieces if you harm anyone in this house!"

"Oh yes, I almost forgot about your men." Sundance, keeping his pistol trained at Hernandez, walked to the window and pulled back the curtains. He whistled shrilly, his signal to Lightning Jack and his men.

From the direction of the bunkhouse came the sound of a door splintering, followed immediately by twin booming explosions of Lightning Jack's big scattergun and the staccato popping of pistols in the night. There were several screams and shouts at first, then only moaning and crying and pleas for mercy could be heard. After a few isolated shots, even the moaning stopped, replaced by an ominous silence.

The bedroom door burst open and the Hernandez children rushed into the room, brought to a halt by the sight of their parents lying on the bed under the gun and knife of the intruders.

Sundance pulled Hernandez out of bed by his hair, and ushered the entire family into a large room in the center of the *hacienda.* He tied Hernandez and his three sons with the rope he brought with him, and sat them on the floor in front of a huge fireplace dominating one wall. His wife and daughters were left huddled in a group in the middle of the room, crying and weeping and clinging together in fear.

El Gato and Lightning Jack sauntered in, Jack reloading his shotgun as he walked. "The men're all taken care of, boss. How're ya'll doin' in here?"

"We got a small problem here, Lightning. Senor Hernandez says he don't have no gold."

El Gato's eyes narrowed and he walked rapidly over to stand before the bleeding man. "No gold?" he asked, his voice thick with sarcasm.

Hernandez glared hate at Gato. "*Bastardo!*" he whispered under his breath.

El Gato kicked him in the stomach, causing him to double over and vomit on the tile floor. His wife and daughters screamed and began to wail even louder. His sons' faces contorted with hate and anger at the big Mexican standing over their father.

"*Viejo! Donde esta el oro?*" El Gato snarled.

"*Chingale, animale!*" Hernandez gasped from his position lying on his side in his vomit.

"Toothpick!" Sundance inclined his head at Hernandez's wife and daughters. Toothpick grinned and drew his blade. He walked to the woman and girls and one by one, slit their nightshirts. Their clothing fell to the floor, leaving them naked and cowering under the lustful gazes of the *desperados*.

Toothpick holstered his knife, put his left arm around Mrs. Hernandez's shoulders, and fondled her breasts with his right hand, whispering filth in her ear about what he was going to do to her.

Tears filled Hernandez's eyes and he hung his head, defeated. "*Si*, you win. If I tell you where the gold is, will you let my family live?"

Sundance squatted in front of the man. "No, I gotta be honest with you, Senor Hernandez. But I will give them a quick and painless death." He shrugged and cocked his head, as if bestowing a favor to a friend. "That's about all you can hope for at this point after lying to us about the gold and all."

Mrs. Hernandez, in a strangled voice whispered, "The gold is in a chest in the bedroom, under some blankets."

Senor Hernandez sobbed and closed his eyes and began to pray softly.

"El Gato, check it out," Sundance ordered, without moving from his position in front of Hernandez.

After a moment, El Gato returned, dragging behind him a chest that was heavy enough to leave gouge marks in the tile floor.

"Senor Sundance, I think we very, very rich now!"

Sundance smiled a kind smile, then drew his pistol and put the barrel against Hernandez's forehead. "You thought with all that preacher-talk old man?"

Hernandez opened his eyes and looked up at Sundance, then he grinned defiantly and spit in his face. Enraged, Sundance cocked and fired, the sound magnified by the room's walls, blowing parts of Hernandez's head into the fireplace, splattering blood and bits of hair and brains all over the wall.

As his sons' eyes spread wide in terror, El Gato pulled both his Colts and emptied them into the boys, the banging of his guns filling the house, making them jump and contort as the hot lead tore through their flesh. The bodies quivered and spasmed for a moment, then became still as death claimed them one at a time.

Sundance sighed and punched out his empty shell, reloading the cylinder as he walked toward the women. "I said we share the money equally, but not necessarily the . . . spoils." He grasped the thirteen-year-old daughter by the back of her neck and pushed her ahead of him toward one of the bedrooms. He called over his shoulder, "You and the rest of the men can take turns with the other two, but I plan to be with this one until dawn. If I finish early, I'll let you know."

As the women continued to cry and moan, Lightning Jack dragged Mrs. Hernandez into a side room, while El Gato grabbed the sixteen-year-old by her hair and pulled her outside to a spot in the yard of the *hacienda* where the rest of the gang waited.

Soon the night was filled with terrified screams from the women and grunts and howls of animalistic passion from the men.

Chapter Nine

The sun was kissing the tops of the western peaks of the Rockies when Pearlie held his hand up and said to Cal, "Well, it's 'bout time to fix us a camp and let the horses blow. The air's pretty thin up here and there's no need to overdo it on our first day."

Cal shook his head. "Pearlie, we got another hour 'fore full dark yet. We can get another few miles, if'n we keep on goin'."

Pearlie narrowed his eyes at the youngster. "Cal, you don't know squat about travelin' in the high country." He walked his horse up to the bank of a small mountain stream gurgling in the twilight, leaned back as the horse dipped his head to drink, and crossed his leg over his saddle horn. He tilted his hat back and began to build himself a cigarette as he talked. "First of all, night comes quick in the up-high, a lot faster'n you think. Second, it takes time to get a camp ready and that's no fun in the dark."

He scratched a match to flame on his pants leg and lit his cigarette, sighing as he exhaled. "There's wood for the fire to gather, water to get to boilin' fer coffee, and since we neglected to take a proper nooning, I've got a powerful hunger on."

"But—"

"No buts, boy. This time of year it's gonna get might near freezin' up here, and I don't intend to turn into no icicle just so's we kin get to Smoke a little sooner." He took his hat off and sleeved the trail dust off his forehead. "Now, you wanted to come up here, so you'll listen to someone who knows just a mite more than you do about travelin' and campin' in the mountains."

He slid off his horse and tied the reins to a small bush near good grass so the horse could graze awhile. "You go gather up some wood—dry, not too green—and I'll arrange a few rocks and build us a campfire that'll work to cook us some dinner and keep us from freezing tonight." He scowled and looked around at the heavy woods surrounding their camp area. "Hell, maybe it'll even keep grizzlies and wolves from eatin' us while we sleep."

After they got the fire burning, and Pearlie sliced and fried some pork fatback and beans and made a pot of coffee and a batch of pan bread, the pair hobbled the horses to stay near camp and settled into their bedrolls in front of the fire.

Pearlie rolled himself a cigarette, then pitched the makings to Cal. "Go ahead and fill you a blanket, after-supper coffee's a lot better with a cigarette." He smiled, "Course, a dollop or two of whiskey in it don't hurt none neither, but I guess we'll do without that tonight."

It took Cal a couple of tries, but finally he put together a makeshift cigarette and lit it off a burning twig from the fire. A deep cough, a gasp, and he was into his first cigarette.

"Pearlie . . ."

"Yeah, kid?"

"How much do you know about Smoke's past?"

Pearlie raised his eyebrows and glanced over at Cal. "Why? You figgerin' to write one of those Penny Dreadfuls like those tenderfeet back East are always doin'?"

Cal took another drag on his smoke and coughed and hacked for a while before he could answer. "Naw, nothin' like that. It's just that ever since Smoke and Miss Sally took me on as a hand, I've been hearin' stories that's hard to believe. Things like he's kilt over two hundred men and all. I's just wonderin' how much of that's true, is all.''

Pearlie chuckled. ''Boy, you kin take anythin' ya' hear 'bout Smoke Jensen and double it, and you might be close to the truth. That *hombre* is a full sixteen hands high and that's no exaggeration.''

''Well, I'm not near sleepy yet. How 'bout you tellin' me what you know about him?''

Pearlie sighed. ''Okay, move that Arbuckles off the fire so it don't git bitter and let me get another butt goin' and I'll tell ya what I know.''

Cal grinned. ''So it don't git bitter? Hell, I almost had to cut it outta the cup with my knife to drink it.''

''Boy, that's real mountain man coffee. If you're gonna run with the big dogs, ya gotta be prepared to eat 'n drink the way they do.'' He held out his cup. ''Now pour me another swig or two and settle back in you're covers for the damndest tale you ever heared.''

Pearlie lay back against his saddle, lit another cigarette, and blew smoke at the stars as he thought about how to begin. ''A few years back, I was in the employ of a man who made the biggest mistake of his life. He decided to go up against Smoke Jensen. After a while, I found I couldn't stomach the things that man was askin' me to do, so I switched sides and joined up with Smoke and his friends.''

''You mean Smoke let you come over to his side after you'd been against him?''

''Yep. Matter of fact, t'was Smoke's idea in the first place. He asked me if'n I was happy workin' fer a scumbag like Franklin. When I said I wasn't, he said he always had room on his payroll for a good worker. So I packed my warbag an' left the same day.''

''What happened then? Was your previous boss mad about you leavin' and all?''

Pearlie snorted as he refilled his tin cup with coffee. He took another puff off his cigarette and as the smoke trailed from his nostrils he continued his story. ''You bet your boots he was plenty pissed at me. He sent a group of the men riding for his brand after me and they shot me up a little bit, then dragged me to hell and back through cactus and rocks and such.''

His eyes narrowed as he recalled how he had to walk almost ten miles with two bullets in him to get to Smoke's place and help. ''Well, Smoke had Doc Spalding yank those lead peas outta my hide, and then put me up in a boarding house in Big Rock to give me time to heal.''

The memory of the pain he went through made his voice husky and he took a long drink of the steaming coffee to clear it. ''That's when I first met Louis Longmont, a long-time *compadre* of Smoke's.

''You mean that dandy gamblin' feller that owns the saloon in Big Rock?''

Pearlie grinned. ''One and the same, though he's no dandy. He's might near the fastest man with a short-gun I ever seen, 'cept for Smoke, o'course. Anyway, he admired the way I stood up to Franklin and took to visitin' me ever day and we'd kinda get to talkin', mostly 'bout Smoke.'' He took a last drag and flipped the butt into the fire. ''Seems he was pretty close friends with Preacher and knew Smoke when he came out West, when he was just a young'un. These stories I'm 'bout to relate to you are the same ones he tole me.''

He shook his head. ''Hell, sittin' here jawin' has got me so jiggered on all that *cafecito* that I'm never gonna git to sleep.'' He rolled to the side and took a pint of whiskey from his saddlebag, hesitated a moment, then poured a small measure in Cal's cup and a much larger one in his.

Cal's eyes got big and he sucked air in his mouth after his drink. ''Whew-eee! That's mighty stout stuff,'' he rasped.

Pearlie chuckled. ''If'n it ain't hairy, it's not worth drinkin'. Now here's what Longmont tole me about Smoke's first years here in the high lonesome, and some of the adventures he and that ole' mountain man, Preacher, had.

''Smoke's dad, Emmett, came back from the War Between the States in the summer of 1865, when Smoke, who was known as Kirby then, was only about fourteen or fifteen years old. Emmett sold their scratch-dirt farm in Missouri, packed up their belongin's, and they headed north by northwest.''

"Why'd they do that?"

"That'll become clear later in the story, but Smoke's dad didn't even tell him why they were goin' west at that time. Anyway, long about Wichita, they met up with an old mountain man who called hisself Preacher. Fer some reason, unknown even to the oldtimer, he took them under his wing when he saw they was as green as new apples, and they traveled together for a spell.

"Soon, they was set upon by a band of Pawnee Injuns, an' Smoke kilt his first couple of men. Longmont says that Preacher tole him he couldn't hardly believe it when he saw Smoke draw that old Navy Colt. Says he knew right off Smoke was destined to become a legend, if'n he lived long enough, that is. That's when Preacher gave young Kirby Jensen his nickname, Smoke, from the smoke that came outta that Navy Colt.

"Right after that, Emmett tole Preacher that he had set out lookin' fer three men who kilt Smoke's brother and stole some Confederate gold. Their names was Wiley Potter, Josh Richards, and Stratton, I don't 'member his first name. Emmett went on to tell Preacher that he was goin' gunnin' fer those polecats, and if'n he didn't come back, he wanted Preacher to take care o' Smoke 'til he was growed up enough to do it fer hisself. Preacher tole Emmett he'd be proud to do that very thing.

"The next day, Emmett took off and left the old cougar to watch after his young'un. They didn't hear nothin' fer a couple of years, time Preacher spent teaching the young buck the ways of the West and how to survive where most men wouldn't. Longmont says Preacher tole him that during that time, though Smoke was about as natural a fast draw and shot as he'd ever seen, the boy spent at least an hour ever day drawing and dry-firin' those Navy Colts he wore."

"Wait a minute," interrupted Cal. "I thought Smoke only had the one Colt. Where'd he get the other one?"

"Oh, I forgot. That first Pawnee brave he kilt was carryin' one, and, naturally, Smoke claimed it fer his own. That's when he started wearin' two guns in that special way he has, with the left 'un butt-forward and the right 'un, butt-backwards.

That's also where he got that big ole sticker he carries in his belt scabbard.''

Pearlie leaned over and refilled Cal's cup, then his own. "And quit interruptin' me if'n you want to hear this story." He drank half the cup down in one draught, fashioned another cigarette, and lay back to continue his tale.

" 'Bout two years later, at Brown's Hole in Idaho, an old mountain man found Smoke and Preacher and tole Smoke his daddy was dead, that those men he went after kilt him. Smoke packed up an' he and Preacher went on the prod.

"They got to Pagosa Springs, that's Injun fer healin' waters, just west of the Needle Mountains, and stopped to replenish their supplies. They rode into Rico, a rough 'n tumble mining camp that back then was an outlaw hangout."

Pearlie took a deep drag of his cigarette, and paused as the smoke drifted toward the stars, imagining how it must have been for the young boy and his old friend in those rough and rowdy days . . .

Smoke and Preacher dismounted in front of the combination trading post and saloon. As was his custom, Smoke slipped the thongs from the hammers of his Colts as soon as his boots hit dirt.

They bought their supplies and turned to leave when the hum of conversation suddenly died. Two rough-dressed and unshaven men, both wearing guns, blocked the door.

"Who owns that horse out there?" one demanded, a snarl in his voice, trouble in his manner. "The one with the SJ brand?"

Smoke laid his purchases on the counter. "I do," he said quietly.

"Which way'd you ride in from?"

Preacher had slipped to his right, his left hand covering the hammer of his Henry, concealing the click as he thumbed it back.

Smoke faced the men, his right hand hanging loose by his

side. His left hand was just inches from his lefthand gun. "Who wants to know—and why?"

No one in the dusty building moved or spoke.

"Pike's my name," the bigger and uglier of the pair said. "And I say you came through my diggin's yesterday and stole my dust."

"And I say you're a liar," Smoke told him.

Pike grinned nastily, his right hand hovering near the butt of his pistol. "Why . . . you little pup. I think I'll shoot your ears off."

"Why don't you try? I'm tired of hearing you shoot your mouth off."

Pike looked puzzled for a few seconds. No one had ever talked to him in this manner. Pike was big, strong, and a bully. "I think I'll just kill you for that."

Pike and his partner reached for their guns.

Four shots boomed in the low-ceilinged room, four shots so closely spaced they seemed as one thunderous roar. Dust and bird's droppings fell from the ceiling. Pike and his friend were slammed out the open doorway. One fell off the rough porch, dying in the dirt street. Pike, with two holes in his chest, died with his back against a support pole, his eyes still open, unbelieving. Neither had managed to pull a pistol more than halfway out of leather.

All eyes in the black powder-filled and dusty, smoky room moved to the young man standing by the bar, a Colt in each hand. "Good God!" a man whispered in awe. "I never even seen him draw."

Preacher moved the muzzle of his Henry to cover the men at the tables. The bartender put his hands slowly on the bar, indicating he wanted no trouble.

"We'll be leaving now," Smoke said, holstering his Colts and picking up his purchases from the counter. He walked out the door slowly.

Smoke stepped over the sprawled, dead legs of Pike and walked past his dead partner.

"What are we 'posed to do with the bodies?" a man asked Preacher.

"Bury 'em."

"What's the kid's name?"

"Smoke."

A few days later, in a nearby town, a friend of Preacher's told Smoke that two men, Haywood and Thompson, who claimed to be Pike's brother, had tracked him and Preacher and were in town waiting for Smoke.

Smoke walked down the rutted street an hour before sunset, the sun at his back—the way he had planned it. Thompson and Haywood were in a big tent at the end of the street, which served as saloon and cafe. Preacher had pointed them out earlier and asked if Smoke needed his help. Smoke said no. The refusal came as no surprise.

As he walked down the street a man glanced up, spotted him, then hurried quickly inside.

Smoke felt no animosity toward the men in the tent saloon: no anger, no hatred. But they came here after him, so let the dance begin, he thought.

Smoke stopped fifty feet from the tent. "Haywood! Thompson! You want to see me?"

The two men pushed back the tent flap and stepped out, both angling to get a better look at the man they had tracked. "You the kid called Smoke?" one said.

"I am."

"Pike was my brother," the heavier of the pair said. "And Shorty was my pal."

"You should choose your friends more carefully," Smoke told him.

"They was just a-funnin' with you," Thompson said.

"You weren't there. You don't know what happened."

"You callin' me a liar?"

"If that's the way you want to take it."

Thompson's face colored with anger, his hand moving closer to the .44 in his belt. "You take that back or make your play."

"There is no need for this," Smoke said.

The second man began cursing Smoke as he stood tensely, legs spread wide, body bent at the waist. "You're a damned thief. You stolt their gold and then kilt 'em."

"I don't want to have to kill you," Smoke said.

"The kid's yellow!" Haywood yelled. Then he grabbed for his gun.

Haywood touched the butt of his gun just as two loud gunshots blasted in the dusty street. The .36 caliber balls struck Haywood in the chest, one nicking his heart. He dropped to the dirt, dying. Before he closed his eyes and death relieved him of the shocking pain by pulling him into a long sleep, two more shots thundered. He had a dark vision of Thompson spinning in the street. Then Haywood died.

Thompson was on one knee, his left hand holding his shattered right elbow. His leg was bloody. Smoke had knocked his gun from his hand, then shot him in the leg.

"Pike was your brother," Smoke told the man. "So I can understand why you came after me. But you were wrong. I'll let you live. But stay with mining. If I ever see you again, I'll kill you."

The young man turned, putting his back to the dead and bloody pair. He walked slowly up the street, his high-heeled Spanish riding boots pocking the air with dusty puddles. *(The Last Mountain Man)*

Cal's eyebrows went up when Pearlie paused in his story to take another sip of whiskey. "How old was he when this happened?"

"I dunno. 'Bout eighteen or so, I guess."

"Jimminy Christmas! That's only a couple 'a years older'n me!"

Pearlie grinned in the darkness. "Yeah, only Smoke was eighteen goin' on thirty, while you're sixteen goin' on ten."

"Aw, Pearlie. That's not fair. I'm pretty good with my irons—you said so yourself."

"No offense meant, kid. Just be glad you ain't never had to kill nobody, it ain't hardly never nothin' to be proud of. You heard how Smoke tried to get those men to back down? He never goes out lookin' fer blood, it just seems to find him more'n most people."

Pearlie turned over, pulled his blanket up over his head, and said, ''Now that's enough stories for one night. Get some shut-eye. Dawn's gonna come earlier than you think, and we got to get on the trail early if'n we're ever gonna ketch up with Smoke.''

Cal stifled a huge yawn. ''Okay, but if'n we don't catch him by tomorrow night, will ya tell me some more 'bout Smoke when he was first startin' out?''

''Yeah, yeah. Now go to sleep!''

Chapter Ten

Smoke smelled a fire long before he could see evidence of it. He figured it was coming from about a mile or so upwind. His horse snorted and shook his head, telling Smoke there was water thereabouts. He stepped out of the saddle and tied his horse and packhorse to a bush where they could graze. Time to get down and dirty, he thought.

He pulled his Henry rifle out of the saddle boot and loosened rawhide hammer thongs on his Colts, then began to creep up the mountain through thick underbrush, toward the fire.

He knew it was much too soon to worry about Sundance and his gang, but in the high lonesome your enemies weren't necessarily known to you. As Preacher had told him on more than one occasion, strangers are always hostile, unless you know both their first and last names.

Moving through the forest so silently most of its wildlife was unaware of his passage, he inched ever closer to the source of a column of woodsmoke above him.

Slowly, so as not to make a sound, he came close to a small clearing and peered from behind a ponderosa pine at the camp. A rough-hewn log cabin of one room sat in the trees. A paint pony grazed nearby, enjoying lush green mountain meadow grass. There was a fire going in front of the shack, with coffee heating on a trestle and a deer haunch roasting on a spit.

Smoke relaxed when he saw the horse, straightened up and walked into the clearing. "Yo, the cabin. Can I join you?" he called, holding his rifle pointed down, his hands in plain sight.

He felt the barrel of a rifle touch his neck seconds after a sixth sense warned him of someone's approach from behind, then a high-pitched chuckle followed. "Heh-heh, thought you's gonna sneak up on old Puma, huh boy?"

Smoke laughed and raised his arms in the air. "Please don't shoot me, Mr. Mountain Man, I'm just a poor pilgrim who's lost his way in the woods."

He turned and the two men embraced, pounding each other on the back, Smoke's pats raising dust and dirt from the old man's buckskins.

"Puma Buck, you old cougar, you get uglier every time I see you," Smoke said around a grin. "And that cayuse has got to be twenty years old if it's a day."

"Smoke Jensen, I thought old Preacher taught you better trail-smarts than that. Hell, I heared you comin' nearly an hour ago, an' that's why I put that there deer on to cook."

Smoke shook his head. "Mighty hard to keep in practice trackin' when you live 'round civilization, Puma. Matter of fact, a body can forget plenty of important lessons if he stays away from the up-high too long."

Puma nodded and threw his arm around Smoke's shoulder, leading him over to the fire. "That's true, boy, that's surely true. Bein' 'round people just purely sucks the smarts right outta a man. Come on, light and set and let me pour you some coffee."

Smoke squatted and held out a tin cup he found near the fire. After Puma filled it, he took a drink. "Yeah, I've missed your cookin' Puma. Been a long time since I had coffee that'd float a horseshoe."

"Takes a long time to cook it just right. Guess you civilized folks don't never take the time to do it right. I been workin' on that pot fer might' near three days now, and it's just about ripe. Maybe another day or two . . ."

Smoke took his knife from its scabbard and sawed a hunk of meat off the deer haunch, handing the first piece to Puma, who took it and nodded his thanks.

There was little more in the way of conversation until both had eaten their fill. Puma grunted once and pitched Smoke some wild onions. They were strong and sweet and went well with wild venison and boiled coffee.

After supper, Smoke trotted back to retrieve his horses and returned to the cabin. The mountain man had his makings out and was about to fashion a cigarette. Smoke said, "Uh-huh, just a minute Puma." He reached in a pouch on his pack horse and pulled out a package wrapped in waxed paper. He pitched it to Puma and stooped to pour himself another cup of coffee.

Puma unwrapped the package and grinned widely, exposing yellow stubs of teeth. "Hoss, it seems like years since I had any store-bought ceegars." He licked one, bit the end off, and lit it with a flaming stick from the fire's edge. "Young'un," he sighed, "this is one of the few things I miss about civilization, ready-made stogies."

He flipped one to Smoke, and they lay back against a log, smoking and drinking coffee and swapping tales until the sun went down and the temperature began to drop.

Puma glanced at clouds covering the peaks turned orange-red by a setting sun. He raised his nose like an old wolf sniffing for his mate. "Smells like snow's on the way. Seems to come earlier and colder every year."

Smoke grunted and grinned in the twilight. "That's just 'cause you're older'n dirt, Puma. You're gettin' a mite long in the tooth to winter up here. Maybe it's time for you to winter in the desert, where the cold don't make your bones as brittle as dead wood."

Puma snorted and ambled into his cabin, returning after a moment with three half-cured bearskin blankets. He threw one over his paint pony and handed the other one to Smoke.

Smoke's nose wrinkled as he wrapped the green hide around his shoulders. "Whew! Puma, you done forgot how to cure skins? This bear's 'bout as ripe as you are."

"That's what's wrong with you city folk. You bathe too

much. That's how I knowed you was a'comin', I smelt soap on you from three miles off, an' me bein' upwind!''

"I brought some extra if'n you'd care to try it."

Puma got a horrified expression on his face. "Hell no. I bathed in the spring. Don't wanna overdo it, might git sick'n die, then who'd be here to teach you the thangs you done forgot 'bout wilderness livin'?''

"Preacher always washed two, maybe three times a year," Smoke answered.

"Yeah, Preacher did git a mite too civilized in his old age. I heared in his later years he kilt a couple'a old boys and didn't even take their hair." He shook his head. "Don't do to git too soft up here or folks'll take 'vantage of ya."

Smoke sobered at the thought of his old mentor. "Puma, do you think Preacher is still alive?''

Puma's gaze shifted to the distant mountains, their snow-covered peaks still burnished pink by the fading sun. "I 'spect so, boy. There's still beaver in them ponds, an' grizzlies still look over their shoulders fer him in fear when they hunt. Ole Preacher ain't about to cross over while there's still game to be had or grizzlies to wrassle." He studied the glowing end of his stogie, blue smoke curling toward stars just becoming visible at dusk. "By the by, speakin' of ole warriors, I heared you was comin' up here to put the war paint on."

Smoke shook his head in wonderment. It amazed him how these old cougars, who thought the up-high was getting too crowded if they saw another white man more than every two or three months, could know what was happening in flat country so soon.

He pitched his cigar into the fire and settled deeper into his bearskin. "Yeah, that's so. A feller back-shot a friend of mine a few years back. I took his ear and sent him on his way with a couple'a ounces of lead in his hide. Now he thinks it's time I paid the fiddler for that little dance."

Puma grimaced. "Shoulda taken his hair, Hoss, then you wouldn't have to be watchin' your back-trail." He took a final drag on his cigar, pinched the ash off, and began to chew the butt. "Man makes hisself enough enemies just livin', without havin' to go out and try to make more."

"I guess so. Preacher told me don't never leave a man alive with your lead in'im. Just makes 'em wanna heal up and give it back to you when you're least 'spectin' it."

Puma chuckled. "Preacher knew which way the stick floats, all right. Took his share o' scalps, too—both white and red." He cut his eyes over at Smoke. "You figger on needin' any hep, or some'un to watch your back in this war your' gettin' ready fer?"

"Well, Preacher also said don't never turn down help when it's offered, though I hope these ole boys are like most flatlanders and don't know nothin' 'bout the high lonesome. I got some surprises planned for 'em that may make 'em think twice 'bout comin' after me."

Puma spit tobacco juice into the fire, making it hiss and crackle. "Don't underestimate the strength of vengeance, Hoss, it be a powerful motivator fer most folks." He spit again. "Gold, women, and blood-feuds kilt more men than all the wars put together. I wouldn't count on those ole boys turning tail and runnin' just cause you tweak their noses a little. You listen to an expert, boy, and don't go halfway. You git a chance, you lift some hair and count some coup, 'cause as sure as beavers build dams, they'll do it to you if'n they can."

"I'll do it, Puma. Now, you think we can get under that shack you call home before my eyeballs freeze, or you gonna stay out here 'til the spring thaw?"

"Heh-heh. You sure be gittin' soft, Smoke. Good thang you come up here to relearn what Preacher and us other ole mountain beavers taught you, afore it's too late. Come on, we'll git covered and git some shuteye and talk more on this war of yours at sunrise." Puma got up slowly and led the way into his cabin.

As snowflakes began to drift down to cover the mountainside in winter's white coat, Smoke snuggled deeper under his bearskins in the unheated room and hoped the coffee he drank wouldn't cause him to have to venture forth into the frigid night air to relieve his bladder.

Lying there, watching his breath frost and disappear in the moonlight coming through a crack in the roof, he began to question what he was doing. "Do I have the right to come up here and endanger my old friends in one of my fights?" he murmured to himself, on the edge of sleep. After all, he thought, he knew when he made his plans to make his final stand in the up-high, mountain men holing up in the area wouldn't permit one of their own to fight against heavy odds alone. Some of the old cougars were likely to get dusted in the upcoming fracas. He considered, for a moment, spreading the word among them that he wanted to kill his own snakes without their help. Of course, he realized almost immediately, that would do no good at all. Asking mountain men, the most independent breed in the world, not to interfere in a fight would almost certainly make them all the more determined to buy chips in his game.

Most of these oldtimers were only a few years shy of going forked-end up anyway, he thought. They'd like nothing more than to go out with rifles and cap and ball pistols in their hands, facing death and spitting in its face.

Sighing, he turned to the side, pulled the skins up over his face, and slid into sleep, still undecided if he was doing the right thing.

After a fitful night of tossing and turning, Smoke awoke before dawn and went out into the snow-covered clearing in front of the cabin. He stoked the campfire embers to life and added more wood, warming his hands in the heat from the flames. He opened his supply pack and took out breakfast makings and began to cook.

A short while later a yawning Puma Buck limped out of the cabin door, cursing his aching bones. "Smoke, I don't know what you're cookin' up over there, but it smells right good enough to eat."

"Light and set, Puma. I made us some *pan dulce,* Mexican sweet bread, fried some bacon and 'taters, and opened a can of sliced peaches for dessert."

Puma glanced over at his paint pony and shook his head.

"Good thang you're not up here very often, Smoke, otherwise old Spot there wouldn't be able to carry me around no more. I'd be so damn overfed I'd break his back."

Smoke poured some steaming coffee into Puma's cup, saying, "Sorry about the bellywash. I had to add a little water 'cause it was so thick it wouldn't come outta the pot."

Puma arched an eyebrow and frowned. "I hope you ain't plumb ruined it, boy. Took a lotta cookin' to git it just right."

To ease his feelings, Smoke cut a chunk of sweetbread out of the skillet and handed the sugary cake to the old man.

Puma tasted it, then smiled and began to chew in earnest.

The pair ate in amiable silence, enjoying the majestic views of mountain peaks, snow-covered valleys and meadows, and white-capped ponderosa pines.

After they finished breakfast, Smoke rolled a cigarette and Puma started on another stogie, both men drinking a final cup of coffee.

Smoke sighed. "You know, Puma, every time I come up here to God's country, I wonder why I ever bother to leave and head back to the flatlands."

Puma grinned, dislodging crumbs of bread from his scraggly beard. "Might be that sweet woman who warms your blankets has more'n a little to do with it."

"She's a big part of it, all right," Smoke agreed. "But I think when this little dust-up is over, I'll bring Sally up here to show her why I can't never get this country outta my heart."

Puma said, "Leave it to Smoke Jensen to call a war with thirty or forty men against him a little dust-up. Well Hoss, if this child is still kickin' when that happens, I'd be honored if you and the missus would make camp with me for a spell." His lips curled in a sardonic smile. "I promise not to tell her too many tales about you in the old days, when your juices were jest startin' to flow."

Smoke clapped him on the back, stood up, and began to put together his pack. "Yours will be the first stop on our journey, Puma. Now, I've gotta get busy if I'm gonna get my surprises ready for that polecat and his gang afore they get up here." He looked over his shoulder as he tied his packs on his pack horse. "You might spread word among the others up here to walk carefully on the trails. I wouldn't want any of my friends to get hurt by my traps."

Puma shook his head. "Boy, if'n a mountain man don't know enough to watch where he's steppin', he don't hardly deserve to be in the high lonesome no-how."

Smoke stepped into the saddle and reined away with only a wave over his shoulder as a farewell.

Chapter Eleven

Sundance Morgan sat on his mount, a cigarette stuck in a face full of stubble, and looked out at his gang gathered before him. They had crossed the border just before dawn, in small groups of five men to avoid being noticed, and gathered at the same grove of cottonwoods on the Rio Bravo where they first met.

The *desperados* were bleary-eyed and surly from a night without sleep. The Hernandez women lasted for hours, until finally Sundance ordered his men to put them out of their misery and ride north.

Two of the Mexicans argued over the scalps, and the loser of the fight now sat with his arm bandaged from a knife wound while the winner proudly displayed bloody hanks of hair on his saddle horn.

Sundance tipped a pint bottle of whiskey at the sky and sleeved the excess off his lips with his forearm before speaking. "*Hombres,* we are like *los corrientes,* the wild longhorns who live in the *brasada,* obeying no man's laws and answering to no one for our actions." He waved his bottle in the air. "From now on, we ride hard and we ride fast. We will take what we want, and send those to the devil who oppose us."

The group nodded and laughed among themselves, too sleepy to work up much enthusiasm at such an early hour. Sundance continued. "We'll ride 'til midday to put some trail between us and Mexico, then find a shady place for a *siesta* and for our nooning."

He pitched the empty whiskey bottle in the air and blew it to pieces with his Colt, the booming echo of the gunshot continuing long after the fragments of glass fell to the ground. "Now, *andale compadres,* shag your mounts! *Vamanos!*

The gang rode north on the trail toward San Antonio for several hours. When the sun reached mid-sky and heat waves danced over the desolate land of the Texas bush country, they pulled off the road into a stand of live oak trees and dismounted. Some men cooked bacon and beans, while others lay in the shade, drinking whiskey and eating jerked meat. A few slumped on the dirt snoring, hats pulled down over their eyes.

Sundance took this time to call a meeting of his lieutenants to plan their next move. Lightning Jack, swigging out of a bottle with no label on it, said, "Sundance, there be a small settlement on the coast just north o' here called Corpus Christi. Not much there, but it might be worth a look or two."

El Gato shook his head. "No, I don't think so. I there last year. It is full o' *campesinos* and fishermen. There no gold in that town."

Toothpick looked up from spooning beans into his mouth, juice running down his chin into his whiskers. "I heared there's a big spread hearabouts." His brow furrowed in thought for a moment. "King Ranch, I think it's called."

Sundance smirked. "You heard right, Toothpick. Trouble is, they's a bunch o' hairy ole boys ridin' fer that brand. Mainly Mexicans, but they all carry sidearms and they all know how to use 'em. Old man King hired him a bunch o' buff'lo soldiers from the Union Army after the war, and them boys ain't afraid of nuthin' nor nobody."

He rolled a cigarette and placed it between his lips. "A bunch o' *pistoleros* from down the border tried to tree that particular spread a few months back." He grinned as he lit his smoke. "What was left of 'em, 'bout a third I reckon, came straggling back through Del Rio with their tails 'tween their legs, lookin' mighty shot up.''

Toothpick shrugged and went back to eating beans. Lightning Jack asked, ''You got a better plan then?''

Sundance tilted his head toward the road, just over a small ridge from their camp. ''Yeah. The noon stage from San Antone is due to come down that trail in a couple o' hours. The station where they change horses for the final leg into Laredo is 'bout three miles north o' here.'' He flipped his butt in the fire. ''After the boys are finished eatin', I figger we'll just mosey on over the hill and be waitin' on that stage when it pulls in.''

Lightning Jack nodded, grinning. ''Yeah, that's a good idee. I'm in need of a fresh mount anyhow.''

Gato threw his empty bottle against a nearby tree. ''And *mas* tequila, eh *compadres?*''

Sundance spent a few more minutes outlining his plan for taking the stage station, then the men were rounded up and they rode north.

Catherine Johanson looked up from her cooking as she heard the door to the way-station slam shut. She peered out the small serving window and saw four disreputable-looking men enter. Something about their manner, swaggering and loud, alarmed her. Frowning, she turned to her teenaged daughter, Missy, and whispered for her to remain hidden in the closet and not to come out until she called her. Without haste, she slipped a Derringer .44 over-and-under into her apron pocket.

Her husband, and station manager, Olaf Johanson, was wiping down the bar when Carlito Suarez, One-Eye Jordan, Curly Bill Cartwright, and Bull burst through the door.

He slipped his hand around a Greener shotgun out of sight beneath the bar and said, ''Howdy gents. Mighty windy out there today, huh?''

Suarez grinned widely, exposing a greenish-yellow front tooth. A dentist in Monterey had told him it was gold, but it turned out to be brass. It was a costly lie. The dentist lived to regret it, and died cursing the day he met Perro Muerte. ''Si,

Senor.'' He took his *sombrero* off and dusted his arms and pants with it. "The dust, she is flying pretty damn *mucho* today.''

One-Eye Jordan turned his head and surveyed the clapboard shack. Along one wall were homemade shelves lined with canned goods, a few bolts of cloth and barrels of dried beans and flour. "This here a store or a dog hole?''

Johanson grinned. "Well, boys, I 'spect it's a bit of both. If you're short of supplies, we can fix you up, at fair prices, and if'n you're thirsty or hungry, we can do something about that, too.''

The men sauntered up to the bar and leaned against it. Suarez ordered a tequila and Curly Bill smiled with his lips, but his eyes never changed. "I'd like a whiskey, with a beer chaser if'n it's not flat.''

"Make that two,'' joined in Bull, in his high voice.

Johanson's lips started to curl in a smile, but the look on Bull's face stopped him cold. He shivered, as if someone had walked over his grave, and reluctantly let go of his shotgun to fix the men their drinks.

Jordan walked to a window and glanced toward a corral behind the building. There were eight horses grazing on hay piled on the ground. "Them the horses for the stage?'' he asked.

Johanson looked back over his shoulder. "Yeah. Should be here any time now, 'less they broke a wheel or something.''

He put the drinks on the bar in front of Bull and Cartwright. "You boys up from Laredo?''

Cartwright threw back his whiskey and followed it with a draught of beer. "Yeah, why?''

Johanson shrugged. "Oh, no reason. A couple of punchers came through from there earlier today and said a Mexican rancher south of there was burned out. All of his hands and family was killed and his wife and daughter was scalped.''

Cartwright smiled and held out his glass for a refill. "Yeah, awful what them greasers do to one another, ain't it?''

Suarez glanced at the kid, death on his face, then grinned, exposing his tooth again. *"Si,* is terrible.''

Johanson looked from one of the men to another, sweat beginning to bead on his forehead.

Bull sipped his whiskey slowly, almost delicately. "You say that stage is due here soon?"

Johanson nodded, his hand searching under the bar for his shotgun.

Bull took another drink. "You work this place all by yourself?"

Johanson glanced quickly over his shoulder and said in a loud voice. "Yes, I'm here alone."

"Lotta work fer one man." Bull sniffed. "Smells like ya left somethin' cookin' in the back room there."

Johanson started to bring the shotgun up, but, faster than the eye could follow, a knife appeared in Cartwright's hand and he swung backhanded across the bar.

Johanson stepped back, looking startled, and reached for his throat. He found a hole he could stick his fist in, before he fell to the floor, gurgling and drowning in his own blood.

One-Eye Jordan stepped quickly into the kitchen and came out a moment later dragging a struggling Catherine Johanson into the room by her hair.

"Hey boys, look what I found me. A wildcat of a woman."

He spun her around and grabbed her head and pulled it toward his face, trying to kiss her. A loud boom sounded in the small room, rattling the walls and filling the area with smoke. Catherine backed out of the gunpowder cloud, holding the Derringer in front of her. Jordan rolled on the floor, cradling his left hand against his stomach. "Jesus, the bitch shot my fingers off!" he cried, adding to the confusion.

When Catherine saw her husband writhing on the floor, his blood spurting in the air, she gasped and put her hands to her mouth.

Bull took two quick steps and slapped her backhanded, knocking her against the wall, unconscious, the Derringer falling beside her.

Suarez bent over Jordan and pulled his hand out where he could see it. It was missing the index and middle finger and was tattooed black from the gunpowder blast. He poured tequila over the hand, causing Jordan to begin wailing again, and wrapped his filthy bandanna around the mutilated stumps. "Git up, *Senor* One-Eye. You cryin' like a woman makin' my head hurt."

"I'm gonna kill that bitch fer what she did to me," he groaned.

Bull stepped in front of Catherine's limp body. He began to undo his belt. "Not just yet, you ain't," he growled. "I got me some business with her first."

Suarez looked over his shoulder at Cartwright. "Curly, go signal Sundance. We must clean floor before stage come."

Cartwright stepped out the door and fired his pistol in the air three times, then returned to the room. He walked to Johanson's body and squatted before it, careful not to step in the blood that pooled the boards around him. Without haste, he pulled the dead man's shiny black boots off and took them across the room to the table. He sat and removed his threadbare boots and put on the station master's newer ones. He stood and shined them on his pants, one at a time, admiring their sheen for a moment. Then, with a jaunty step, he pitched his old boots onto Johanson's body and dragged it out the rear door and covered it with some firewood he found there.

Sundance entered the room to find Suarez throwing dirt over the bloodstains and Jordan sitting propped against a wall, rocking back and forth with his wounded hand against his stomach, swigging whiskey with the other, tears streaming down his face.

Cartwright was in the kitchen, eating some of the food that Catherine had been preparing. Sundance glanced around the small enclosure. "Where's Bull?"

Suarez shrugged. "He in other room. Say he have business with lady there."

Sundance grimaced and shook his head. "Lord save me from galoots who think with their balls 'stead o' their brains."

He pointed to Jordan. "Git off your ass and pull the mounts around back and outta sight. The stage'll be here any minute an' we don't have much time."

Once the blood was covered and the horses were hidden, he

stationed Suarez and Cartwright behind the door to the building and told Jordan to stay in the kitchen. Bull strolled in from the Johanson's living quarters, fixing his pants, sweat running down his face and making rivulets in the dirt.

"Where're the rest of the boys, boss?"

"I left them outta sight over that ridge yonder. I figger we got enough to do what we need right here."

"What you want me to do?"

Sundance inclined his head toward the back door. "You station yourself behind the corner of the building. The stage driver will send the passengers in while he and the man riding shotgun change horses. They's your responsibility."

Bull tipped his hat and drew his shotguns, breaking them open to check the loads as he ambled out the door.

A few minutes later, the stage pulled up outside amid a squealing of wheel-brakes and a cloud of dust. There was much excited talking and laughing as four passengers unloaded and headed for the station, anxious to get out of the stifling Texas heat and to stretch muscles cramped from the jolting ride.

Sundance was behind the bar, wearing an apron he had liberated from the kitchen. The first person through the door was a middleaged white man, dressed in black, carrying a brown case worn yellow in spots. He looked like a drummer to Sundance. He was followed by three women, all appearing past forty years of age and wearing heavy makeup and brightly colored dresses with hats and carrying small parasols to ward off the sun. Saloon girls, unless I miss my guess, thought Sundance as they approached the bar.

Sundance inclined his head. "Mister, ladies. How can I help you?"

The man put his case down and leaned his elbows on the bar-rail. "Whiskey, if you please, my good man."

Two of the women asked for beer, and one ordered whiskey. Sundance grinned as he fixed the drinks, thinking he was the most expensive bartender these folks would ever meet.

As he set the glasses down, there came a loud double-explosion from behind the building, shaking dust out of the ceiling, to fall and settle like snow on the bar top. The women screamed and the man reached inside his coat, stopping when he felt the barrel of Cartwright's Colt against his ear.

Sundance raised his hands, palms out. "Settle down, now, folks. Finish your drinks and nobody'll get hurt."

Suarez put his arms around two of the women. "Especially you ladies," he murmured, dropping his hands to caress their breasts.

From outside came a single scream, followed by a sound like a watermelon falling off a table onto the floor. A moment later, Bull walked in, wiping blood and hair off the butt of his shotgun with a dusty bandanna. He raised his eyebrows at Sundance's look. "The driver didn't wanna die, so I helped him along a little. Weren't no need to waste a shell on 'im, so I jist tapped him on the head." He frowned, looking down at his gun. "Damn near broke my stock."

One of the women moaned softly and sunk to the ground in a faint. The other two shut their eyes and began to pray to themselves, evidently hoping for more mercy than they typically gave their clients.

Sundance glanced at the drummer. "What's in the case?"

He sleeved sweat off his forehead before answering, then placed the case on the bar. "Airtights." He opened the case to reveal several tin cans bearing the names Beef Biscuit, Meat Biscuit, and Condensed Milk. "I work for the Gail Borden company. She's trying to expand her market to the southwest." He continued, sweat pouring off his face. "It's really quite popular up north."

Cartwright picked up one of the cans, sniffing it to see if it had a smell. "Mister, that's 'bout the dumbest thang I ever heared." He waved his hand at the window. "Look around, pardner. There ain't nothin' out there 'ceptin' beeves. We got pretty near all the meat and milk we want, jest fer the takin'. What fer we need beef in a can?"

Suarez laughed. *"Si,* is said, only fool eats his own meat in this country."

The drummer stammered, "But this is different. You can carry these tins with you in your saddlebags and not have to eat bacon and beans with every meal. We even have tinned peaches and tomatoes so you can have them in the winter.''

Bull pushed his way into the group. "Hey, I like peaches. You got any of those in there?''

Sundance jerked his Colt and shot the drummer in the face, the booming of his gun causing the others to curse and cover their ears, and the drummer to be thrown backwards, landing spread-eagled on his back on top of a small rough-hewn table in the middle of the room.

''Enough of this chatter. Bull, put that tin down and go out to the stage and see what's in the strongbox. We need to git outta here 'fore anybody else decides to come visitin'.''

The women began crying and begging Suarez and Cartwright to let them live. "We won't tell anyone anything,'' one said, rubbing her hand up and down Cartwright's arm, pleading for her life. ''I can make you happy, just give me a chance,'' she purred, tears on her cheeks and terror in her eyes.

''Well darlin','' he drawled, no life at all in his eyes, ''I intend to give you that chance.''

Bull walked into the room, a metal strongbox looking small on his shoulder. He dropped it to the ground with a loud thump. ''H'yar it is, boss.''

Sundance inclined his head at Suarez. "Carlito,'' he said.

Suarez walked to the box and drew his pistol, then shot the lock off. His bullet ricocheted off the metal and buried itself in the wall next to Bull's head, causing him to curse and duck. ''Goddamn, Suarez, watch what you're doin'!''

Suarez grinned. "Sorry, *amigo*. I aim a little better next time.''

Bull nodded, then frowned and glowered at Suarez through narrowed eyes, wondering just what he meant by that remark.

Sundance toed the box open with his boot, revealing a pile of letters and two canvas bank bags. He reached down and picked out the bags, holding them up in front of Cartwright. The kid drew his knife and slit them without a word, letting handfuls of greenbacks and double-eagle gold coins fall to the floor.

Sundance's face broke into a toothy grin. ''Okay, boys, fun's over. Pack that *dinero,* saddle up some of those broncs out back, set fire to this place, and let's git outta here.''

Cartwright said, ''Hey, wait a minute. What about the women?'' He rubbed his crotch in an obscene gesture. ''I'm not finished here jest yet.''

Sundance said, ''Hell, bring 'em along.'' He waved his hands at the corral behind the building. ''We got plenty of horseflesh to carry 'em on.''

One of the women groaned and said, ''Oh no.''

Cartwright put his palm against her cheek. ''It's your choice, darlin'.'' He glanced at the cooling body of the drummer, still leaking blood and gore out of his skull. ''We kin leave ya here, if'n ya want.''

Sundance started to leave, hesitated, and pointed over his shoulder at the shelves against the far wall. ''Bull, before you torch this place, pack up any supplies we might need and bring 'em along. It might be awhile 'fore we git to town again.''

Cartwright, his arm around the woman's shoulder, asked, ''Where we headed, boss?''

Sundance raised his eyebrows. ''Why, north, of course. We're heading for Smoke country. I got me a score to settle, boys, and I'm tired of waitin'.''

As the group mounted and rode off, no one noticed a small figure scramble out the back door of the burning building, her dress on fire.

Chapter Twelve

Cal hollered, "Gosh darn it, Pearlie. Why for do we have to do this?"

He and Pearlie were standing waist deep in a small brook three quarters of the way up the mountain they'd been climbing. Pearlie had ordered Cal into the water with him, and was now standing behind him, picking ticks and fleas off his hide. Cal was shivering and shaking and had turned a light blue color in the near-freezing stream.

"Listen up, pup," Pearlie answered, as though talking to a small child. "If'n we don't git these critters off'n our skin now, they'll fester up and cause itchin' like you never had before in your born days."

"Aw, Pearlie. I had ticks afore. They didn't bother me none. Hell, anybody who herds beeves gits used to ticks 'n fleas and such."

Pearlie shook his head. "Yeah, boy. You've had ticks before, but these'r high mountain ticks. They's a difference. Kinda like the difference 'tween a tame shorthorn you're always dealin' with, an' a rangy ole longhorn out in the bush. These here critters'll eat you fer lunch, and carry off your horse fer dessert."

The two men had ridden through very thick underbrush for the last halfday, switching back and forth and trying to find a trail through the dense undergrowth. The ride left them covered from head to toe with hundreds of thick, voracious mountain ticks, and not just a few fleas.

When it came time to pitch camp, with still no sign of Smoke Jensen, Pearlie stripped down to his longjohns and told Cal to do the same. With much protesting, Cal followed him into the frigid water.

After picking each other as clean of the pests as they could, Pearlie made Cal take a curry comb to both mounts to try and rid them of some of the ticks, while he made a fire and prepared their supper.

Cal, with a blanket thrown over his shoulders, walked to the campfire, still grumbling about never having taken so many baths in his life until he met up with Smoke and joined his crew.

Pearlie grinned and tossed him a steaming biscuit. "Here, young'un, eat this sinker and maybe it'll take your mind off'n your troubles fer a spell."

Cal juggled the hot biscuit from hand to hand, trying to keep it from burning him. Finally, with a deep sigh, he shoved the entire thing in his mouth and began to chew as if he hadn't eaten for days. "Hmmm, I swear Pearlie, your damn near as good a cook as Miss Sally is."

Shaking his head, Pearlie poured them both cups of coffee as black as Mississippi mud. "You only think that 'cause you're 'bout starvin' to death, being as how it's been mite near six hours since we last ate."

Cal squatted before the fire, took his tin plate and heaped it full of beans and fried fat-back, and piled three more biscuits on top of that. After a giant draught of coffee, he began to shovel food into his mouth as fast as he could, making Pearlie grin in disbelief.

"I don't know how you do it, boy. If'n you ate any faster, you wouldn't need teeth a'tall. You could jest git an ole kerosene funnel and put it in your mouth and pour the food down your gullet."

Cal tried to smile, but his bulging cheeks wouldn't allow it, so he continued to eat, ignoring Pearlie's remarks. Finally, satiated, he put his plate and empty coffee cup down and leaned back against his saddle. He raised his eyebrows and inclined his head toward Pearlie's saddlebags. "How about throwin' me your fixin's and gittin' that there bottle of Kaintuck whiskey out'n your bag and let's have us a little smoke and a drink or two?"

Pearlie put his head in his hands and mumbled, "Oh God, Smoke is gonna kill me. I've done gone and corrupted this poor young'un and taught him evil ways."

With a sigh, he handed Cal his pouch of Bull Durham and a packet of papers. "You'll have to git your own fire," he mumbled sarcastically to the boy.

While Cal fumbled and cursed, spilling more tobacco than he managed to roll in the paper, Pearlie poured small amounts of whiskey into their cups and passed one over to Cal.

They smoked and sipped the harsh alcohol in amiable silence, enjoying the sight of the sun easing down behind mountain peaks to the west.

"You know, Pearlie?" Cal drawled, sprawled back against his saddle, snuggled in his blanket. "I wish I could draw pitchers like I seen in Mr. Smoke's cabin. That sunset sure produces some pretty colors in the clouds when it's settin'."

Pearlie leaned back, hands behind his head, and stared at the orange and yellow snow-clouds playing around the peaks. "Yeah, that'd make a right pretty picture all right. I seen some drawin's once in a magazine from back East. Drawn by a feller name of Remington, if I recollect correctly. Showed some punchers ridin' hard, bein' chased by Injuns, firing their Colts over they shoulders, dodgin' arrows."

He grinned, his teeth glittering in the flickering firelight. "I swear, he made it look almost like fun, the way they was ridin', mounts sweatin', guns shootin', and the Injuns yellin' and waving they hands in the air."

Cal frowned. "Bein' chased by Injuns don't sound like fun to me, Pearlie."

Pearlie nodded. "It ain't, boy, it ain't and that's a fact."

Cal flipped his cigarette butt into the fire. "How 'bout you tellin' me more 'bout Smoke's 'ventures when he was first come out West?"

Pearlie expertly rolled another cigarette and lit it off the butt of his first. He lay back, watching his smoke trail toward the stars and thought about how to begin.

"After Smoke shot and killed Pike, his friend, and Haywood, and wounded Pike's brother, Thompson, he and Preacher went after the other men who kilt Smoke's brother and stole the Confederates' gold. They rode on over to *La Plaza de los Leones,* the plaza of the lions. T'was there that they trapped a man named Casey in a line shack with some of his *compadres.* Smoke and Preacher burnt 'em out and captured Casey. Smoke took him to the outskirts of the town and hung him."

Cal's eyebrows shot up. "Just hung 'em? No trial nor nuthin'?"

Pearlie flicked ash off his cigarette without taking it out of his mouth. "Yep, that's the way it was done in those days, boy. That town would never have hanged one of their own on the word of Smoke Jensen." He snorted, "Like as not they'd of hanged Smoke and Preacher instead. Anyway, after that, the sheriff of that town put out a flyer on Smoke, accusin' him of murder. Had a ten thousand dollar reward on it, too."

"Did Smoke and Preacher go into hidin'?"

"Nope. Seems Preacher advised it, but Smoke said he had one more call to make. They rode on over to Oreodelphia, lookin' fer a man named Ackerman. They didn't go after him right at first. Smoke and Preacher sat around doin' a whole lot o' nothin' fer two or three days. Smoke wanted Ackerman to git plenty nervous. He did, and finally came gunnin' fer Smoke with a bunch of men who rode fer his brand . . ."

At the edge of town, Ackerman, a bull of a man, with small, mean eyes and a cruel slit for a mouth, slowed his horse to a walk. Ackerman and his hands rode down the street, six abreast.

Preacher and Smoke were on their feet. Preacher stuffed his mouth full of chewing tobacco. Both men had slipped the thongs from the hammers of their Colts. Preacher wore two Colts, .44's. One in a holster, the other stuck behind his belt. Mountain man and young gunfighter stood six feet apart on the boardwalk.

The sheriff closed his office door and walked into the empty cell area. He sat down and began a game of checkers with his deputy.

Ackerman and his men wheeled their horses to face the men on the boardwalk. "I hear tell you boys is lookin' for me. If so, here I am."

"News to me," Smoke said. "What's your name?"

"You know who I am, kid. Ackerman."

"Oh yeah!" Smoke grinned. "You're the man who helped kill my brother by shooting him in the back. Then you stole the gold he was guarding."

Inside the hotel, pressed against the wall, the desk clerk listened intently, his mouth open in anticipation of gunfire.

"You're a liar. I didn't shoot your brother; that was Potter and his bunch."

"You stood and watched it. Then you stole the gold."

"It was war, kid."

"But you were on the same side," Smoke said. "So that not only makes you a killer, it makes you a traitor and a coward."

"I'll kill you for sayin' that!"

"You'll burn in hell a long time before I'm dead," Smoke told him.

Ackerman grabbed for his pistol. The street exploded in gunfire and black powder fumes. Horses screamed and bucked in fear. One rider was thrown to the dust by his lunging mustang. Smoke took the men on the left, Preacher the men on the right. The battle lasted no more than ten to twelve seconds. When the noise and the gunsmoke cleared, five men lay in the street, two of them dead. Two more would die from their wounds. One was shot in the side—he would live. Ackerman had been shot three times: once in the belly, once in the chest, and one ball had taken him in the side of the face as the muzzle of the .36 had lifted with each blast. Still Ackerman sat in his saddle, dead. The big man finally leaned to one side and toppled from his horse, one boot hung in the stirrup. The horse shied, then began walking down the dusty street, dragging Ackerman, leaving a bloody trail.

Preacher spat into the street. "Damn near swallowed my chaw."

"I never seen a draw that fast," a man spoke from his store front. "It was a blur."

The editor of the paper walked up to stand by the sheriff. He watched the old man and the young gunfighter walk down the street. He truly had seen it all. The old man had killed one man, wounded another. The young man had killed four men, as calmly as picking his teeth.

"What's that young man's name?"

"Smoke Jensen. But he's a devil."

Cal whistled through his teeth. "Wow! That was somethin'! What did they do next, Pearlie?"

"Well, they both had some minor wounds, and there was a price on Smoke's head, so they took off to the mountains to lay up fer a while and lick their wounds and let the heat die down."

Pearlie cut his eyes over at Cal. " 'Cept it didn't work out exactly that way. They chanced upon the remains of a wagon train that'd been burned out by Injuns, and rescued a young woman. Nicole was her name. She was the lone survivor of the attack. There wasn't nothin' else they could do, so they took her up into the mountains with them where they planned to winter."

Cal's eyes were big. "You mean Smoke and Preacher took a woman with 'em up into the mountains?"

Pearlie frowned. "What'd ya expect 'em to do, leave her out there fer the Injuns to come back and take? Course they took her with them."

"Where'd they live?"

"Way I heared it, Smoke built 'em a cabin outta 'dobe and logs, and they spent two winters and a summer in that place, up in the high lonesome. After the first year, Smoke and Nicole had a kinda unofficial marrying, and by the second winter she had Smoke a son.''

"I didn't know Smoke had no son."

Pearlie sighed. ''That there's the sad part of the story. When the boy was about a year old, Smoke had to go lookin' fer their milk cow that wandered off. When he came back, he found some bounty hunters had tracked him to the cabin and were in there with Nicole and the baby.''

"Jimminy! What'd he do?"

"Same thing any man'd do . . .''

Some primitive sense of warning caused Smoke to pull up short of his home. He made a wide circle, staying in the timber back of the creek, and slipped up to the cabin.

Nicole was dead. The acts of the men had grown perverted and in their haste, her throat had been crushed.

Felter sat by the lean-to and watched the valley in front of him. He wondered where Smoke had hidden the gold.

Inside, Canning drew his skinning knife and scalped Nicole, tying her bloody hair to his belt. He then skinned a part of her, thinking he would tan the hide and make himself a nice tobacco pouch.

Kid Austin got sick at his stomach watching Canning's callousness, and went out the back door to puke on the ground. That moment of sickness saved his life—for the time being.

Grissom walked out the front door of the cabin. Smoke's tracks had indicated he had ridden off south, so he would probably return from that direction. But Grissom felt something was wrong. He sensed something, his years on the owlhoot back trails surfacing.

"Felter?" he called.

"Yeah?" He stepped from the lean-to.

"Something's wrong."

"I feel it. But what?"

"I don't know." Grissom spun as he sensed movement behind him. His right hand dipped for his pistol. Felter had stepped back into the lean-to. Grissom's palm touched the smooth wooden butt of his gun as his eyes saw the tall young man standing by the corner of the cabin, a Colt .36 in each hand. Lead from the .36's hit him in the center of the chest with numbing force. Just before his heart exploded, the outlaw said, "Smoke!" Then he fell to the ground.

Smoke jerked the gun belt and pistols from the dead man. Remington Army .44's.

A bounty hunter ran from the cabin, firing at the corner of the building. But Smoke was gone.

"Behind the house!" Felter yelled, running from the lean-to, his fists full of Colts. He slid to a halt and raced back to the water trough, diving behind it for protection.

A bounty hunter who had been dumping his bowels in the outhouse struggled to pull up his pants, at the same time pushing open the door with his shoulder. Smoke shot him twice in the belly and left him to scream on the outhouse floor.

Kid Austin, caught in the open behind the cabin, ran for the banks of the creek, panic driving his legs. He leaped for the protection of a sandy embankment, twisting in the air, just as Smoke took aim and fired. The ball hit Austin's right buttock and traveled through the left cheek of his butt, tearing out a sizable hunk of flesh. Kid Austin, the dreaming gun-hand, screamed and fainted from the pain in his ass.

Smoke ran for the protection of the woodpile and crouched there, recharging his Colts and checking the .44's. He listened to the sounds of men in panic, firing in all directions and hitting nothing.

Moments ticked past, the sound of silence finally overpowering gunfire. Smoke flicked away sweat from his face. He waited.

Something came sailing out the back door to bounce on the grass. Smoke felt hot bile build in his stomach. Someone had thrown his dead son outside. The boy had been dead for some time. Smoke fought back sickness.

"You wanna see what's left of your woman?" a taunting voice called from near the back door. "I got her hair on my belt and a piece of her hide to tan. We all took a time or two with her. I think she liked it."

Smoke felt rage charge through him, but he remained still,

crouched behind the thick pile of wood until his anger cooled
to controlled, venom-filled fury. He unslung the big Sharps
buffalo rifle Preacher had carried for years. The rifle could drop
a two thousand pound buffalo at six hundred yards. It could
also punch through a small log.

The voice from the cabin continued to mock and taunt Smoke.
But Preacher's training kept him cautious. To his rear lay a
meadow, void of cover. To his left was a shed, but he knew
that was empty, for it was still barred from the outside. The
man he'd plugged in the butt was to his right, but several fallen
logs would protect him from that direction. The man in the
outhouse was either dead or passed out, his screaming had
ceased.

Through a chink in the logs, Smoke shoved the muzzle of
the Sharps and lined up where he thought he had seen a man
move, just to the left of the rear window. He gently squeezed
the trigger, taking up slack. The weapon boomed, the planking
shattered, and a man began screaming in pain.

Canning ran out the front of the cabin to the lean-to, sliding
down hard beside Felter behind the water trough. "This ain't
workin' out," he panted. "Grissom, Austin, Poker, and now
Evans is either dead or dying. The slug from that buffalo gun
blowed his arm off. Let's get the hell outta here!"

Felter had been thinking the same thing. "What about Clark
and Sam?"

"They're growed men. They can join us or they can go to
hell."

"Let's ride. There's always another day. We'll hide up in
them mountains, see which way he rides out, then bushwhack
him. Let's go." They raced for their horses, hidden in a bend
of the creek, behind the bank. They kept the cabin between
themselves and Smoke as much as possible, then bellied down
in the meadow the rest of the way.

In the creek, in water red from the wounds in his butt, Kid
Austin crawled upstream, crying in pain and humiliation. His
Colts were forgotten—useless anyway; the powder was wet.
All he wanted was to get away.

The bounty hunters left in the house, Clark and Sam, looked

at each other. "I'm gettin' out!" Sam said. "That ain't no pilgrim out there."

"To hell with that," Clark said. "I humped his woman, I'll kill him and take the ten thousand."

"Your option." Sam slipped out the front and caught up with the others.

Kid Austin reached his horse first. Yelping as he hit the saddle, he galloped off toward the timber in the foothills.

"Your wife don't look so good now," Clark called out to Smoke. "Not since she got a haircut and one titty skinned."

Deep silence had replaced the gunfire. The air stank of black powder, blood, and relaxed bladders and bowels. Smoke had seen the men ride off into the foothills. He wondered how many were left in the cabin.

Smoke remained still, his eyes burning with fury. Smoke's eyes touched the stiffening form of his son. If Clark could have read the man's thoughts, he would have stuck the muzzle of his .44 into his mouth and pulled the trigger, ensuring himself a quick death, instead of what waited for him later on.

"Yes, sir," Clark taunted him. He went into profane detail of the rape of Nicole and the perverted acts that followed.

Smoke eased slowly backward, keeping the woodpile in front of him. He slipped down the side of the knoll and ran around to one wall of the cabin. He grinned. The bounty hunter was still talking to the woodpile, to the muzzle of the Sharps stuck through the logs.

Smoke eased around to the front of the cabin and looked in. He saw Nicole, saw the torture marks on her, saw the hideousness of the scalping and the skinning knife. He lifted his eyes to the back door, where Clark was crouching just to the right of the closed door.

Smoke raised his .36 and shot the pistol out of Clark's hand. The outlaw howled and grabbed his numbed and bloodied hand.

Smoke stepped over Grissom's body, then glanced at the body of the armless bounty hunter who had bled to death.

Clark looked up at the tall young man with the burning eyes. Cold, slimy fear put a bony hand on his shoulder. For the first time in his evil life, Clark knew what death looked like.

"You gonna make it quick, ain't you?"

"Not likely," Smoke said, then kicked him on the side of the head, dropping Clark unconscious to the floor.

When Clark came to his senses, he began screaming. He was naked, staked out a mile from the cabin, on the plain. Rawhide held his wrists and ankles to thick stakes driven into the ground. A huge ant mound was just inches from him. And Smoke had poured honey all over him.

"I'm a white man," Clark screamed. "You can't do this to me." Slobber sprayed from his mouth. "What are you, half Apache?"

Smoke looked at him, contempt in his eyes. "You will not die well, I believe."

He didn't. *(The Last Mountain Man)*

Cal's face glowed red in the light of the campfire. "That's a tough way to die, but those bastards deserved it for what they did to Nicole and his son."

Pearlie raised his eyebrows. "Cal, deserve don't hardly have nothin' to do with how you die out here in the wild country. Those men died that way 'cause they crossed Smoke Jensen, and he was twice as mean and tough as they was. That's the long and the short of it. Don't never bite off more'n you can chew, and you'll never choke on it."

He rolled over, his back to the fire. "Now it's time to sleep. We got to catch up with Smoke tomorrow sometime."

Cal slid down against his saddle and pulled his hat over his eyes. "Night, Pearlie."

"Night, Cal."

Chapter Thirteen

Monte Carson was in his usual position in front of the jail, leaning back in a chair with his hat down over his eyes and his feet crossed on the hitchrail. A barefoot boy of nine or ten ran up to him and tugged on his shirt sleeve. "Mr. Carson, Bob over at the post office said fer me to give you this." He stuck a wrinkled envelope in Monte's hand.

Monte pushed his hat back and scowled at the boy in mock anger for a moment. "Didn't your momma ever teach you not to wake a man when he's sleepin'?"

The kid frowned, then his eyes started to tear. "But, Mr. Bob said to give it to you right away, an' not to go messin' 'round 'til I done it."

Monte grinned and winked. "I'm just funnin' with you, Jeremy. Here, this is for doin' such a good job of deliverin' messages." He reached in his pocket and handed Jeremy a coin.

The boy's face lit up with happiness. "Wow! A whole dime! That'll git me ten peppermint sticks over at the store."

Monte waggled his finger in Jeremy's face. "Now, don't you go eating all of 'em at one time and gittin' a bellyache. Your momma will have my hide if you do."

"Yessir, Mr. Carson, I mean, no sir!" He said it over his shoulder as he high-tailed it toward a group of boys playing in a mud hole down the street.

Monte sighed, trying to remember when he had been that young and life had been simple. He slit the envelope with a thumbnail and pulled the letter out. As he read it, his face wrinkled in a frown over its contents. After a moment he rested the piece of paper in his lap and sat there, eyes unfocused, thinking about what he should do.

Finally, he got up and stretched, groaning like an old dog forced to move from in front of a fireplace. "I'll be over at Longmont's if you need me," he called through the door to Jim, his deputy.

"Okay, boss. I'll holler if'n anyone tries to rob the bank," he replied, grinning around his plug of tobacco.

Monte walked down the street toward Louis Longmont's saloon, his gunfighter's eyes scanning buildings and the citizens of Big Rock he was sworn to protect. He was about to put them in more danger than they had ever been in before.

Walking slowly through batwing doors, he paused for a moment out of habit, to let his eyes adjust to the semi-darkness.

A deep voice called from the gloom. "You may enter, Monte. There isn't anyone here waiting to bushwhack you."

Monte grinned. Louis, an expert gunman himself, had recognized and appreciated his caution when entering a room without knowing who might be waiting inside. "That's mighty easy for you to say, Louis. You ain't walkin' around town with a tin target pinned to your chest."

Louis shook Monte's hand without rising from his corner table, one reserved for the owner of the saloon and gambling house. "Can I have Andre fix you something to eat, or are your taste buds permanently ruined by eating that fire-food down at Maria's *cantina* on the edge of town?"

Monte raised his eyebrows. "Sure, I'd love some grub, long as it ain't frogs or snails or any of those other French delicacies your man is always trying to push on me."

Louis chuckled and called over his shoulder. "Andre, how about fixing the sheriff some real Western cuisine? Something like a beefsteak, burnt black and charred, fried potatoes, and some of those vine-ripened tomatoes we were saving for someone special."

Monte added, "And a pot of coffee. Hot, black, and strong. We're gonna need it."

Louis cocked his head, staring into his friend's eyes. "Bad news? Not about Smoke, I hope."

Monte handed him the letter. "Here, read this and then we'll talk."

Louis took the paper and read out loud. "To Sheriff Monte Carson, Big Rock, Colorado. From Texas Ranger's branch office in San Antonio. Dear Sheriff Carson, In answer to your inquiry of last week, there has been some news of the gunfighter Sundance Morgan. He and a gang of about twenty or thirty men are alleged to have robbed a stage line office in South Texas and killed the stationmaster, his wife, the stage driver and shotgun guard, and a passenger. Apparently, three female passengers were taken with the men when they fled. The stationmaster's daughter, a girl of thirteen, managed to hide and escape serious injury when the station and stage were set on fire. She didn't see much, but remembers the name Sundance being mentioned several times by the bandits. When they left, she said they rode off to the north. She says she also heard the name Smoke Jensen mentioned. Regards, Ranger Captain Ted Longley."

Louis looked up from the paper just as Andre placed a plate with a large steak, potatoes, tomatoes, and a hunk of fresh-made bread in front of Monte. A young man brought out a silver coffee server and placed it along with two china cups and saucers in front of them.

Louis folded the letter neatly and laid it on the table. "Looks like Smoke was right. This Sundance character is on the prod for him, and has an abundance of help."

Monte nodded around a mouthful of steak. "Yep," he mumbled, "my guess is that they'll be here within a week. That letter is dated ten days ago, so the gang could be over halfway here by now. I don't figger Sundance is gonna let any grass grow under his feet lookin' for Smoke. Vengeance is a powerful motivator.''

Louis poured them both coffee, adding a dollop of fresh cream and two spoonfuls of sugar to his cup. He took a sip, then pulled a long black cigar out of his vest pocket and lit it with a lucifer. When he had it going to his satisfaction, he pointed it at Monte and said, ''And, unless I miss my guess, you have a plan for when the gang arrives in Big Rock.''

Monte grunted and held up his hand. ''Just let me finish this steak and I'll tell you all about it.''

While the sheriff ate, Louis leaned back and smoked his cigar, thinking about all the times he and Smoke had pulled iron together. He wished Smoke had dealt him into this hand, but he supposed he respected the man's desire not to get any of his friends hurt because of his actions.

Finally, Monte was through with his meal. ''Jesus, Louis, but that Andre can cook a mean steak. If you ever want to get rid of him, he can come live with me and the missus.''

Louis grinned. ''Not likely, Monte, not while I still have teeth an' can chew. Now, tell me what you have planned for Sundance if he and his men ride into Big Rock.''

Monte shook his head, frowning. ''Not if, Louis, but when. I know that snake will come here lookin' for Smoke first. He don't know the area, and I doubt if he's smart enough to find out where Smoke's ranch is without trying here first.''

Louis smoothed some ash into a pewter ashtray on the table. ''You aren't planning to try to handle twenty to thirty men with just you and your three deputies, are you?''

''No, not exactly. I intend for the good citizens of Big Rock to take care of Sundance Morgan and his gang. With your help, if you're willin'.''

Louis smiled and puffed his cigar until the end glowed red, sending blue clouds of smoke spiraling toward the ceiling. ''Monte, I think I know what you have in mind, and I like it.''

''Meet me on the field where we had the Fourth of July picnic, at five o'clock. I'm callin' a town meeting.''

He reached in his pocket for money, but Louis waved a dismissive hand. ''No, Monte, the meal's on me. I'll close the saloon and have all my employees come with me. We'll need every gun we can get.''

The fall sun was inching toward the horizon, casting long, cool shadows by the time the town's inhabitants had all gathered at a large field just beyond the city limits. Every store and commercial establishment was closed, with hand-written notes in most windows, ''Gone to the meeting.''

Monte stood on a small wooden bandstand and addressed the crowd. ''Good citizens of Big Rock, we've got trouble headed our way, and unless we stand together, we're gonna be in for a tough time.''

Al Jamison, owner of the livery stable, was standing in the front row. He held up his hand like a kid in school. Monte nodded at him. ''Al?''

''What kinda trouble, sheriff?''

''You all remember that little fracas we had here a few years back, when Tilden Franklin attacked the town? Well, one of the gunmen he hired at the time, man name of Sundance Morgan, is on the prod and wants some revenge for what happened that day.''

A lady in the middle of the crowd cried, ''Is he comin' for you, Sheriff Carson?''

Monte shook his head. ''No. Matter of fact, he's not coming for anyone in this town. He's got him a gang of thirty or so men and he aims to kill Smoke Jensen.''

Al Jamison spoke again. ''But Smoke ain't here. He headed on up into the mountains. Left several days ago with Miss Sally. He tole me he was taking her to the train to go back East and he was goin' huntin' up in the high lonesome.''

Monte spoke louder, to make himself heard over the murmur of the crowd. ''That's true. Trouble is, Sundance Morgan don't know that. I figger he and his men will head here to find out where Smoke's ranch is, and to see if he happens to be in town.''

A man near the front of the crowd shouted, "If that's so, why do you think the town's in for trouble. Seems to me, the onliest one in trouble is Smoke Jensen."

Monte scowled. "Cyrus, just what do you think thirty of the toughest desperados this side of Texas are going to do when they get to town and find out Smoke Jensen ain't here? Go to church, maybe?"

Monte gave the crowd time to stop laughing at the blushing Cyrus, then he continued. "Hell no, they're not. They'll try to ride roughshod over this town and all its citizens. At the very least, they'll shoot up the place to send Smoke a message about how tough they are."

He paused a moment, then pointed at a young lady carrying a parasol. "Mary, you want bullets flying around town while Jeremy and his friends are playin' in the street? Or do we just lock ourselves in our houses and let this Texas trash come up here and scare us into being cowardly moles, hidin' in the dark until they go on their way?"

"Hell no," a couple of men shouted, to be joined after only a few moments by most of the others. Soon everyone quieted and one of the men asked, "Monte, you sound like you have some idea about what we oughta do 'bout these skunks that're on their way up here."

Monte held his hands over his head to quiet the townspeople. "I do. I've been thinkin' on it and I've come to the conclusion that the best way for us to survive this invasion by gunfighters, is to be ready for them when they hit the outskirts of town."

A voice shouted from the crowd. "Whatta you mean, ready for 'em?"

"From this day on, I want every person in town, 'cepting the children, to go armed at all times. I want volunteers to station themselves on top of some of the buildings where they can command a good line of fire into the street."

A woman with a soft, almost timid voice, said, "What about those of us who don't know how, or don't want to use a gun, Mr. Carson? What can we do to help the town?"

Monte smiled. "You're right, Miss Kathy, lots of folks don't know nothin' 'bout shooting other folks. After all,'' he spread his arms, "this is a civilized town."

At that comment, most of the citizens laughed, realizing that Colorado in the late 1880s was anything but civilized.

"Anyway," Monte went on, "those of you who don't want to use firearms can help the men on lookout by bringing them water and food and such so they don't have to leave their posts every time they get the urge. A few of you, and the children, can help out by staying a couple of miles out of town on that ridge down there to the south, and rushing back here to give the rest of us some warning when they see the others comin'. Thirty men on horseback will kick up quite a dust cloud and they should be visible long before they get here."

"What about those of us who want to help, but don't have no money nor job so's we can buy a gun?" asked a grizzled, poorly dressed oldtimer known to spend most of his time hanging around the saloon, caging drinks.

Louis Longmont climbed on the bandstand next to Monte. "I will provide every man in this town with a pistol, rifle, or shotgun who will agree to use it to protect his fellow citizens." He pointed to Gus McRae, owner and operator of the shop with the largest selection of firearms in town. "Gus, you have my pledge, in front of the entire town. I will stand good for any guns you sell for this purpose. Just keep a list and I'll settle with you after all this is over. That includes ammunition, too."

"Wait just a minute." A sour-faced woman stepped forward, pushing and shoving her way through the crowd. When she arrived in front of the platform on which Monte and Louis stood, she pointed at them with a bony finger. "Why should the good, law-abiding citizens of Big Rock go out of their way to help a known gunfighter and killer like Smoke Jensen?" She faced the crowd. "I'm asking all of you women out there, especially those of you in the Sunday school class that I teach, to go home to your husbands and tell them you won't abide their taking part in this violence." After she spoke, her face turning red and beading with sweat although the early evening air was cool, she stood there, hands on hips, looking righteous in her anger.

Monte looked down on her with a pitying expression. "Oh, I can see your point, Miz Jones, I surely can." He looked out over the gathering of his friends and neighbors. "Why should we go out of our way to help Smoke and Sally Jensen? What have they done for us that should make us stand behind them in their time of need?"

He searched the faces for a moment, then pointed to Reverend Jackson. "Reverend, tell the good folks here about the fund for widows and orphans."

The man's naturally deep and sonorous voice boomed when he spoke. "Well, right after Smoke founded Big Rock, and Miss Sally had her folks get a bank set up that has, over the years, given most of you loans to set up your businesses or buy crop seed and horses in bad times, Smoke came to me and gave me ten thousand dollars." There was a murmur of surprise from the group, most of whom would never see that amount of money in their entire lives. "He said it was cash he'd been paid for going after a few outlaws awhile back, reward money. He said he wanted it to do some good, so he gave it to me and told me to parcel it out to anyone I thought needed a helping hand. No restrictions other than they needed it." He paused for a moment and rubbed his cheek as he thought. "Oh, one more thing. He asked me to keep quiet about it, said he didn't want anyone to know where it came from, other than the church and good folks of Big Rock."

Monte said, "Thank you, Reverend. Now, how about you saying a few words, Miss Goodlaw."

Priscilla Goodlaw, the schoolmarm, raised her face and took off her bonnet so she could be heard. "Miss Sally Jensen came to me right after I arrived from New York. It seems she and Smoke had paid my way out here and guaranteed my salary for five years, plus they built the school house out of their own funds and provided most of the books and other teaching materials that I use to teach your children how to spell and cipher. Miss Sally also takes over the class when I'm sick and can't teach, as most of you know, and she gives me money each and every month to give to those kids I see who don't have enough to eat, or who don't have proper clothes or shoes to come to school in. She made me promise to give the money to the children in private so they wouldn't have to be embarrassed about taking charity, and to never tell them where it came from.''

Monte grinned and said, "Thank you, Miss Goodlaw." Turning his eyes back to the group, he said, "I could go on for hours about all the things Smoke and Sally Jensen have done for Big Rock—all the drunks and down-and-outers he's taken out of my cells and put to work on his ranch so's they could feed their families, all the children that've gotten ponies to ride to school and back on, all the businesses he's bailed out of trouble when times were lean. But I won't. If there's anybody in this town," he inclined his head downward toward Miz Jones, "other than Miss Fiona there, who don't know who this town's best citizen and best friend is, then they ought to move on down the line, 'cause they've been livin' here with their heads buried in the sand. I say we do this not so much for Smoke Jensen, though God knows he deserves it, but for Big Rock and ourselves. If it ever gets known that our town can be treed by a bunch of sorry gunslicks who ride the owlhoot trail, then we might as well burn down the buildings ourselves and settle somewhere else, 'cause it'll happen again.''

The crowd let out a cheer and some of the men threw their hats in the air. Fiona Jones whirled and hurried off toward her house, where she lived alone. It was rumored only her cats could put up with her sour disposition.

Monte said, "See my deputy, Jim, for your assignments and stations. He'll also keep track of who's gonna be on lookout for the gang's arrival."

Louis shouted, "After you talk to Jim, come on over to my place for a free round of beer."

This caused a louder cheer than before and a general movement back toward town, especially of the men.

Monte put his hand on Louis's shoulder. "Thanks for your help, Louis."

"Don't mention it, Monte. I owe Smoke my life, on several

occasions.'' He grinned. ''And even more important than that, he's my friend.''

The two men walked back toward town, where, together, they would plan how best to defend their small community and make it a fortress against Sundance Morgan and his gang.

Chapter Fourteen

Smoke Jensen was enjoying his time alone in the up-high. The sight of wild game, the explosion of color in the late-blooming fall wild flowers, and the extreme wildness of the high country recharged his soul and brought him inner peace.

"Horse," he said to his mount as they traversed the mountainside, pack horses trailing behind, "this is surely the most beautiful country God ever made."

Horse snorted and waggled his ears, as if in agreement with his master.

Smoke rode with his Henry rifle slung across his saddle horn, eyes scanning the mountain above him for just the right place to make his stand. The air was crisp and cold, but not bitterly so, and smelled of pine needles and fresh snow on the way. Patches of ice-covered snow had gathered in shady areas, but most of the trail was still clear, with occasional small boggy mud holes from previous ice-melts.

Smoke had removed his buckskin shirt and hat, taking advantage of the bright afternoon sun to tan his hide even darker than it already was. He didn't want any pale skin to reflect moonlight and give his position away in the nighttime fighting he knew was coming.

On the second day after he left Puma Buck's camp, he found what he was looking for. A natural fortress only a few hundred yards below the top of the mountain. Backed on three sides by sheer rock walls extending skyward, the place had a level meadow dotted with large ponderosa pines and a ridge in front. From there, the ground fell off at a steep angle downward to end along a single trail up the mountain.

There were few trees or boulders large enough to provide cover for his enemies between his fort and the path the men would have to take to get to him. He had a clear line of fire, and the grade was too steep for the outlaws' horses to climb with riders on their backs. They would have to approach him on foot, if they dared.

Leaving Horse down below on the trail, he pulled and tugged his pack horses up the hill, one at a time. Once there, he unloaded some of his supplies. He whistled as he unpacked his gear. After he had it all laid out on the ground, he planned how he wanted it distributed and set various rifles and guns and bundles of dynamite in different spots. He knew he was likely to take some lead in the upcoming fight and he feared he might not be as mobile as he wanted to be. It was essential that he have weapons in several locations because he didn't know where he might be if he got hit.

He made a mark, a blaze with his knife, down low on each of the trees behind which he hid weapons. His bright mark on the wood would show up well in either moon or starlight. With each bundle of dynamite he secreted some lucifers wrapped in wax paper to keep them dry in the event of snow.

After a while, when he was certain he had done all he could to prepare his battleground, he took the pack animals back down the hill to where he had left Horse. He removed his saddle and bridle from Horse and gave him an apple while he spent a moment rubbing his mount's neck. He knew his gelding would find its way back to Sugarloaf and that there was plenty of sweet grass in the meadows along the way, and sooner or later one of the mountain men or miners who knew Smoke would find him and take him back to the ranch.

He slapped Horse on the rump and watched as he trotted off

down the slope. Smoke saddled one of the pack horses and began to make his way back down the mountain. He had a few surprises to construct, and he didn't know how much time he had before the gang would arrive.

It was full dark when he reached the lower regions of the mountain, where it first began its steep climb toward the summit. He built a small fire and cooked some of the venison Puma had smoked for him, made some pan-bread, and fixed a pot of strong coffee. The air would get very cold, even at this lower elevation, and he wanted something warm in his stomach to get him through the night.

When he was finished eating, he rolled two cigarettes and smoked them both with the last of his coffee. He put out the fire and moved his camp a mile over to the south, not wanting to sleep where there had been any light from his cooking fire.

He picketed the pack horses and snuggled down in his bed-roll, covered with an additional layer of pine boughs and leaves. His breath sent frost-smoke from his nostrils and small beads of ice formed on his eyebrows as large, fluffy flakes of snow began to drift down from clouds overhead.

At dawn, he began working without taking the time to cook breakfast. He shared some apples and sugar and some cold mountain water from his canteen with the horses and then got busy. Finding a muddy, boggy area, he squatted and got large handfuls of mud and smeared it over rolls of lariat rope and rawhide he brought from the ranch. Once covered with the black mud, the rope blended in perfectly when laid on the ground or wound around a tree. It couldn't be seen from more than a foot or two away. He left one roll of the rope uncovered. This particular rope he wanted to be noticed.

He cut down a bunch of young saplings, five to six inches in diameter, and ranging from five to ten feet in length. Using a small hatchet, since he didn't want to dull his tomahawk on the tough trees, he sharpened each end of the spear-like lengths of wood, then tied them to a pack horse. They would be needed later.

As he moved along the trail, he stopped and gathered all the wild pumpkins and gourds he could find, storing them in a gunny sack tied to the side of his pack horse. Whenever he came to a rock fall, he picked up as many of small, fist-sized rocks as he could find, throwing them in the sack with the gourds and pumpkins.

Several times, he stopped at narrow places on the trail and got his shovel out and dug holes, about twice the diameter of a horse's hoof and two feet deep. In the bottom of these, he would place a sharpened wooden stake, then fill the hole with pine needles, making it look as though it was part of the trail. If stepping in the hole didn't break a horse's leg, the stake would impale its hoof and make it unable to carry any weight. Smoke hated the idea of injuring innocent animals, but in this case, it was them or him. He needed any advantage he could create, and putting flat-landers afoot in these altitudes would quickly sap them of their strength and will to fight.

In some places, next to drop-offs and cliffs, he dug parts of the side of the trail away, then made a frame of small branches covered with more dirt and pine needles to hide the defect. Any bronc stepping on these would stumble to the side, carrying its rider over the edge with it.

Some heavy limbs were pulled back, with the help of the horses, and tied so that anyone passing would release them and be smacked in the chest, breaking ribs and arms and sowing more confusion.

Fear was to be Smoke's strongest ally. These men were completely unused to being afraid of anything. Most were certainly not afraid of dying, at least not in ways familiar to them. But, give them a situation in which they felt they were not in control, a situation where they didn't know what was going to happen to them next, where they were continually seeing their comrades-in-arms dying or being injured without warning, and even the strongest of them was liable to break and head back home.

As Smoke made his rounds, laying traps and setting deadfalls and other surprises for his pursuers, he occasionally came upon lone mining camps and small enclaves of miners and trappers. He felt it was his obligation to warn them of the impending battle. Most of the occupants just shrugged and said they'd take their chances, not having much that would interest the outlaws. Some immediately packed their meager belongings and headed down the mountain, figuring on a short vacation before the snow made their mining impossible anyway.

The following morning, as Smoke was riding through pine forest, familiarizing himself with the layout of the area, he saw smoke rising from just over the next ridge. He loosened the rawhide thongs on his Colts and shucked a shell into his Henry.

With eyes even more alert, scanning the woods and underbrush to either side as he rode, he walked his mount to the top of the hill to take a look. He saw an old, weathered miner's cabin in flames, with two bodies lying nearby in a small clearing in front of a makeshift tunnel in the side of a mountain.

He spurred his horse and loped down toward the burning building. Before dismounting, he took another look around, but saw no one in the area. Swinging down from his saddle, he approached the bodies, the Henry cocked and ready.

There were two corpses, an older, bearded man who looked to be sixty years old or so, and a younger, clean-shaven boy who had some facial resemblance to the first. "Father and son, probably," thought Smoke, as he bent and checked for signs of life. There were none. Both men had been shot through the head and were dead as yesterday's news.

Smoke examined the area. Tracks and boot prints indicated four to six men and their mounts. The majority of the prints led to and from the mine entrance in the side of the cliff. He laid his rifle down, filled his hands with Colts, and walked slowly toward the black hole in the mountain.

His boots kicked up small puffs of dirt, and smoke from the cabin swirled around him, ruffling the fringe on his buckskin shirt and stinging his eyes and nose.

Turning sideways to present less of a target when he was backlighted in the entrance, he slipped into the cool darkness of the tunnel. He could hear a soft sound a short distance down the shaft, like rats scrabbling for food or prey.

He parted his lips and breathed through his mouth to lessen the sound, crouched, and inched his way along, feeling his way in the darkness.

Sensing a movement in the still air, he dove to the ground just as a shadowy figure appeared before him and swung a two-by-four at his head. He heard the board whistle past his ear, and tackled his attacker, the two of them rolling in the dirt and rocks of the tunnel floor.

A woman's scream pierced the gloom, yelling that she was going to kill him and all his damned friends. After a brief struggle, Smoke managed to subdue the woman, sitting on her with her arms pinned to the ground.

She flung her head from side to side and tried to bite his hands where he held her. When she realized he had her under complete control, she relaxed and went limp, mumbling the Lord's prayer to herself.

Astonished and surprised, Smoke helped her to her feet and managed to convince her that he meant her no harm. She began to cry hysterically and told him to help her mother-in-law, pointing farther down the tunnel.

Smoke holstered his pistols and went in search of the other lady. He found her fifteen yards deeper in, and picked up her limp and unresponsive body and carried her to the mine's entrance.

After finding she was unconscious from a severe beating, but had no life-threatening injuries, he got his bedroll and bundled her in it, just inside the mine shaft. When he had the sleeping lady wrapped and protected from the chilly air, he asked the younger woman what had happened.

She sleeved tears and dried blood off her face, patted her ratted and disheveled hair into some semblance of order, then held out her hand. "I'm Jessica Aldritch, and she is my husband's mother, Aileen Aldritch."

Smoke took her hand and said softly, "I'm sorry about your husband and his father. There was nothing I could do for them."

Jessica nodded, straightening her shoulders and standing

straight. "I know. The outlaws killed them before they took us and . . ." She began to cry again, unable to finish her sentence.

She didn't have to. Smoke could tell what had happened by the ladies' torn dresses and the bruises and streaks of blood on their thighs.

He found his teeth clenching so hard his jaws ached. "How many were there, and when did this happen?" he asked, his mild voice betraying none of the emotion he felt.

Jessica looked out the tunnel entrance and watched their cabin burn for a moment before she answered. Finally, in a hoarse whisper, she said, "They came to the cabin yesterday, six of them, and asked for food and water. While my husband and his father gathered up some supplies, two of the men grabbed them and two others shot them." She paused to take a deep breath, "Then they took Aileen and me down into the mine." Her eyes looked haunted. "They kept at us 'til this morning, then took off, leaving us for dead."

"I was wondering why they didn't kill you."

"Aileen passed out hours ago, and I pretended to faint, hoping that would stop them." She wiped at her eyes. "It didn't."

Smoke walked to his horse and took two extra pistols out of his saddlebag. He gave them to Jessica. "You know how to use these?"

She opened the loading gate of the Colt, spun the cylinder to check the loads, then snapped it shut with a flick of her wrist. "Yes, sir, I do."

Smoke smiled, thinking, this one would do to ride the river with, all right. He didn't feel that about many women other than his Sally.

"I'm going to go after them, then I'll come back here and see that you two get down to town. Okay?"

"What's your name, mister?"

"Smoke Jensen."

"Mr. Jensen, if the chance avails itself, I'd appreciate it if you could manage to bring the red-haired one back with you, alive."

Smoke raised his eyebrows. "Any particular reason why you want that one?"

Her eyes bored into his. "He's the one who shot my husband." Her eyes flashed, reflecting the shimmering flames of her burning home. "I would like to discuss that act with him, and watch his face while I kill him."

Smoke nodded. "You got every right, I guess. If it's possible, I'll be back before sundown."

As he turned to go, she touched his arm. "Mr. Jensen, do you have a shovel with you? I'm afraid they burned ours."

Smoke left the ladies with his shovel and rode off, bending low over the saddle to follow tracks the killers left.

It was almost noon when he found their camp. The sleepless night must have made them exceedingly tired, as they were all sprawled around their campfire snoring. No one was standing watch.

Smoke slipped off his mount and walked on cat feet up to the camp, slipping his knife out on the way and filling his other hand with iron.

At the edge of their campsite, next to a saddle, he found a leather bag with the name Aldritch stamped into the leather. That settled it as far as Smoke was concerned; these were the men he was hunting.

He squatted between two of the sleeping men, and quick as a rattler striking, he slit their throats with his big knife. One of the men only moaned, and lay there bleeding his life out into the dirt. The other squealed like a gut-shot pig and sat up, his hands at his throat, blood pumping and squirting from his neck, glistening scarlet in the bright afternoon sunlight.

Two of the desperados came instantly awake, clawing at their sidearms. Smoke cocked and fired, hitting one in the chest and the other in the abdomen, his second bullet punching through flesh, blowing out part of the gunman's spine. The gunshots were so close together they sounded like one noise. As his big Colts exploded, shots booming and echoing off the mountains, two of the others shook their heads and stared groggily around them, trying to make sense of what was happening.

Smoke stepped over and kicked one in the side of the face, snapping his head around and shattering his jaw. The other, the red-haired one Jessica had told him about, Smoke grabbed by the throat and jerked to his feet.

The dazed man looked around him, a puzzled expression in his eyes. "Why . . . why did you do this mister? We ain't done nothin' to you."

Smoke pulled the killer's face close to his. "Did you enjoy what you did to those women last night?"

The outlaw's eyes widened, then narrowed to slits as he glared at Smoke. "Why . . . what the hell do you mean?"

Smoke's lips curled in a sardonic grin, but his eyes were dark with hate. "I want you to reflect on it. I want you to remember how much *fun* you and your friends had, killing two men who were trying to help you; how *good* it felt to rape and beat their defenseless wives all night."

The killer's expression became defiant. "Why should I do that . . . and what business is it of your's anyway?"

The mountain man picked the two hundred pound man up effortlessly and threw him face-down over one of the horses. As he tied his feet to his hands beneath the nervous animal's belly, Smoke leaned down and spoke quietly in his ear. "I just hope it was worth it for you. That little episode of fun is going to have to last you an eternity."

"What do you mean?" the man stammered, fear-sweat dripping off his face.

"You got about an hour left to live. I'm taking you to meet the grim reaper, and she can't wait to say hello."

When he started blubbering and pleading for his life, Smoke left him and put the gent with the broken jaw across his horse the same way. After he was certain they were both securely tied, he began to move around their camp, searching carefully for anything that might belong to the Aldritch women.

The leather satchel contained a quantity of gold dust and nuggets, and in addition, he found almost ten thousand dollars, some in old bills and some in new ones. Figuring it was probably stolen from other folks like the Aldritchs, Smoke gathered up the gold and money and put it all in the satchel.

The ammunition and guns that he could use, he packed on one of their horses.

Finally, when he had taken everything of use, he strung the rest of their horses together and dallied them to his saddle horn. As he pulled out, headed back to the Aldritch mine, the two killers continued to beg and plead with him to let them go. They promised him untold wealth if he'd only relent and let them live.

Smoke spoke to them one last time over his shoulder. "Your rotten lives aren't mine to give. I'll let you ask the women you raped, whose husbands you shot, what should be done with you."

His final comment sentenced the outlaws to spend their last hours on earth thinking about their miserable lives, and wondering just how they were going to die.

It was almost dusk by the time Smoke and his prisoners arrived back at the Aldritch place. Aileen Aldritch was awake, and was eating soup that Jessica had heated over a small camp-fire in the clearing. The cabin fire was almost out, though several logs were still smoldering and smoking, and likely would be for days.

Jessica glanced over her shoulder at the procession, and paled when she saw who was on the horses. She handed the soup bowl to Aileen, stood and smoothed her dress, and waited for Smoke with crossed arms.

Smoke dismounted and inclined his head at the red-haired prisoner. "Now what? It's your call," he asked Jessica.

She grabbed the man by his hair and bent his head up where she could look him in the eyes. She smiled, and the sight of it sent chills down Smoke's spine. He knew then the man was going to die very painfully.

"Mr. Jensen, if you would be so kind as to tie this coward to that tree over there, I'd be much obliged."

"Oh Jesus, oh Jesus, don't let her do nothin' to me mister! Just shoot me right now! Please!"

Without changing expression, Jessica slapped the gunman across the face, the sound like a gunshot in the quiet afternoon air. "You miserable coward! You never had the decency to live like a man your entire life, at least try to have the courage to die like one."

Smoke bent and cut the rope beneath the horse's belly, leaving the killer's hands and feet tied together. He flipped the end of the rope attached to his wrists over a low-hanging branch and pulled the man upright.

The gunman's eyes were wide with fright, tears were running down his face while he was crying and shouting and yelling for mercy.

Before Smoke could move, Jessica slipped his knife out of his scabbard and stepped in front of the red-haired cowboy. "Aileen, you can watch or not, it's up to you," she called over her shoulder.

After a moment, mother-in-law and daughter-in-law were standing side by side in front of the hysterical outlaw. Aileen took the knife and stepped up to him. "Forty-three years. We were together longer than you've lived, young man. You might as well have shot me when you killed my man. One thing is certain, you'll never make another woman a widow." She held the knife out and with a flick of her wrist slashed his belt and waistband. His pants fell to the ground. He wasn't wearing any underwear or longjohns.

Aileen handed the knife to Jessica and stepped aside. Jessica said, "When I was a young girl, my father told me that when a stallion, a bull, or a male dog gets vicious or bad, there's only one cure. Do you know what that is, mister?"

"No ... no ... no!" he screamed, twisting his body back and forth, trying to protect his private parts from the women. "You're plumb crazy ... you can't do this to me!" He turned his head toward Smoke. "Mister, for God's sake! Stop her!"

Smoke shrugged and grinned. "I told you, she couldn't wait to say hello."

Jessica laid the razor-sharp edge of Smoke's knife underneath the outlaw's testicles, and it was over in one quick upward motion.

The killer looked down at his parts on the ground and screamed. Jessica moved to the side to avoid the stream of blood, and wiped the blade on his shirt. She handed the knife to Smoke and pulled one of the Colts he had given her out of her dress pocket.

Without hesitating, she placed the barrel against the head of the man still tied to his horse. "I don't recall your name mister, but I do recall that you weren't as brutal as the others." She smiled down at him. "That deserves some leniency."

As he smiled hopefully up at her, she pulled the trigger, blowing most of his skull out over the ground.

As the horse bucked and danced in fear, she handed the Colt to Smoke and put her arm around Aileen. "Let's go finish that soup before it gets cold, dear."

Smoke looked at the bodies of the two men and thought, "God, protect me from the wrath of a woman!"

Chapter Fifteen

Sundance Morgan removed his hat and sleeved sweat off his forehead. Though the air was cooler the farther north they rode, a mid-afternoon sun in a cloudless sky was brutally hot. In the last few days on the trail they hadn't come near a town of any size and his men were getting testy and short-tempered. Three days with no whiskey or females was beginning to cause problems.

The saloon women they had taken from the stage line station lasted only a few days. Two were killed trying to escape, the other, two days later, had taken her own life. While one of the outlaws was having his way with her, she pulled his Colt from its holster, shot him, and then put the barrel in her mouth and pulled the trigger, ending her torture. They left their companion to die in the dirt beside the bullet-torn body of the prostitute.

Sundance knew if they didn't come to a town soon, there would be trouble—blood trouble. Lightning Jack had taken to taunting some of the Mexican riders, calling them greasers and chili-eaters. It was only a matter of time before one of them, or Perro Muerte himself, stuck a knife between someone's ribs, and that would be the end of the uneasy alliance of the desperados.

Just when he was about to call the gang to a halt for their nooning, Sundance topped a ridge and saw a small group of buildings in the distance. He twisted in his saddle and waved his hat at his followers. *"Mi compadres,* a town!"

The killers perked up and spurred their horses to a trot, anxious to sit on something that didn't move and drink something stronger than water.

On the outskirts of the village was a hand-lettered sign nailed to a pole: Hell's Hole, Colorado Territory.

The place was little better than a mining camp, with more tents than buildings. The good news was a large tent with a board front attached that had the word Saloon printed in large block letters at the top.

Sundance held up his hand. "Okay men, I know you're ready for some whiskey and women, but we got to get the horses cared for first. Take 'em to the livery stable and get 'em fed and brushed down before headin' for the dog hole."

His pronouncement was greeted with several hoots and groans, but he scowled them into silence. "Don't forget who's in charge here! We got us a ways to go yet 'fore we get to Smoke's stomping grounds, and I don't want no broncs pullin' up lame." He whirled his mount around and headed toward the far end of town where corral stables were visible from high ground. "We've got plenty of time to get alkalied, and to get laid if that's what you're hankerin' for," he added.

They rode off the ridge at a short lope.

After leaving their horses in the care of an elderly man at the livery, the entire group of paid gunmen walked down a dusty street to the saloon.

The townspeople didn't pay them much attention, since the town was full of characters not much different from Sundance's gang. Typical of many of the small mining camps in the Colorado mountain regions, it was full of rowdy, rough miners, few ladies other than camp-town whores, and not a few outlaws and men riding the owlhoot trail looking for a place to hide until their reputations died down.

Sundance paused before pushing through the batwings and looked at a sign, painted in blood-red paint which had dripped down the wall next to the entrance. "The Hole," he read out loud, with a chuckle. "Then I guess it'll be 'bout right for this group, huh, El Gato?"

The big Mexican grunted and pushed past him into the darkness of the saloon. "Only if it has *tequila.*"

Even though it was early afternoon, the place was full of hard-looking men. Sundance let his eyes adjust to the gloom, then walked to the far rear corner of the room and stood before two large tables, occupied by six men wearing denim jeans and thick shoes common to miners. They appeared to be well on their way to being drunk.

Sundance smiled, looked over his shoulder at his men, then back to the seated miners. "Sorry gents, it appears we're gonna need these tables."

One of the men looked up, too deep in his whiskey to see the menace in Sundance's eyes. "That's too bad, mister. These here seats're taken," he slurred, and reached for a liquor bottle in front of him.

Sundance spoke softly, "Carlito."

Suarez pushed through the crowd to stand next to his boss and slowly slipped his knife out of its scabbard and stood there, caressing the blade. His brass tooth gleamed in the meager light from a kerosene lantern overhead.

Sundance leaned down, placing his hands on the table with his face near the miner's nose. "Do you speak Mexican, mister?"

Red-rimmed, bloodshot eyes looked up at Suarez. "Yeah, a little. Why?"

"Do you know what they call my friend here?"

"No, what?"

"Perro Muerte."

The man thought for a moment, then his eyebrows raised. "Dead dog? What kind of name is that?"

In spite of himself, Sundance had to laugh, causing Suarez to take a step toward the drunk. Sundance held him back with a gesture. "No, no. It means 'Hound of Death.' Now, how do you suppose he got that name?"

The man snorted, a sarcastic expression on his face. "By killin' dogs?"

Before the miner could laugh at his own joke, Suarez stepped forward and buried his blade in soft flesh, slitting the drunk's throat so deeply that his neck was almost severed.

As his head flopped back and blood spurted, the other men at the table jumped back. Sundance planted a boot in the dead man's chest and kicked him over backwards. He called to the bartender, "Get this trash outta here and bring us some drinks."

By the time the gang was seated at the recently vacated tables, the barman had dragged the body out the door and brought several bottles of liquor to set before them.

"Will there be anythin' else?" he stammered.

El Gato took a swig of the whiskey, then leaned over to spit it on the floor, where it mixed with the pool of coagulating blood. He looked up, eyebrows knitted together in anger. "*Si!* Tequila and womens."

"We only got two whores, and they's busy in the rooms out back."

El Gato shrugged. "Make them less busy, *pronto,* or El Gato do it."

"Uh . . . yes sir. I'll go git 'em myself. And I don't have no tequila, but I got some *mescal.* That do?"

Lightning Jack asked, "You got any limes?"

"Limes?"

"Never mind," interrupted Sundance, "just get the girls and get the *mescal* and come back real soon."

"Yes sir!"

As the barkeep scurried back to the bar, a tall, rangy man walked into the saloon, a Greener cradled in his arms and a Colt slung low on his hip. "All right, everybody just stay calm! Now," he said, pushing back his hat, "I want to know who's been killin' people and leavin' 'em layin' on my street, bleedin' all over the place."

Sundance stood, and his men, all thirty-two of them, swung in their chairs, clearing their gun sides for action and letting their hands rest on wooden butts worn smooth by use. Even in the semi-darkness, the cowboy with the shotgun could be seen to pale. He glanced at the men, then down at his two-shot Greener, apparently realizing it would bring him nothing but a short ride to Boot Hill if he tried to use it.

"Are you the sheriff of this town?" asked Sundance.

"Name's Jake," he said uneasily.

"Well, Jake, I guess I'm the one you got to blame for that body out there. Seems he insulted my man here," he inclined his head at Suarez. "Called him a dirty name."

"Well, I—"

Sundance spread his arms. "We don't want no more trouble, Sheriff. If there's a fine for littering, or anything like that, I'd be glad to pay it."

Sweat beaded the lawman's forehead. "Yeah . . . okay. Fine for litterin's two dollars."

"Two dollars?" Sundance frowned.

"Uh, yeah, but since you're new to town, I'll overlook it this time. How's that?"

Sundance stepped up to the cowboy and slapped him on the back. "Jake, I knew when you walked in you was a reasonable man. How about havin' a drink with us?"

"Sure, why not?" he replied, his voice thin, a bit shaky.

El Gato moved his chair to make room for Jake to sit, and Lightning Jack poured him a tumbler full of whiskey.

"Just what do you folks do in this town for fun, Sheriff?" asked Bull.

Jake did a double-take at Bull's high voice and slight lisp, but wisely decided not to mention it. "There's only two things to do around here after dark. You're already doin' one of 'em, an' that's drinkin'."

As the sheriff spoke, two women, dressed in well-worn, once brightly colored but now faded and shabby dresses, emerged from the back of the tent.

Jake nodded in their direction. "And there's the other." He leaned forward and whispered, " 'Ceptin' drinkin's more fun than those two. They're mighty well used, if you git my drift."

Lightning Jack laughed and slapped the man on the shoulder, Jack's big arm almost knocking the man off his chair. "After a week on the back of a bronc with nothin' better to look at than the butt of the horse in front of ya', I don't 'spect we'll be too choosey, my friend.''

The women walked toward Sundance's men, stopping when they got within range of the smell of the group. One turned to the other and wrinkled her nose, rolling her eyes. Sundance noticed the look and grunted. He took a leather pouch out of his pocket and threw a handful of double-eagles on the table. "We might not smell too good, ladies, but I'll bet the odor of this gold'll take your minds off that right quick.''

The whores smiled, showing teeth that would have made a horse trader wince, and joined right in, throwing arms around any man they could reach. "Mescal for everybody, Roy," one called to the bartender. "Let's get this party going!''

Bull stood and swept the heavier of the two women up in his arms. He glared at the others. "I'm goin' first this time. Any objections?''

"Not as long as you don't take too long. I got me a powerful thirst for woman-flesh, and I don't aim to wait 'til tomorrow," yelled Lightning Jack, with a grin.

Toothpick smiled. "Don't you worry none, Lightnin'. Bull's a lot faster on the draw with a woman than he is with those two cannons he carries.''

"His load's a mite smaller with that weapon, too," chimed in one of Jack's Southerners.

As Bull went through the door into a back room, he could be heard to say, "Yeah, but this one's good fer more'n two shots at a time.''

While his men proceeded to get drunk and man-handle the remaining whore, Sundance drew the sheriff to a quieter corner of the room for a private talk.

"What's your full name, Sheriff?''

"Jake Best.''

"Well, Jake Best, I'm pleased to meet you. My men and me're on the way up north. I got me a score to settle with a town, and a feller up there.'' He poured Jake another slug of whiskey. "I was wonderin' if you got any men in this town who might like to make a little money. I need men that don't mind gettin' shot at, nor shootin' back when it comes right down to it.''

Jake rubbed his chin whiskers, downed his drink in one quick swallow, then nodded. ''There might be a few who'd be interested in a deal like that. We got a few hereabouts that're meaner than a polecat.'' He smirked and motioned for a refill. ''Only not so smart.''

Sundance tilted the bottle over his glass. ''Brains ain't exactly what I'm lookin' for, Jake. I got enough brains for all of us. What I need is mean *hombres.*''

''Oh, they're plenty mean all right. Some of these boys'd shoot their mamma if she burnt their supper. Trouble is, they might be a mite hard to control.''

Sundance's teeth flashed in the shadows. ''That's not a problem. If'n money don't make 'em mind, then Mr. Colt will.''

Jake's eyes shifted to the pistol tied down low on Sundance's hip. ''Then I'll spread the word you're lookin' to hire some men. I'll tell 'em to meet you here in the saloon tomorrow after lunch.'' He looked around at the amount of whiskey the men were drinking. ''I don't 'spect you'll be up and about much 'fore then.''

Sundance glanced at the whore sitting on Lightning Jack's lap. El Gato was standing between her legs with his hand stuck down her bodice. ''No, Jake,'' Sundance mused, his lips curling in a slight smile. ''We've all got some catchin' up to do, too.''

The sun was directly overhead the next day when Sundance slouched into the saloon. His forehead was wrinkled and his eyes squinted against the power of the headache sending lightning bolts through his skull. His groin was sore and had begun to itch, adding worry about the health of his private parts to the agony of his hangover.

''Roy,'' he croaked, throat raw from whiskey and cigars he had consumed through the night, ''bring me some coffee. As strong as you got.''

''You want me to fetch some eggs or steak from the boardin' house across the street, Mr. Sundance?''

Stomach rolling at the thought of putting anything solid in it, Sundance shook his head and moaned as the motion caused pain to awaken behind his eyes. "No, just coffee, and water, if you got any worth drinkin'. My mouth's dry as Correo County back home in Texas."

After three cups of boiled bellywash, with pieces of eggshells used to settle the grounds still floating in it, Sundance was feeling slightly more alive. His two trips to the outhouse out back had relieved his gut some and eased his poor disposition a little.

It wasn't long before some of the roughest looking men he had ever seen began to drift into the room. They all wore pistols tied down low, and several carried rifles or shotguns slung over their shoulders.

When seven men were seated at his table, Sundance ordered beer all around, more to settle his stomach than to be sociable.

He rolled a cigarette and stuck it carelessly between his lips. Striking a lucifer on the hammer of his Colt, he lit his *cigarillo* and peered at the men through a cloud of smoke.

"Okay gents, here's the deal. My men and me are headed up into the mountains to a town name of Big Rock. I intend to tree that town and kill a man up there who did me dirt."

One of the cowboys, with eyes as old and hard as coal, raised his eyebrows. "Big Rock? Ain't that the town where Smoke Jensen hangs his hat?"

Sundance's eyes narrowed. "And who might you be, mister?"

"Name's Evans." He had one Colt in a low slung holster, another stuck behind his belt, and an American Arms ten gauge scattergun across his back on a rawhide sling.

"And I'll bet you be Sundance Morgan," he continued, the right side of his mouth curling in a sneer.

"What makes you say that?"

Evans picked up his mug of beer and drank, using his left hand. His right lay on his thigh, inches from his pistol. He sat the glass down and sleeved the foam off his moustache with his left forearm.

"I was down in Mexico last year, near Chihuahua, and ran

into a Mex named Carbone. He told me 'bout an *hombre* who fancied himself a gunhawk, and how Smoke Jensen shot off his ear to teach him a lesson.'' Evans reached for his beer and took another swig, his eyes never leaving Sundance's. ''He also said not to never turn my back on this particular gunslick— 'cause he's a back-shooter.''

''Why you ...'' Sundance grabbed for iron, only to find himself looking down the barrel of Evans's Colt before he could clear leather. He forced a sickly grin and put his hands flat on the table. ''You got it wrong, mister. Smoke Jensen bushwhacked me when I wasn't lookin'. It weren't no fair fight.''

''That's not the way I heard it, pilgrim, and I heard it from more'n one person.'' He grinned insolently. ''You're more famous than you realize, Sundance. Folks're laughing at you and your one ear from Mexico to the Canadian border.''

Evans stepped out of his chair, his gun barrel never wavering an inch. As he backed toward the door, he said, ''I don't know 'bout you other fellers, but this is one galoot who'd rather go to bed with a grizzly than trust Sundance Morgan.''

Sundance's face turned blotchy red as Evans backed through the batwings and disappeared into the sunlight. He slammed his fist on the table and asked, ''Who was that asshole?''

The man sitting next to him said, ''That there was Jessie Evans. Made himself quite a name in the Lincoln County war a few years back.'' The cowboy cut himself a chunk of tobacco from his plug and stuffed it in his mouth, then took a long drink of his beer. ''Said to have killed more men than he has fingers and toes.''

One of the others added, ''He supposedly backed down Billy Bonney, but, since he's been dead, most everybody claims that nowadays.''

Sundance took a deep breath, trying to calm his anger. ''Hell, I don't need him anyway.'' He raised his eyebrows and looked around the table. ''You men interested in makin' some money, and havin' some fun along the way?''

The man with the chewing tobacco leaned to the side and spit on the floor. ''How much money we talkin' about?''

"We split up the take evenly among those that survive, but I'll personally guarantee you each a hundred dollars a month, and I pay all expenses."

"Including whiskey and women?"

"All you can stand of both."

The men looked at each other, thought a moment, then one by one they nodded. "Count us in. Hell, it's got to be better'n scrabbling on our knees tryin' to dig gold outta them mountains."

Sundance gave each of the men two double-eagle gold pieces. "Here's an advance, boys. We're gonna leave in the mornin', so see if you can round up any more men who want a few of these in their pockets and the chance to tree a town and kill a sonofabitch at the same time."

The next day, the gang gathered in the saloon. Sundance stood and banged the butt of his Colt on the table for attention. "Men, we've got some new partners who have agreed to come along to Big Rock with us."

He pointed to a table aside from the ones where the original members sat. "The man on the end, with the scalps hangin' from his belt, is Blackjack Walker." Sundance looked around the room, "He says he's not particular, he'll scalp anybody, red, brown, or black."

As the men laughed, Sundance said, "The black man next to Walker is Moses Washburn. Moses was a buffalo soldier for the North, but I don't want that to put your men off, Lightning Jack. He deserted 'fore killin' any Southerners. He came out here and spent most of the war killin' Injuns."

"Next to Moses is Slim Johnson, he's from over New Mexico way, but says he don't wanna go back there 'cause there's more'n one noose waitin' on him."

He inclined his head toward two men sitting off by themselves at another table. "Over there we have George Stalking Horse and Jeremiah Gray Wolf. They used to scout for the Army, but had to leave suddenly after killin' one of their officers. He walked up on 'em while they was enjoyin' a little white woman lovin'. Seems she wasn't enjoyin' it quite as much as they was. They claim to be able to track a side-winder through a sandstorm." He smiled, "We'll see. We might just need some good trackers if Jensen's forted up in the mountains."

The gang stood and began to mill around the newcomers, introducing themselves and trading stories about mutual acquaintances. After a little while, Sundance said, "Okay boys, time to dust the trail. Load up on what you like to drink and eat, and let's saddle our mounts."

Chapter Sixteen

As dawn broke and the sun peered over peaks to the east, Cal and Pearlie walked their mounts up a narrow mountain trail. It was little more than a path, winding through dense ponderosa pines, with underbrush and small shrubs tugging at their legs on either side.

The air became thinner and colder the higher they climbed, and occasional small flurries of snow fell and dusted their hats and shoulders and their horses.

Cal sighed deeply, sending clouds of fog from his mouth to stir and mix with early morning ground mist still hanging low around them. "I swear, Pearlie," he said, "if'n we climb much higher, we're gonna have to look under rocks and such to find enough air to breathe."

Pearlie shook his head, flinging small flakes of snow off his hat. "Yeah, and we're only 'bout halfway to the top. It's gonna git worse 'fore it gits any better." He coughed as he shivered in his fur-lined coat. The dampness of the mist caused small beads of moisture to form in his moustache, glistening and sparkling in sunlight.

They rounded a bend, where tall pines thinned out into a small clearing next to a sheer drop-off. Pearlie, who was in the lead, leaned sideways and glanced over the edge at a two hundred-foot drop straight down. His horse, nervous at being so close to the cliff, whinnied loudly and began to side-step and dance away into the brush on the right side of the trail. "Whoa boy, easy there!" Pearlie cried, sweat popping out on his forehead as he fought his frightened animal.

When he finally had his mount under control, he swung his leg over the cantle and stepped out of his saddle. He spent a moment rubbing the horse's neck to calm its fear. "Cal, we'd better walk our mounts through this narrow place. Mine's actin' a might skittish."

Cal reined up and jumped to the ground, only a few feet from the precipice. "Yep," he said, "that looks to be one helluva long fall."

Pearlie grunted. "It ain't the fall that kills 'ya, kid. It's the landin' that messes up your innards."

They stood there, looking across snowy mountains and enjoying the view. Emerald-green pines and junipers interspersed and mingled with brilliant, sun-brightened white snow on peaks and in the valleys.

Suddenly, without warning, a piece of bark on a nearby pine tree in front of them exploded with a resounding thump, followed seconds later by a booming echo of a gunshot from trees to their right.

"Holy shit!" yelled Pearlie, as he dove beneath the belly of his snorting, rearing horse. He scrabbled on his hands and knees into nearby bushes, followed closely by Cal.

"Jesus, Pearlie! Someone's shootin' at us!"

Pearlie crouched in thick weeds and grass and small shrubs, looking around, trying to get a fix on where the bullet had come from. "That sounds like a Sharps Big Fifty."

"What's that?" asked Cal, both hands full of Colts.

"It's a buffalo gun." Pearlie said. He sprang from cover and jerked his Henry rifle out of his saddle boot, then hurried back into the brush, panting, his chest heaving as he thumbed a shell into the chamber. "I ain't seen one since Smoke's mountain men friends came to the ranch two year ago. Those old coots are 'bout the onliest ones who still carry 'em."

Dirt next to Cal's boot erupted, spewing a geyser of soil and pine needles into the air, followed again by an explosion that made their ears ring as it reverberated off the mountainside.

A voice called from a distance, "Come on out, boys, or I'll put the next one up your nose."

Fear-sweat dripped off Cal's face and his eyes were wide. "What'll we do now, Pearlie?"

Pearlie swiveled his head, but could see nothing except trees and forest all around them. "Don't look like we have much choice, Cal. That Sharps will cut through this brush like a hot knife through lard." He sighed and laid his Henry on the grass. "Holster them Colts, kid. You can't hit what you can't see."

He stood and raised his hands, stepping into the clearing with the back of his neck tingling. Cal followed, looking around in hopes of catching sight of whoever fired at them.

"Grab some sky, fellers, or I'll ventilate your ribs," the voice cried.

As Cal and Pearlie stood there, hands lifted over their heads, a ghost-like figure appeared out of the mist. He was leading a pinto pony and carrying a rifle that looked to be as long as he was tall.

Cal whispered, "Jumpin' Jimminy." He had never met one of the special breed called mountain men. The oldtimer was clad in buckskin shirt and pants, moccasins, with leggings up to his knees, and wore what appeared to be a beaver-skin hat. His grizzled whiskers were snow white, and his grin revealed yellow stubs of teeth. The barrel of his Sharps ended in a hole that seemed big enough to put a fist in, and it was pointed straight at the two cowboys.

"Howdy gents. Name's Puma Buck." The mountain man's eyes narrowed to slits and his grin faded. "Just what the hell are you two pilgrims doin' up here in my backyard?"

Pearlie smiled with relief, removed his hat and sleeved sweat off his face.

Puma's Sharps moved to aim between his eyes. "Why're you grinnin' like a she-wolf in heat, boy? You starin' death plumb in the face."

"We're right glad to meet up with you, Mr. Buck. I met

you 'bout two years ago at Smoke Jensen's ranch, when you and the other mountain men came down to Sugarloaf." He put his hat back on and lowered his hands. "Cal and me work for Smoke, an' we came up here to see if 'n we could find him." Pearlie paused a moment, hoping the old man hadn't forgotten the occasion, then continued, "Seems Smoke's got hisself a little problem."

Puma lowered his long rifle and nodded. "I 'member now." He peered closely at Pearlie. "You be the puncher that eats anythin' that ain't tied down."

Pearlie blushed as Puma chuckled. "Smoke spoke right highly of you, boy. Said you was a lot like him when Preacher took him to raise. Your name be Pearlie, if 'n I recollect correctly."

"Yes sir, Mr. Buck."

Puma frowned and gave the men an irritated look. "My name be Puma, boy, but only my daddy was called Mr. Buck." He raised his eyebrows. "So you two pilgrims came traipsin' up here to see if 'n you could help Smoke out, huh?'

"Yes sir."

Puma smirked, cocking his head. " 'Pears you young'uns don't have much faith that ole Smoke can take care of hisself."

Cal blurted out, "That's not it at all, Mr. Puma! It's jest that there's thirty or more gunslicks on their way here, settin' out to kill Smoke."

Pearlie nodded. "We just figgered a couple more guns wouldn't do no harm."

Puma chuckled. "You boys've got it all wrong. It ain't the number of guns you got with ya' or agin ya' that counts in a business like this. It be what you got deep inside that makes the difference in who rides out and who gits carried out facedown across a horse." He rubbed his whiskers and leaned on his Sharps as he looked out over the mountains. "I been knowin' Smoke since he weren't nothin' more'n a tadpole, and I'm here to tell you boys somethin'. He had fire in his belly and steel in his spine even then."

Puma paused to fire up one of the stogies Smoke had given him. After a few puffs, with smoke trailing out of his nostrils, he continued, "Ole Preacher recognized that fact right off." The mountain man wore a dreamy expression on his face as he remembered his old friend. "Preacher was tough and mean as a coon with rabies, but he had a soft spot in him for young'uns." He winked at Cal, " 'Specially those with bark on 'em. Smoke must have got some of that particular weakness from his ol' teacher. He tole me the other day he and Sally had taken in a button that would be famouser than him someday." The oldtimer smiled around his cigar. "I guess that'd be you he was talkin' 'bout, Cal."

Pearlie smothered a laugh by getting his makings out and rolling a cigarette, while Cal's face turned red as sunset.

"That's why I'm here, Mr. Puma. I owe Smoke an' Sally Jensen 'bout everything a body can, and I aim to pay 'em back by putting as much lead in Sundance Morgan's gang as I'm able."

Puma put his hand on Cal's shoulder. "Now, don't git your fur in a tangle, boy. Everybody was young onc't upon a time. Ain't no shame in bein' green as a new sapling when you's first startin' out." He picked a piece of tobacco off his lip. "Shame is not learnin' from those that can teach ya' what ya' need to know."

He leaned his head to the side and said, "Come on over here and follow me, both of you." He walked twenty yards up the trail and squatted, pointing at the ground. "Reason I shot at you boys wasn't to scare ya' . . ." he paused a moment, with a twinkle in his faded blue eyes, and said, "leastways, not the onliest reason."

He wrapped his gnarled, arthritic hand around a branch lying in the dirt, partially covered with leaves and pine boughs. When he raised it, the men could see where the trail had been dug away and the trap had been set.

"If'n your mounts had stepped on this," he said, looking a few feet away to the edge of the cliff, "you'd be buzzard bait, splattered all over them rocks down there by now."

Pearlie whistled low under his breath as Puma reset the trap. "I didn't even see that." He looked back over his shoulder at the path they had been on. "It don't look no different from the rest of the trail."

Puma pinched the fire off his cigar and stuffed the rest into his mouth and began to chew. "Hell fire, boy, that's the whole idee! Don't do much good to set a trap fer an animal if'n the critter can see it."

Cal whispered in a hoarse voice, "That don't look like no animal trap to me."

Puma spit tobacco juice into the dirt. "It's fer the most dangerous and cunnin' animal there is, boy. The two-legged kind."

Puma stood up slowly and stretched, as if his old legs had stiffened in the short time he squatted. "Well, I guess if you young'uns are bound and determined to help your friend, the least I can do is make sure you survive long enough to pop a cap or two." Shaking his head in disgust, he climbed into his saddle. "You damn sure don't have enough trail-sense to make it on your own."

He turned his pinto into the woods and trotted off, avoiding the trail, without looking back. He called over his shoulder, "Follow me, boys, if'n you can manage it without gittin' yourselves killed."

Puma led the men on a tortuous journey up the mountain. He rarely used trails or paths, winding in and out among trees and underbrush in no discernable pattern. When Cal and Pearlie would think they were at a dead end, Puma would pull a branch aside and there would be an opening just big enough for the horses and men to squeeze through.

Cal whispered, "Jimminy, Pearlie, he must know 'bout every tree and rock on this here mountain. I'd have sworn there weren't no way up this hill 'ceptin' the trail."

Pearlie grunted. "Yeah, but that old man's been roamin' these mountains since long 'fore either one of us was born. He oughtta know his way 'round by now."

After two hours of climbing, just when the men thought their horses weren't going to be able to go any longer, Puma led them into a small clearing in front of his cabin. He twisted in his saddle and said, "Here be home, boys. Light and set and I'll git some *cafecito* goin'. Looks like you could use some."

As they stepped off their mounts, Puma disappeared into his lean-to. After a moment, he came out carrying a bag of Arbuckle's coffee and a pot that looked as old as the mountain man, and as black as if it hadn't been cleaned since he bought it.

He filled the pot half full of grounds, added a small amount of water, and hung it from a trestle over the campfire coals. Stirring the glowing embers with his moccasin, he threw some dry grass and twigs on top. After a moment, small flames began to flicker and then he added a couple of short logs.

Puma glanced at the sun, dimly visible through the snow-clouds overhead, and said, "Looks close enough to noon fer me to eat. How 'bout you boys?"

Pearlie grinned and rubbed his belly. "Sounds good to me, Mr. Puma. I'm so hungry my stomach thinks my throat's been cut."

Cal shook his head. "Boy, Puma sure had you pegged, Pearlie. You'd fight a buzzard fer its leavin's if'n you ever missed a meal . . . which you sure as hell haven't since I've knowed ya'."

Puma raised his eyebrows. "I've got some two-day-old venison in the cabin, which should be okay since it's been so cold lately, or I can rustle up some quail eggs, fatback, and make some pan-bread. It's your call, men."

Cal spoke up quickly, "If'n it's all the same to you, Mr. Puma, I'd like some of that venison." He glanced over at his friend. "Pearlie's a fine cook an' all, but I'm gittin' a mite tired of fatback and biscuits."

Pearlie frowned. "You sure as hell didn't seem to mind when it came time to dish it outta the pan, least not so's I noticed when ya' piled it so high it took both your hands to lift your plate."

Puma chuckled. "You boys make me miss havin' a woman 'round to jaw at." He rubbed his whiskers, "Huh, must be goin' on ten years or more since my last squaw died on me."

Cal's forehead wrinkled. "How'd she die, Mr. Puma? Killed by outlaws?"

"Naw, nothin' like that. Was in the middle of winter, and she got outta the blankets to go an' heat us up some coffee. One of those high-mountain squalls blew in kinda sudden-like, an' next thing I knowed, she was froze solid, squattin' in front of the fire with the coffee pot in her hand."

Pearlie said, "Jesus, that musta been awful."

With a twinkle in his eye, Puma nodded. "Yeah, it was. I had to wait fer the spring thaw to git the coffee pot outta her hand 'fore I could use it." He grinned, "It's a long winter without *cafecito,* boys, let me tell ya'."

It was only when he laughed and slapped his knee that the men knew he was funning with them. He went into the cabin to get the deer meat, and Pearlie jabbed Cal in the side with his elbow. "I knowed he was just havin' us on all the time."

Cal laughed, "Sure you did, Pearlie, sure you did."

The men all pitched in to cook lunch. Cal peeled some wild potatoes and cleaned the dirt off onions Puma had in a burlap sack, and Pearlie poured coffee all around while Puma put the venison on a spit to heat it up.

Cal dumped the potatoes and onions in a pot to boil, then took a drink of coffee Pearlie handed him. After sucking in his breath and swallowing a couple of times, he said, "That's some bellywash."

Puma sipped his coffee and sighed. "Just 'bout right, I reckon." He looked over at Pearlie. "I wouldn't leave it in the cup too long, boy. It's liable to eat its way right through the tin."

He drew one of the largest knives Cal and Pearlie had ever seen out of his scabbard and sliced off hunks of steaming meat and piled it on their plates, then speared potatoes and onions and added them to the venison. "Dig in men, 'fore the flies and mosquitoes carry it off."

As they ate, Cal said, "Mr. Puma, Pearlie's been tellin' me some stories 'bout when Smoke was first up here, when he was with Preacher."

Puma nodded. "Those were the good days. The only law

up here then was the law a man carried in his holster or in his saddle boot. The rivers was full of beaver, the woods was full of wolves an' grizzlies, and the plains was full of Injuns. Hell, if'n I saw another white man more'n twice a year, I'd move 'cause the area was gittin' too civilized.''

Pearlie spoke up. ''I was tellin' Cal 'bout how Smoke went after Potter, Stratton, and Richards, the men who killed his brother and stole the Confederates' gold.''

Puma held a large piece of deer meat in both hands, chewing it as fast as his stubby teeth would allow. ''Yep. That was a right smart fracas, all right.''

''Can you tell me about how he got 'em, Puma?''

The old man looked up, over his venison, and grinned. ''Soon's I finish this here meat, boy. Never could eat 'an talk at the same time.''

Chapter Seventeen

The three men sat around the campfire eating quietly, enjoying their meal. Occasional small flurries of snow fell, hissing and crackling in the flames, while frigid mountain air ruffled fringe on the old man's buckskin shirt and caused the younger men to hunch their shoulders in their heavy coats.

Pearlie noticed the mountain man didn't seem to mind the cold. His blood must be thick as molasses after all these years up here in the high lonesome, he thought.

Puma finished his venison, wiped his greasy hands on his buckskin shirt, and fished a stogie out of his pocket. He lit it with a burning twig from the fire and laid back against a log, coffee tin in one hand and cigar in the other.

"That were the last battle fer some of my ol' friends, Dupre, Greybull, and the midget, Audie. They'd come out of the mountains to help their friend, Preacher, and his young boy, Smoke, to git his revenge. T'was near the town of Bury, but the final fight took place at an ol' ghost town, name of Slate."

He took a few pulls on the cigar, getting it going just right, then sipped his coffee and began his tale.

* * *

The ever-shrinking band of outlaws and gunhands looked toward the west. Another cloud of black smoke filled the air.

Lansing began cursing. "How in the hell are those old men doin' it?" he yelled. "We're fightin' a damned bunch of ghosts."

"Are you stayin' or leavin'?" Stratton asked.

"Might as well see it through," the man said bitterly. Those were the last words he would speak. A Sharps barked, its big slug taking the rancher in the center of his chest, knocking him spinning from his saddle.

"I've had it!" a gunhand said. He spun his horse and rode away. A dozen men followed him. No one tried to stop them.

"Look around us," Brown said.

The riders examined the land. A mile away, in a semicircle, ten mountain men sat their ponies. As if on signal, the mountain men lifted their rifles high above their heads.

Turkel, one of the most feared gunhawks in the territory, looked the situation over through field glasses. "That there's Preacher," he said, pointing. "That 'un over yonder is the Frenchman, Dupre. The one ridin' a mule is Greybull. That little bitty shithead is the midget, Audie. Boys, I don't want no truck with them old men. I'm tellin' you all flat-out."

The aging mountain men began waving their rifles.

"What are they tryin' to tell us?" Reese asked.

"That Smoke is waitin' in the direction they're pointing," Richards said. "They're telling us to tangle with him—if we've got the sand in us to do it."

Potter did some fast counting. Out of what was once a hundred and fifty men, only nineteen remained, including himself. "Hell, boys! He's only one man. There's nineteen of us!"

"There was about this many over at that minin' camp, too," Britt said. "Way I see it is this, we either fight ten of them ringtailed-tooters, or we fight Smoke Jensen."

"I'll take Smoke," Howard said. But he wasn't all that happy with his choice.

The mountain men began moving, tightening the circle. The gunhands turned their horses and moved out, allowing themselves to be pushed toward the west.

''They're pushin' us toward the ghost town,'' Williams said. Richards smiled at Smoke's choice of a showdown spot.

As the abandoned town appeared on the horizon, located on flats between the Lemhi River and the Beaverhead Range, Turkel's buddy, Harris, reined up and pointed. ''Goddamn place is full of people!''

''Miners,'' Brown said. ''They come to see the show. Drinking and betting. Them mountain men spread the word.''

''Just like it was at the camp on the Uncompahgre,'' Richards said with a grunt. *(The Last Mountain Man)* ''Check your weapons. Stuff your pockets full of extra shells. I'm going back to talk with Preacher. I want to see how this deal is going down.''

Richards rode back to the mountain men, riding with one hand in the air.

''That there's far enough,'' Lobo said. ''Speak your piece.''

''We win this fight, do we have to fight you men, too?''

''No,'' Preacher said quickly. ''My boy Smoke done laid down the rules.''

His *boy!* Richards thought. Jesus God. ''We win, do we get to stay in this part of the country?''

''If'n you win,'' Preacher said, ''you leave with what you got on your backs. If'n you win, we pass the word, and here 'tis. If'n you or any of your people ever come west of Kansas, you dead men. That clear?''

''You're a hard man, Preacher.''

''You wanna see just how hard?'' Preacher challenged.

''No,'' Richards said, shaking his head. ''We'll take our chances with Smoke.''

''You would be better off taking your chances with us,'' Audie suggested.

Richards looked at Nighthawk. ''What do you have to say about it?''

Nighthawk made no sound.

Richards looked pained.

''That means haul your ass back to your friends,'' Phew said.

Richards trotted his horse back to what was left of his band. He told them the rules of engagement.

Britt looked uphill toward a crumbling store. "There he is."

Smoke stood alone on the rotted boardwalk. The men could see his twin .44's belted around his waist. He held a Henry repeating rifle in his right hand, a double-barreled express gun in his left hand. Smoke ducked into the building, leaving only a slight bit of dust to signal where he once stood.

"Two groups of six," Richards said, "one group of three, one group of four. Britt, take your men in from the rear. Turkel, take your boys in from the east. Reese, take your people in from the west. I'll take my hands in from this direction. Move out."

Smoke had removed his spurs, hanging them on the saddle horn of Drifter. As soon as he ducked out of sight, he ran from the building, staying in the alley. He stashed his express gun on one side of the street in an old store, his rifle across the road. He met up with Skinny Davis first, in the gloom of what had once been a saloon.

"Draw!" Davis hissed, hunkering down.

Smoke cleared leather and put two holes in the gunman's chest before Davis could cock his .44's. The thunder from his Colts echoed across the valley.

"In Pat's Saloon!" someone shouted farther down the street.

Williams jumped through an open, glassless window of the saloon. Just as his boots hit the floor, Smoke shot him, his .44 slug knocking the gunslick back out the window to the boardwalk. Williams was hurt, but not out of it yet. He crawled along the side of the building, one arm broken and dangling, useless, blood pouring from a gaping bullet wound in his shoulder.

"Smoke Jensen!" Cross yelled. "You ain't got the guts to face me!"

"That's one way of putting it," Smoke muttered savagely, taking careful aim and shooting the outlaw, feeling his pistol slam into his palm. A ball of lead struck Cross in the stomach, doubling him over and dropping him to the weed-grown, dusty road.

The miners had high-tailed it to ridges surrounding the town. There they sat, drinking and betting and cheering. The mountain men stood and squatted and sat on an opposite ridge, watching.

A bullet dug a trench along a plank, sending tiny splinters flying, a few of them striking Smoke's face, stinging and bringing a few drops of blood from his cheeks.

Smoke ran out the back of the saloon and came face to face with Simpson, a gunhawk with both hands filled with .44's.

Smoke pulled the trigger on his own .44's, the double hammer-blows of lead taking Simpson in his lower chest, slamming him to the ground, dying from two mortal wounds.

Quickly reloading, Smoke grabbed up Simpson's guns and tucked them behind his gunbelt. He ran down the alley. The last of Richards's gunslicks stepped out of a gaping doorway just as Smoke cut to his right, leaping through an open window. A bullet burned Smoke's shoulder. Spinning, he fired both Colts, one bullet striking Martin in his throat, the second taking the gunnie just above his nose, almost tearing off the upper part of his right cheek.

Smoke caught a glimpse of someone running. He dropped to one knee and fired. His slug shattered Rogers's hip, sending the big man sprawling in the dirt, howling and cursing. Reese spurred his horse and charged the building where Smoke was crouched. He smashed his horse's shoulder against a thin plank door and thundered in. The horse, wild-eyed and scared, lost its footing and fell, pinning Reese to the floor, crushing his belly and chest. Reese screamed in agony as blood filled his mouth and darkness clouded his eyes.

Smoke left the dying man and ran out a side door.

"Get him, Turkel!" Brown shouted.

Smoke glanced up. Turkel was on the roof of an old building, a rifle in his hand. Smoke flattened against a building as Turkel pulled the trigger, the slug plowing up dirt at Smoke's feet. Smoke snapped off a shot, getting lucky as the bullet hit the gunhand in his chest. Turkel dropped the rifle and fell to the street, crashing down to a rotted section of boardwalk. He did not move.

A bullet from nowhere nicked a small part of Smoke's right ear. Blood poured down the side of his face. He ran to the spot where he had hidden his shotgun, grabbing it and cocking it just as the door frame filled with men.

Firing both barrels, Smoke cleared the doorway of all living things, including Britt, Harris, and Smith, buckshot knocking men off the boardwalk, leaving them dead and dying in the street.

"Goddamn you, Jensen!" Brown screamed in rage, stepping out into the empty roadway.

Smoke dropped his shotgun and picked up a bloody rifle from the doorway. He aimed quickly and fired, catching Brown in the stomach. Brown jerked and fell to the street, both hands holding his stomach.

Rogers leveled a pistol and fired, his bullet ricocheting off a support post, a chunk of lead striking Smoke's left leg, dropping him to the boardwalk. Smoke ended Roger's life with a single shot to his head.

White-hot pain lanced through Smoke's side as Williams shot him from behind. Smoke toppled off the boards, turning as he fell. He fired twice, his bullets taking Williams in the neck, causing Williams's head to twist at an unnatural angle.

Smoke scrambled painfully to his feet, grabbing a fallen scattergun with blood on the barrel. He checked the shotgun, then quickly examined his wounds. Bleeding, but not serious. Williams's slug had gone through the fleshy part of his side. Using the point of his knife, Smoke picked out a tiny piece of lead from Rogers' gun and tied a bandanna around the slight wound. He slipped farther into the darkness of the building as spurs jingled in an alley at the rear of the old store. Smoke thumbed back both hammers on the coach gun. He waited.

The spurs jingled once more. Smoke followed the sound with both barrels of the express gun. Carefully, silently, he slipped across the floor to a wall fronting the alley. He could hear heavy breathing somewhere in front of him.

He pulled both triggers, the charge blowing a bucket-sized hole in the weathered plank wall.

The gunslick was blown across the alley, hurled against an outhouse. The outhouse collapsed, while the gunhand fell into a pit where the outhouse had been.

Silently, Smoke reloaded the shotgun, then reloaded his own .44's and the ones taken from the dead gunman. He listened as Fenerty called for help from his companions.

There was no reply.

Fenerty was the last gunhawk left.

Smoke located the voice, just across the road in a decaying building. Laying aside the shotgun, he picked up a rifle and emptied its magazine into the storefront, explosions ending a brief moment of silence. Fenerty came staggering out, shot in chest and belly. He died face-down in a corpse-littered street.

"All right, you bastards!" Smoke yelled to Richards, Potter, and Stratton. "Holster your guns and step out where I can see you. Face me, if you've got the guts."

The sharp odor of sweat mingling with blood and gunsmoke filled the still summer air as four men walked out into the sunshine.

Richards, Potter, and Stratton stood at one end of the town. A tall, blood-smeared figure stood at the other. All their guns were in leather.

"You son of a bitch!" Stratton screamed, his voice as high-pitched as a woman's. "You ruined it all." He clawed for his .44.

Smoke drew and fired before Stratton's pistol could clear leather. Potter grabbed for his Colt. Smoke shot him dead, gunshots echoing off empty buildings, then he holstered his gun, waiting.

Richards had not moved. He stood with a faint smile on his lips, staring at Smoke.

"You ready to die?" Smoke asked, a sardonic grin creasing his face.

"As ready as I'll ever be, I reckon," Richards replied. There was no fear in his voice. His hands appeared steady. "Janey gone?"

"Took your money and pulled out."

"Been a long run, hasn't it, Jensen?"

"It's just about over now."

"What happens to all our holdings?"

"I don't care what happens to the mines. The miners can have them. I'm giving all your stock to decent, hard-working punchers and homesteaders. They've earned it."

A puzzled look spread over Richards's face. "I don't understand. You did . . . all this," he waved his hand, "for nothing?"

Someone moaned, the sound coming from up the street.

"I did it for my pa, my brother, my wife, and my baby son."

"But it won't bring them back!"

"I know."

"I wish I'd never heard the name Jensen."

"You'll never hear it again after this day, Richards."

"One way to find out," Richards said with a smile. He drew his Colt and fired. He was snake-quick, but hurried his shot, lead digging up dirt at Smoke's feet.

Smoke shot him in the right shoulder, spinning the gunman around. Richards grabbed for his lefthand gun and Smoke fired again, his slug striking Richards in the left side of his chest. He struggled to bring up his Colt. He managed to cock it before Smoke's third shot struck him in his belly. Richards sat down hard in the bloody dirt. He toppled over on his side and died instantly.

Smoke looked up at the ridge where the mountain men were gathered.

They were leaving as silently as the wind. *(Return of the Mountain Man)*

Puma finished his cigar at the same time he finished his story. He flicked it into the fire and stared silently at the flames, remembering his old friends and their last battle.

A voice called from the edge of the forest, startling the three men. "You boys believe anything that old coot has to say and you'll be sorry."

Smoke grinned and walked into the clearing, a Colt in each fist hanging at his side. "I heard you had company, Puma, so I slipped up here to see if they were friendly."

Cal and Pearlie both jumped to their feet and slapped Smoke on the back and shoulders. "Boy are we glad to see you, Smoke. We came up here lookin' for ya', to see if we could help out against Sundance and his gang," blurted Cal in a rush of words.

Smoke raised one eyebrow. "Uh-huh, and you end up listening to that old coot over there, the ugliest living mountain man in all Colorado territory, tell you some of his lies."

Puma frowned. "Weren't no lies, Smoke Jensen." He paused and grinned at his friend. "Leastways, not too many anyway."

Smoke threw his arm around Puma's shoulder and said to his punchers, "Boys, would you run up that trail, just over the next ridge, and fetch me the buckboard I left back yonder?"

As Cal and Pearlie turned to go, Smoke added, "Oh, and be careful, it's got a couple of women in it who've had a hard time."

After the Aldritch women were brought to Puma's cabin and were given some venison and coffee, Smoke asked Pearlie if he would escort them down to Big Rock to see Doc Spalding.

Pearlie raised his eyebrows. "What about Cal?"

"I reckon he can stay up here for a while. Maybe Puma can teach him some trail-craft while I set my traps and prepare for the arrival of Sundance and his gang."

"But Smoke," Pearlie said, obviously not wanting to leave his friends.

Smoke held up his hand. "No butts, Pearlie. You know Cal can't manage that buckboard by himself, and you can. Now, the sooner you get gone, the sooner you can get back up here." He paused, then said, "I wouldn't want you to miss all the excitement."

Pearlie grinned. "Yes sir, Smoke. I'm on my way already."

Both the Aldritch women thanked Smoke, causing him to

blush mightily. "You tell Doc Spalding to give you anything you need," he called to them, as Pearlie drove the wagon away.

Puma shook his head and spit into the campfire. "I ain't never had so much company at one time in all my born days. It's gettin' too damned crowded around here."

Chapter Eighteen

Sundance Morgan reined in his mount and sat with his palms resting on his saddle horn, staring ahead through the heat waves and dust devils on the trail, thinking about what lay before him. His gang pulled their horses to a halt and they gathered around him. The animals' sides heaved and they shook sweat from their necks, exhausted from the ride. El Gato took a long pull from his canteen, wiped his moustache with the back of his hand, and asked, *"Senor* Sundance, why we stop?"

Sundance removed his hat and sleeved trail dust and sweat off his forehead. "Just over that next ridge is the town of Big Rock. I'm decidin' how we should handle it."

Perro Muerte grinned, his brass tooth gleaming in the sunlight. He pulled a Colt from his holster and held it up, barrel pointed at the sky. "This be one way. It sure to get their attention."

Sundance frowned. "I don't think so, not just yet. I believe we oughtta just ride in, peaceable as can be, and get the lay of the land first." He put his hat back on and settled it low. His eyes sparkled with hatred and remembered shame. "Then, if we don't get what we want, we'll have some fun and do some damage."

He spurred his bronc, and the others followed, raising a cloud of dust in still, dry air.

Matt and Timmy O'Leary, thirteen- and fourteen-year-old brothers, pulled their ponies up in front of Sheriff Monte Carson's jail in Big Rock.

"Sheriff Carson, Sheriff Carson, come quick," the younger boy cried from his saddle.

Monte stepped to the door of the jail, pipe in one hand and cup of coffee in the other. "Okay boys, calm down and tell me what's got you so riled up."

Matt, the older of the two, pointed over his shoulder toward the city limits. "Big cloud of dust, 'bout five or six miles out of town. Looks like it might be that gang we was watchin' for."

Monte's eyes narrowed as he looked south. "You boys did good. Ride on down to the blacksmith shop and ring the fire bell like we planned. That'll let everyone know the time has come."

"Gee, Mr. Carson, you're gonna let us ring the bell?"

Monte smiled. "Sure. You gave the warning, so you get to ring the bell. Tell Smitty I told you to do it. He'll understand." He pointed with the stem of his pipe. "Afterwards, you get your butts on home and stay off the street 'til I tell you it's okay to come out."

"Sure thing, Sheriff. Let's go, Timmy. I'll let you ring it first, then it's my turn." The boys rode off, kicking their ponies to a gallop.

Monte took a deep drag on his pipe, then he spoke to his deputy. "Jim, looks like it's about that time. Hand me my Greener, will ya'? We got to get to our stations as soon as we can."

Monte took his ten gauge scattergun from Jim and sat in his chair on the boardwalk in front of the jail. He put his coffee cup down, loosened the rawhide thongs to his Colts, and leaned his chair back against the wall. He placed the Greener across his lap, both hammers jacked back, stuck his pipe in his mouth, and waited. I hope we're doing the right thing, he thought, worrying about what could happen to his town.

Louis Longmont drew three cards to a pair of queens. As he spread them out, he noticed he had drawn two sevens and another queen. Other than a shallow breath, he displayed no emotion at all over his good fortune. He picked up his cigar and fingered a stack of chips, ready to bet his hand, when he heard the fire bell begin to ring.

He rolled his eyes and swore softly to himself. Yet another reason to hate Sundance Morgan. He flipped the pasteboards to the table face-down and said to the man seated across from him, "Your pot, James. Game's over."

Coming to his feet, he motioned to his barkeeper and the women around his saloon to take their places. Two of the girls took small belly-guns out of their handbags and sat at tables on either side of the batwings. His young waiter took an old shotgun with rusted barrels off a rack and went upstairs, finding a spot next to a window overlooking the street below. Jonathan, the barkeep, put a .44 Colt in his waistband behind his back and stood, wiping the bar with a rag and whistling to himself.

Louis drew his pistol and opened the loading gate, spinning the cylinder to check his loads. After he finished, he holstered his gun and called, "Andre. Come out here please."

When the chef appeared, apron tied around his ample stomach, Louis said, "Andre, under no circumstances are you to come out of the kitchen. Do you understand?"

"But sir," Andre answered, "I want to do my part. What if you get shot? What will I do?"

Louis smiled. "Andre, the world can easily do without a gambler and roustabout like me, but civilization can ill afford to lose a master chef of your talent. Believe me, I will not abide you risking your life in this matter." Louis hesitated, sniffing the air. "Now, if my nose does not deceive me, you have a souffle in the oven that needs your immediate attention."

Andre smiled at the compliment and departed to his beloved kitchen, swaggering as he walked away.

* * *

Sundance rode into Big Rock, his men spread out behind him, riding six abreast, forty-three men in all. They were a rough bunch and he knew it. All wore their guns tied down low, and most carried rifles or shotguns braced upright on their thighs or lying across saddle horns.

Something is terribly wrong in this place, he thought. He had ridden through dozens of Western towns in his years on the owlhoot trail. Some were big, and some small enough to throw a stone from one end to the other, but none was like this one. There were no people on the streets, no children or dogs, and no cowboys on horseback or folks in buckboards loading supplies.

George Stalking Horse spurred his mount up to trot side-by-side with Sundance. "Boss," he said out of the corner of his mouth, eyes narrowed and suspicious. "I'm beginnin' to feel like Custer must have felt ridin' into Little Bighorn."

"I know the feeling, George. Something ain't right here, that's for sure." Sundance looked to one side as they neared the jail, and saw the only sign of life in town. A man was sitting, his chair tilted back and legs outstretched on the hitching rail. His pipe was emitting a thin trail of smoke, and his hand was on the shotgun in his lap.

Bull, riding on Sundance's other side, whispered, "Boss, take a peek at his short-guns."

Sundance turned and saw the rawhide thongs pulled back from the hammers of a pair of Colts. He gritted his jaw. He didn't like the looks of things.

Pulling his mount to a halt, he thumbed his hat back and grinned at the man with a badge pinned to his shirt, the effort hurting his lips. "Howdy, Sheriff. How're things?"

The lawman raised his head, glaring at the riders from under his hat brim. "Hello, Sundance. Things are just fine. How about with you?"

Sundance was startled when the sheriff called him by name, and suddenly he realized that meant he probably had known they were on the way and the reason for his visit. He remembered the sheriff's name. "Tolerable, Sheriff. Carson's your handle, ain't it?"

Carson let his chair fall forward until all four legs were on the porch. While doing so, he slowly let the barrel of the shotgun lean over until it pointed directly at Sundance's belly. "Yep. I'm honored that you remember." He laughed derisively, low in his throat. "Last time you was here, you left in such a rush, I didn't get to give you your ear back."

Sundance sucked in his breath and his face blanched at the insult. His hand twitched and hovered over his Colt, but the end of the Greener never wavered an inch, and Carson's eyes burned a hole in his face.

Carson continued, a smirk on his lips. "I tried to save it for you, but a dog ate it before I could get to it."

Sundance did his best to bridle his temper. Those twin barrels of the scattergun looked like cannons. "Speakin' of that incident, Sheriff, where is Smoke Jensen these days? I'd kinda like to pay him a visit." His voice broke when he spoke, making him even more angry that he'd lost control.

Carson said, "I know you'd like to pay him a social call, Sundance, but I bet he'll like it a whole bunch more'n you will." He tilted his head toward the mountains. "He heard you were coming, so he went up into the high lonesome to wait for you. Said to give you his regards, and to tell you he'd be somewhere close to that tall peak to the east." Carson spat on the ground, as if talking to the gunman gave him a bad taste in his mouth. "Course, don't none of us who know you think you'll have the guts to go up after him." He glanced at the assortment of riders behind Sundance. "No matter how many men you have backin' you up."

Sundance turned his horse to face Carson and leaned forward in the saddle. "You know, Sheriff Carson," he muttered, venom in his voice, "you shouldn't let your mouth overrun your ass. I got over forty men with me here, and you got . . . what? Two shots in that express gun of yours?"

Carson continued to smile insolently at the outlaw. "I'm not worried. You see, the first barrel, the one on the right here, is loaded with buckshot. That's for you. I figger there won't be enough of you left to fill a coffee cup after I unload on your belly." His smile turned to a snarl when he saw sweat running down Sundance's cheeks, staining the bandanna around his neck. "The second barrel, the one on the left is also loaded with buckshot, but it's for that big, stupid-looking gent ridin' next to you, the one with the jug-handle ears."

Bull's eyes widened, and his hands clenched and unclenched in helpless anger. He knew that if he drew, he'd be dead before he cleared leather. In his high, woman's voice, he spat, "What about the rest of these men, Sheriff. They'll kill you where you sit, before you reach for those pistols."

Carson laughed, infuriating Sundance even more, but clearly making the rest of his gang edgy. What was this man so confident about? Sundance wondered. He was facing forty men with guns.

"We've been ready," Carson said, continuing to chuckle over Bull's voice. He yawned elaborately, covering it with the back of his hand. "You asked about the rest of your men?" He put two fingers in his mouth and whistled shrilly.

Doorways all along the street filled with citizens armed to the teeth with rifles, shotguns, and pistols. Heads popped up on roofs and behind eaves and elevated store fronts, and gun-toting men appeared in alleys and between buildings.

From behind, Sundance heard a deep voice say, "Hey, back-shooter, remember me?"

Sundance twisted in his saddle to glance over his shoulder. He saw a tall, slim man, dressed in a black split-tail coat and a ruffle-front shirt, with two Colts slung low on his hips. Then he recognized him as Louis Longmont, hands hanging at his sides, fingers flexing in anticipation.

"That's correct, Lester Morgan, I'm calling you a coward." Louis shrugged his shoulders minutely, then the gambler proceeded to give the outlaw a solid cussing.

Sundance cursed under his breath, looking wildly around at all the townspeople and their guns. "Now's not the time, Longmont," he answered hoarsely, trying to control his jittery horse.

Longmont spread his arms. "When is the proper time for

you, coward? How about those sons-of-whores who ride with you? Are they chickenshit like you? Don't any of you *men* have any balls?'' he added sarcastically.

Several of the men on horseback yelled and cursed and drew their weapons, unable to take the insults any longer. Sundance held up his hands, trying to stop them, warning it was a trick, but his men were too angry to listen.

The street erupted with the sound of gunfire, booming and echoing off buildings while both men and horses screamed, some hit hard by flying lead. Clouds of gunsmoke billowed away from flaming gun barrels, filling the town with deafening noise.

Carson's scattergun exploded as he pulled both triggers and rolled out of his chair, scrambling quickly behind a nearby water trough. His shot cut one of the outlaws almost in half, blowing him out of his saddle.

Bull filled his hands with iron, two sawed-off shotguns both firing at Carson, molten buckshot tearing into the water trough, sending water and splinters into the air. Pellets penetrated the wood to lodge in Carson's left arm and shoulder, knocking him backward, spinning him around. He grunted in pain and rolled on his side, clawing for his Colts.

Sundance leaned over his horse's neck and spurred hell-for-leather down the street, firing twice at Louis as he galloped by. One of his slugs took Louis's hat off, the other burning a path across his waist, cutting a shallow gouge in his flesh.

Louis did not flinch from the pain, standing calmly while he took careful aim, firing both his Colts at Sundance, one after the other. Shots came so fast they sounded like one continuous explosion. One of his .44 bullets sliced a chunk out of Sundance's butt, the only target he gave Louis as he spurred away. Sundance screamed in pain and dropped his Colt to grab his ass, although he managed to stay in his saddle.

Bull, his shotguns empty, reined his horse into an alleyway, hitting a man with the animal's shoulder, knocking him to the dirt. Bull jumped off his mount and grabbed the stunned man's rifle, then stood over him and shot him in the head. Wheeling, he grabbed his saddle horn in one huge hand and made a running vault onto the galloping horse's back. As he rode out of town, he fired the rifle one-handed at a figure silhouetted in a window, showering him with bits of glass and splinters, missing his target.

Perro Muerte was having his own troubles. Wounded in the arm and thigh in the initial volley of gunfire, his horse shot out from under him, he was kneeling in the dusty street, firing his Colt at anything that moved. When his hammers clicked on empty chambers, he reached down into the bloody mess that had been the man Carson blew to pieces. He picked up a blood-splattered rifle and wheeled around. A member of the gang, Charley Wilson, was riding by, firing pistols with both hands. Without hesitation, Perro Muerte swung the rifle in a horizontal arc, slamming Wilson backwards out of his saddle and shattering his jaw. Perro Muerte got lucky and managed to grab the mount's reins. Dropping his rifle, he stepped into the saddle and clung to the frightened animal's side for dear life as it galloped down the street.

Slim Johnson didn't have to worry about returning to New Mexico and being hung. As he was riding out of town, firing over his shoulder, one of the ladies who sang in the church choir stepped out of a doorway, leveled her husband's Henry repeating rifle, and blew him to hell. The bullet entered the killer's left ear and exited his right, taking most of the side of his head with it. Johnson was dead before his body hit the ground, to bounce and tumble in the dirt like a rag doll.

As Toothpick spurred down the street, ducking and leaning to the side to avoid bullets, he saw Louis standing on the boardwalk shooting at Sundance. Toothpick drew his long knife from its scabbard and threw it at Louis with all his might as he passed. He laughed with delight when he saw the blade imbed itself in Louis's chest, knocking him backward. He fell on the boardwalk.

The battle of Big Rock lasted only a few minutes, but when it was over, twelve desperados lay dead or dying. Three townspeople were killed and six were wounded.

* * *

Monte Carson got to his knees, his Colts and express gun empty, and peered through the gunsmoke, nose wrinkling at the smell of cordite and blood and voided bowels. Moaning, crying, and pleas for help echoed down the street, but his attention was drawn to his friend, Louis, whose body he could see lying on the boards with a knife stuck in his chest.

"Oh no! God, don't let this be," Monte cried as he stumbled and limped painfully around the bodies of men and horses, running to see if he was too late to help.

He bent over the body and grabbed Louis's shoulders, blood from his own wounds dripping onto his friend's chest. "Louis, Louis, can you hear me?" he yelled, shaking the unconscious man.

Slowly, after a moment, a hand came up and touched Monte on the shoulder, "Of course I can hear you, Monte. I'm wounded, not deaf."

"What . . . ?"

Louis grabbed Monte's arm and pulled himself to a sitting position. He grunted and jerked the knife out of his chest, then reached into his coat and removed a sterling silver flask with a knife hole in it. "Damn," he said with feeling, as amber liquid spilled in the dirt, "that was twelve-year-old scotch."

Monte grinned and sat down hard next to the gambler. "Well, Louis," he rasped though a raw throat, "how'd we do?"

Louis glanced at the number of bullet-ridden bodies lying in the street. "This town did fine, my old friend, just fine."

He gazed toward mountain peaks in the distance. "The rest is up to Smoke Jensen."

Chapter Nineteen

Pearlie heard booming echoes of shotguns and higher pitched cracks and pops of short guns being fired in the distance while he was still several miles from Big Rock.

Jessica Aldritch, sitting next to him on the buckboard seat, cocked her head. The sky at these lower altitudes was a brilliant azure blue with small puffs of white clouds scattered from horizon to horizon like tufts of cotton waiting to be picked.

"Mr. Pearlie, what is that noise? It sounds like thunder, but I don't see any storm clouds."

Pearlie's eyes narrowed, a frown on his face. "T'weren't thunder, Mrs. Aldritch. That there was gunfire . . . a lot of it, and it's comin' from Big Rock."

"Big Rock? Isn't that where we're going?"

"Yes ma'am."

"Do you think it might be Indians?"

"Not likely, ma'am. What few Injuns we got left 'round here might attack a small party if they was hungry enough, but there ain't hardly a band anywhere in these parts big enough to try to take on a whole town."

He shook his head, torn between his desire to whip the horses into a gallop and rush to help his friends in town, and his duty to protect the two women Smoke entrusted to his care.

He hesitated a moment, unsure how much he should tell the widows about their present situation. He drew back on the reins and brought their wagon to a halt.

Aileen Aldritch, bundled in back under bearskins and wrapped in a buffalo robe Pearlie borrowed from Puma Buck, raised her head and looked around, a dazed expression on her face. She was not yet fully recovered from the ordeal she endured at the hands of the men at the mine. "Jessica, why are we stopping? Have we arrived at our destination already?"

Jessica twisted in her seat. "No, Mamma Aldritch." She looked at Pearlie with a quizzical expression. "Mr. Pearlie is just giving the horses a rest. You go on back to sleep. We'll wake you when we get there."

Pearlie sat still, reins in his hands, forehead wrinkled in thought, considering his options. Finally, he decided his best course of action was to relate his concerns to Jessica.

"Mrs. Aldritch, I think those gunshots are from a band of desperados, a bad bunch from down South."

"You mean outlaws?"

"Yes ma'am. We got word a couple of weeks ago they was on their way up here from Texas. They're lookin' fer Smoke Jensen, and intend to kill him."

"They want to kill Mr. Jensen? But . . . why?"

Pearlie shook his head in exasperation. He knew they didn't have much time. "It's a long story, ma'am. I'll tell ya' later, when I git you two to town safe and sound." He looked around, trying to find a suitable place to hide the buckboard and women.

"Trouble is, if'n those men survive the fightin' in town, they're gonna be comin' this way, headed up into the high country lookin' fer Smoke."

Jessica's eyes widened. "Oh, I see. You're concerned that if they see us, they might do us some harm."

Pearlie nodded, lips drawn tight. "You can near 'bout count on it, ma'am. Those men are some of the low-downest, meanest God ever put on this earth." He peered into her eyes, not wanting to frighten her, but knew he had to make her aware of the danger they were in. "If they see us," he said quietly, "they'll kill us sure." He hesitated, "At least, they'll kill me. I 'spect they'll have other plans fer you and your mamma-in-law."

She put her hand to her mouth, face blanching at his implication. "Oh dear God!"

He touched her shoulder. "Not to worry, ma'am, they got to find us first." He surveyed the area again, eyes flicking back and forth.

They were near the boundary of the forest. Another quarter mile and they would be on the plains surrounding Big Rock, wide, sweeping expanses of short grass with no cover to conceal them.

He pulled hard on the reins, turning the team in a wide circle, and headed back the way they had come. After a hundred yards he came to an overgrown path leading off the main trail to the east. It wasn't much more than a mule trace, once used by miners to pack supplies from town up to their camps on the upper peaks.

It would be a tight fit, but he thought they might just be able to squeeze through the narrow spots.

He leaned over and whispered in Jessica's ear, "It's gonna git a might bumpy. Why don't you git in the back with your mamma and help hold her while I try to git us outta sight?"

She nodded, and without another word scrambled into the rear of the wagon to wrap her arms around Aileen. "Mamma Aldritch, Mr. Pearlie is going to take a shortcut through the forest. Hold onto me, dear, because it may get a trifle rough."

Slowly, harness horses whinnying and shaking their heads in protest, he drove them up the path, holding his reins in one hand and the side of the buckboard with the other to keep from being thrown off as it tilted and rocked over rocks and mud holes along the trail. Branches scratched along the sides of the wagon, and twice he had to climb down and clear piles of brush and deadfall out of the way.

When he had gone a half-mile deeper into the piney woods, he pulled the team to a halt. Reaching behind the seat, he grabbed his Henry repeating rifle and jumped to the ground.

"I'm goin' back down the road to cover our backtrail." He paused. "If'n anything happens, an' I don't come back . . ." He turned, pointing down the mountain, "Big Rock is 'bout three or four miles in that direction. Just unhitch the horses and ride on in." He smiled reassuringly. "Folks there'll take good care of you."

Jessica nodded. "Mr. Pearlie, don't you worry about us. We're miners' wives, we can take care of ourselves. But," she looked into his eyes, worry evident, "you be careful, you hear? We don't want anything to happen to you on our account."

"Oh, I'll be careful as a tomcat in a roomful of rockin' chairs, Mrs. Aldritch. An' I'll be back for you, I promise."

He turned, drew his knife from its scabbard, and cut a low-hanging branch off a nearby pine tree. Using it like a broom, he backed down the path, sweeping dirt with the branch to obliterate any signs of their passage.

When he got to a turn off the mountain trail, he piled dead branches and bushes over his wagon tracks, hiding them from sight. Finally satisfied the buckboard's prints were erased as well as they could be in such a short time, he walked to a bald knob and looked back toward Big Rock. Shading his eyes with his hand, he could see a dark blot of men on horseback in the distance, riding hard toward the mountain and raising a sizable dust cloud.

He moved a hundred yards farther up the trail and slipped into the forest, hiding himself behind a large bush. He worked the lever on his Henry, jacking a shell into the chamber, and loosened the thongs on his Colts. He intended to fire on the group only as a last resort, if they looked like they were about to find the road they had taken or if any of them turned toward the spot where he had hidden the Aldritch women.

After a short wait he peered through the branches and leaves covering his hiding place to watch riders slow their mounts to a walk as they entered the forest.

Pearlie's heart pounded and light sweat beaded his forehead, running down his cheeks when the band stopped and several of the gunhawks dismounted a few yards from the hidden turn-off to the mule path.

He brought his Henry to his shoulder and drew a bead on a man who seemed to be the leader of the gang. As he prepared to give his life to protect the women Smoke entrusted to his care, he thought, if nothin' else, I can blow Sundance Morgan back to hell where he came from. Maybe then the rest of his men'll go on back to Texas and leave Smoke alone.

Sundance, wincing in pain, eased off his mount, holding a blood-soaked bandanna to his butt. He limped over to El Gato's horse and jerked a bottle of tequila out of his saddlebag. Dropping his pants and longjohns to his knees, Sundance poured the fiery liquid over his wound.

"Goddamn that hurts!" he yelled, dancing around, drawing a few grins and smirks on dusty, sweat-rimmed faces of several of his gunhands.

Lightning Jack helped Perro Muerte off his bronc and laid him on his back in the dirt. After a cursory examination of his thigh, Jack said, "You got lucky, Carlito. Looks like the bullet missed the bone."

He took Carlito's bandanna off his neck and tied it in a knot around his leg, slowing the flow of blood to a trickle. He grinned at the Mexican, who clamped his eyes shut in pain. "Good thing there ain't no Confederate sawbones with us, Carlito, or they'd try an' hack that leg off real quick."

The *bandido* rasped through pain-tightened lips, *"Senor* Sundance, give me tequila, *rapido!"*

Sundance splashed more tequila on his bandanna and poked it gingerly in his bullet wound, then handed the half-empty bottle to Carlito. "You want me to pour some on your leg?" he asked.

"No." Suarez raised himself on one elbow and tilted the bottle to the sky, draining the rest of the liquid in two large swallows. He gasped and sucked air in through his teeth, his face turning beet-red. "Works better from inside."

* * *

As the rest of the men attended to their wounds and reloaded their weapons, Pearlie silently lowered his Henry. "Come on you bastards, git a move on," he whispered to himself.

Even from this distance, he could see where ruts from the buckboard wheels and his team's hoofprints ended, just short of the path. He mouthed a silent prayer the gang wouldn't notice how the tracks suddenly disappeared.

After another ten minutes Sundance climbed on his horse, grunting at the pain his effort caused. "Let's go, men. We'll ride 'til we find a suitable place to make camp. I figure a day or so to heal up and lick our wounds, then we can plan on how to take care of Smoke Jensen." Pearlie could hear them talking at a distance.

One of the men cleared his throat. "Mr. Morgan, I didn't plan on gittin' the crap shot out of me when I joined up." The gunslick removed his hat and wiped his forehead as he looked around at the others. "I think I'll just mosey down the trail and look fer an easier way to make some money."

Sundance's eyes narrowed and his jaw clenched in anger. He shifted sideways in his saddle to take his weight off his backside. "Bull," he said, pointing his finger at the big man, "I want you to kill any sonofabitch who tries to leave!" He glared at his men. "You bastards took my money and agreed to do a job. Nobody quits 'til that job is done, an' that means 'til Smoke Jensen's been dusted, through and through. You got two choices. You can ride with me and maybe get shot later, or you can try to leave and damn sure get killed now." He whirled his mount, eyes glittering hate. "Any arguments?"

Bull sat rock-still, his hands on the butts of his sawed-off shotguns, watching closely as Sundance's men nodded agreement one by one.

"Okay," Sundance growled, teeth bared in a solemn grin, "let's go."

* * *

Pearlie sighed with relief and mopped his face with his bandanna as the gang rode off up the trail. He let the hammer down on his Henry when the outlaws disappeared from sight. He stood and stretched cramped legs, then walked along the path toward the spot where he left the women.

As he made a bend in the trail, he saw Jessica lying on her stomach in the buckboard, aiming a Colt over the side at him. He raised his hands, grinning. "It's okay, ma'am, it's jest me."

It took him almost an hour, sweating and fighting his team, to get the wagon turned around in the narrow passage. While on their way down the mountain, he had Jessica keep an eye on their backtrail in case the outlaws returned. After another hour and a half, they drove up at the outskirts of town.

When Pearlie pulled his team into Big Rock, he found Monte Carson and Louis Longmont standing before a collection of bodies, lined up like cord wood on the boardwalk for viewing. Monte had his left arm in a sling, and Louis had his coat off, wearing a white shirt with a deep red stain in front.

Pearlie introduced Jessica and Aileen Aldritch to the men, and explained briefly what had happened to them in the mountains and how Smoke had sent them down to Big Rock for medical attention.

Louis removed his hat and bowed deeply. "Ladies, Doctor Spalding is busy now—he's removing some bullets from citizens injured in our little fracas. If you'll permit me, I'll escort you to my establishment and have my chef prepare you some nourishment. By the time you finish your meal, I'm sure the doctor will be able to see you."

Louis extended his hand to help the ladies off the wagon. Once they were down, he turned to Pearlie. "Monte can fill you in on what happened here. I'll take the ladies with me and see that they're cared for properly, then I'll arrange for them to stay at the boarding house." As he turned to go, he winked at Pearlie and said, "I'll also have Andre throw a couple of beefsteaks and some potatoes on the fire for you. You look like you could use some food."

He walked off, saying to Jessica, "Do you ladies care for French cuisine, by any chance?"

Pearlie eyed the corpses of the gunslicks. " 'Pears y'all had a little excitement here."

Monte pulled his pipe out of his sling where he had stashed it and put it in his mouth. After he got it going to his satisfaction, clouds of smoke swirling around his head, he grunted, "Yep. These ole boys never knew what hit 'em." He cut his eyes to Pearlie. "I figure we softened 'em up a little for Smoke."

Pearlie nodded. "That you did, and he's gonna need it. I ran into the gang after you got through with them, and they look like some of the hardest lookin' men I ever see'd."

Monte's lips curled in a smirk. "As hard as Smoke?"

"Ain't nobody alive as hard as Smoke Jensen."

"What're you gonna do now, Pearlie?"

"I'm gonna eat those steaks Louis offered, then I'm headin' back up the mountain to see if I can be of any assistance to Smoke."

Monte's eyebrows raised. "You be careful, son. Try not to find Sundance 'fore you locate Smoke."

"Don't worry, I'm gonna take the back way up—Puma told me how to git up there without goin' by a clear trail."

"Well, you take care anyway. An' let Smoke know the whole town's prayin' for him."

Pearlie grinned wickedly as he turned toward Louis's place. "Y'all'd do better prayin' fer them outlaws. I've got a feelin' Smoke's gonna be doin' some fall planting, an' the crop's gonna be dead Texicans!"

Chapter Twenty

Smoke and Cal rode side-by-side through a ponderosa pine forest, their mounts at an easy walk, discussing the upcoming battle. "Just how much do you know about Indians, Cal?" Smoke asked.

"I know they's dangerous, sneaky, and unpredictable as hell. One time they can be friendly and neighborly, and the next time you meet up with 'em, they'll try an' take your scalp."

Smoke remembered his past. "Yeah, they can be real changable. Preacher used to call it being 'notionable.'" He reined his mount to a stop and fished in his pocket for tobacco. As he began to build a cigarette, Cal coughed lightly and said, "Do ya' think I could have one of those myself?"

Smoke turned his head and regarded the teenager with raised eyebrows. "When did you take up smoking?"

"On the trail up here with Pearlie. He allowed as how if'n I was old enough to fight bandits and outlaws and carry firearms, I was old enough to smoke if'n I had a mind to."

Smoke frowned for a moment, then grinned and shook his head. "Hell, I guess Pearlie's right. You're a man full grown in this country, Cal, and that means you got a right to make up your own mind how you're gonna live your life." He handed him his tobacco pouch and papers. As Smoke struck a lucifer and lit his cigarette, he said, "Course, that don't mean you're always gonna make the right decisions, but you sure as hell have the right to make your own mistakes." He exhaled a cloud of smoke. "The trick, my young friend, is to learn from mistakes and try never to make the same one twice."

Cal stuck a rumpled cigarette in his mouth and handed Smoke back his makings. "Yes sir, Smoke, that's what Pearlie said when we was drinkin' whiskey the other night."

Smoke broke into a laugh. "I can see I need to have a talk with Pearlie. Sometimes a good idea can be taken too far." He raised his canteen, pulled the cork, and took a long draught of cool water before passing it to Cal. "Sorry it ain't whiskey, but from now on, water and coffee are all we're gonna be drinking. Liquor and altitude don't mix. Here in the up-high, one drink is like two or three in the flat-lands, an' we need to keep our senses sharp and our minds clear if we're to stand a chance against Sundance Morgan and his gang."

Smoke sat his horse, palms on his saddle horn, looking out over the high lonesome. "Cal, this country is perfect for the type of fighting Indians showed us."

A puzzled expression flitted across Cal's features. "What do ya' mean, Smoke? I thought Injuns fought just like everybody else, 'ceptin' they used bows an' arrows 'fore they had rifles."

Smoke shook his head. "No, Cal, that's where you're wrong. Indians and white men have completely different ideas about how to wage a war. The white man has always put his faith in superior numbers and better weapons to defeat an enemy." He took his cigarette from his mouth, pinched out the fire, and scattered remnants of tobacco and paper into the wind. "An Indian, on the other hand, uses stealth and fear, and knowledge of the countryside to make up for fewer numbers and more primitive weapons."

Cal frowned. "But isn't our way better? After all, we've managed to beat the Injun tribes and damn near wipe 'em out."

Smoke smiled, a sad expression on his face. "You're right, Cal. In the long run, larger numbers of soldiers and better guns and rifles will eventually win out. But, in the short run, the Indians' tactics of hit and run, sneak attacks at night, avoiding pitched battles, exacts a horrible toll on the winners.'' He took a deep breath, thinking back to his early days in the mountains, when he and Preacher fought Indians on what seemed like a daily basis. "That's why, long ago, mountain men adopted the Indians' way of fighting. It was the only way to survive against them.'' He paused, then continued. "Hell, when you think on it, I'll bet red men have killed ten or more whites for every brave they lost in battle. If we didn't have a steady stream of settlers coming here from back East, the Indians would've run us off years ago.''

Cal thought for a moment. "So, what you're sayin' is that to beat Sundance and his gang, we're gonna have to fight him like we was Injuns?''

Smoke's lips curled, teeth gleaming and eyes glittering in a fierce smile. "That's exactly what I mean, Cal. There's simply no way two or three of us stand a chance in a battle with thirty or forty experienced gunhands if we play by their rules. So, we fight this war like an Apache.''

Cal interrupted, "What does that mean?''

"It's something an old Indian taught me last time I was up here fighting a bunch of bounty hunters who had us out-manned and out-gunned. Me and Louis Longmont took them on, one by one and two by two, and managed to kill or run every one of them off. We fought smart and cautious and used these mountains and forests of the high lonesome to help us whip them.''

"But Smoke, I don't know nothin' 'bout fightin' like some Injun.''

"You'll learn, Cal, 'cause I'm going to teach you, just like the best Indian fighter who ever lived—Preacher, who taught me.''

"When do we start?''

"We've already started. Did you notice what I did with my cigarette butt?''

"Uh . . . yeah.''

"I did that for two reasons. One, we don't want any fires

up here, they might trap us and leave us with nowhere to run, and second, we leave no traces of our passage. When we move through an area, no one can know we've been there, unless we want them to know.''

"Oh, I see. You mean, like coverin' our tracks and such.''

"Yeah, but it's more than just that. It's making sure that we don't break branches or twigs, we walk our mounts around boggy or muddy spots so we don't leave prints, and we never camp where we make our fires.'' He thought a moment, "Matter of fact, when the going gets hot and heavy, we'll probably be eating cold food more often than not and doing without fires.''

Cal glanced at dark, snow-filled clouds overhead. "I guess that means bein' cold ourselves most of the time, too.''

Smoke nodded. "If you're gonna wage war in the high lonesome, being cold is part of it. But you'll get used to it before those galoots from Texas do. They're more used to frying in the heat than shivering in the cold, and that'll be to our advantage when the time comes. Let's go, we're burnin' daylight.''

Smoke wheeled his mount to ride up the mountain and began moving toward the peaks. "I'm gonna take you to where we'll make our last stand, assumin' we both live long enough to get there. On the way, I'll show you some of the traps and falls I've set up, and how to spot them if you have to get out of here on your own.''

"I don't much like it when you talk like that, Smoke, 'bout us maybe not surviving and such.''

Smoke agreed. "I can see where it'd bother you, Cal, but it's the truth of the matter.'' He looked at the boy. "I want you to understand what we're going up against here, 'cause this ain't no Sunday school picnic, and it sure as hell ain't no kid's game where you get up after you're shot bad to try again. This here's for real.'' He sighed deeply. "Cal, only a few men are gonna ride out of this fracas forked-end down. I hope it's you and Pearlie and Puma and me, but it's liable to be Sundance who pisses on our graves, not the other way 'round.''

"Smoke, I ain't afraid of dyin', I'm more afraid of not bein' good enough, or of doin' more harm than good by bein' up

here with you. I don't want you to get hurt 'cause you're havin'
to look after me.''

Smoke chuckled. "Don't worry about that, son. Everybody
gets a mite nervous 'fore a battle, but once the lead starts to
flying, your natural instincts will take over and you'll do just
fine. If I didn't believe you were up to what's gonna happen,
I wouldn't let you stay—and I'm a damn good judge of character.''

Cal sat a little straighter in his saddle and began to look for
traps Smoke had set. He wanted to find some without Smoke
having to show him where they were, to prove to his friend he
was worthy of his trust.

After a few miles he reined up, asking, "What's that ahead
of us?''

Smoke turned his head. "What are you lookin' at?''

"Right there, near the pine tree. That pile of leaves and pine
needles don't look natural—kinda looks like it was piled up
there on purpose.'' He stepped out of his saddle and walked
slowly up to the tree, squinting before it, leaning down. "Uh-
huh, here's a rope, covered with mud or something, wrapped
'round the trunk.'' He followed the rope with his hands where
it ran along the ground across the trail to encircle another tree
and finally to where it was tied to a branch, holding it back
under tension. "Jumpin' Jimminy, Smoke. If we'd tripped this
here rope, it would've let that branch go and it would've damn
near taken our heads off!''

Smoke smiled. "You're learning, Cal. That's exactly what
it's meant to do. Let's hope the gunslicks aren't as keen-eyed
as you.''

Cal walked to his horse and swung into the saddle, blushing
over the compliment. "I'd never have seen it if'n I weren't
lookin' fer it,'' he said quietly.

"Don't let up,'' Smoke added, "there's a few more between
us and our destination.''

Cal managed to find two more of three traps on the way to
where Smoke had left his supplies. Smoke had to stop him

before he walked his mount onto a thin covering over a pit Smoke dug in the middle of a mountain path. Even after he was shown the trap, Cal stated he could not tell it from what looked natural.

They came to Smoke's fort, as he called it, at noon. Smoke figured it would be a good time to take their nooning.

"Want me to gather wood fer a campfire?" Cal asked.

Smoke frowned. "Remember what I told you. We don't make a fire where we're gonna camp."

"But Smoke, they ain't hardly had time to get up here yet," Cal protested.

Smoke shrugged. "You're probably right, Cal, but are you willing to bet your life they haven't sent a scout or a party of gunmen on ahead, ridin' hard to try and catch us unawares?"

"When you say it like that, I reckon not."

"No, and I'm not, either. This is a game with high stakes, life or death, and it don't do to underestimate your opponent. We won't get any second chances, so we'd better be right every time."

They staked their horses on the trail below and hiked up the steep incline to a level spot at the top, stumbling some on loose soil. They surveyed the approach, and Smoke said, "I picked this place for its defense." He pointed down. "We got an unobstructed view in front and both sides, and our back is covered by those cliffs behind us. A rock slide some time back took out the trees and brush on the hill to the front, and there aren't any boulders or tree trunks big enough for our attackers to hide behind while working their way up here. We've got over a hundred and fifty yards of clear space they'll have to cross to get to us, on foot 'cause it's too steep for horses." He pointed left and right, "Not quite as good over on the sides, there's some good-sized rocks and a couple of fallen trees over there, but I'm gonna let you hide a few surprises in that cover there in case our friends decide to try and use 'em."

Cal's forehead wrinkled, "What kind of surprises?"

Smoke shook his head. "You'll get no help from me. I'll show you what we got to work with, and you let your imagination take it from there. Hell, if you can't cook up something mean, then I may have to change my opinion of the natural contrariness of young men.''

Cal rubbed his chin a moment, thinking. "You say you got some extra dynamite and a few cans of black powder?''

"Yep, and there's a pile of gourds and small pumpkins and rocks I gathered the other day, if you're planning what I think you are.''

Cal pointed to several areas and explained in detail what he had in mind to Smoke, causing the older man to grin in anticipation. "You know, Cal, you almost make me hope some of those outlaws make it this far, just so we can see if your plan works.''

"Me too, boss,'' Cal said.

Smoke opened his saddlebags and broke out some jerked meat and biscuits he had saved from breakfast, along with a few dried apples. They washed their food down with water from canteens. After they finished eating, Smoke gave Cal a tour of his caches of guns, rifles, and shotguns, ammunition, and explosives he had placed in various locations around his plateau. "I've spread the supplies around 'cause I don't know how many are going to be coming up after us and I don't have any way of knowing if we're gonna be wounded or able to move around much, if they're firing on us real heavy.''

Cal followed Smoke as he showed him where everything was located, nodding his head at the meticulous planning that had gone into the arrangement. "Looks like you thought of most everything, Smoke,'' he said.

"I doubt it, because you can never anticipate all the possibilities, but I'm damned if I can think of anything else to do up here to prepare for an assault.'' Smoke packed up the remnants of their lunch and said, "Now, we set about making more tricks for Sundance and his gang. That's the other part of fightin' like Indians—instilling fear of the unknown in your adversaries.''

They slipped and slid down the embankment to their horses and mounted up. Smoke inclined his head at his bed roll. "I've got an extra pair of moccasins and some buckskins in there, so remind me to give 'em to you later. We're gonna be doing some sneaking around and I want you to be as quiet as a mouse, and as close to invisible as I can make you in the dark. Get rid of your spurs, and anything else that jangles or clinks when you're crawling around on your hands and knees. We'll also get you some mud to put on your weapons, just in case the clouds clear and we get some moonlight. It won't do to have anything that'll cause a glare or reflection to give us away."

"You mean we're gonna go right into their camp?"

"Maybe. There's nothing makes a man more nervous than to wake up and find the gent next to him with his throat cut and his scalp gone." He grinned at Cal's wide-eyed expression. "Makes it a mite tough to get to sleep the next night, and tired men don't fight real well or think too clear."

The balance of the afternoon was spent setting more traps, undermining areas of the trail, and digging pits and placing sharpened stakes in the bottoms. Smoke was amazed at how quickly Cal grasped the ideas behind creating fear and terror in their enemies, and how innovative he was at thinking up his own surprises for the gang.

At dusk, Smoke called a halt to their preparations, and they made camp a few miles from Smoke's fort. The hat-sized fire was small, and placed up against some rocks so the flames couldn't be seen from more than a few yards away. Smoke cooked the last of Puma's venison, made pan-bread and a pot of boiled coffee, which Cal said was considerably weaker than Puma's.

Smoke's eyes twinkled in the firelight as he said, "I want you to get some sleep tonight, and real mountain man coffee will keep somebody who isn't used to it awake for a spell— like two or three days."

Cal asked, "Why'd you make so much. Ain't no way we're gonna drink all that."

"I brought a couple of spare canteens. What we don't drink tonight, we'll put in those. Cold coffee ain't high on my list of favorite things to drink, but it'll help keep us alert if we aren't able to make a fire to warm it."

Cal was about to answer, when suddenly Smoke held up his

hand. A Colt appeared in Smoke's fist as if by magic, so fast that Cal never saw him draw. "Keep talking, like I'm still here," Smoke whispered, and slipped out of camp as silently as the breeze.

Cal continued to talk, until a few minutes later when Smoke reappeared, leading Pearlie's horse by the reins, with a blushing Pearlie still in the saddle.

"Cal," Smoke said, barely visible at the edge of the firelight, "we're coming in, so don't shoot."

Cal holstered the Colt Navy he was holding and stood up to welcome his friends back to camp. "Hey, Pearlie, glad you found us," he said

"Shucks, I didn't find you. Smoke found me. I figgered if I rode around up here makin' enough noise, y'all'd hear me sooner or later."

Smoke said, "What if it'd been Sundance's gang who heard you?"

Pearlie shook his head. "Naw, I passed their camp over five miles down the mountain. You can't hardly miss it, since they got a fire big enough to roast a cow, although they seem to be drinkin' their supper instead of eatin' it."

"That's good—drunk and hungover men have a tendency to be careless about keeping their scalps in a fight. Did you get the Aldritch women down to Big Rock?" Smoke asked.

"Yes sir. Just missed meetin' up with the outlaws, though."

"Oh?"

"Yeah." Pearlie squatted before the fire, piled some deer meat and bread and beans on his plate, and poured a cup of coffee. While he ate, he told Smoke and Cal about the gunfight in Big Rock.

Smoke shook his head. "I can't believe those fools tried to tree that town."

Pearlie grinned. "I don't know if the fight was strictly the outlaws' idea, boss. 'Pears to me that Monte Carson and Louis Longmont set them up where they didn't exactly have any choice in the matter. Monte said the town wanted to soften 'em up a mite fer ya'."

"I'd certainly call killing a dozen hardcases softening 'em

up,'' Smoke said, "though I wish my friends hadn't taken such a chance on my account.''

"Turned out alright. Those gents will think twice 'bout ridin' back though Big Rock any time soon.''

Smoke's eyes, reflected in the campfire, radiated hate. "I don't intend to give them that chance, Pearlie. Every one of the sorry sons of bitches is going to be planted right here, in the up-high, or I will.''

Cal added softly, "You mean, *we* will, Smoke. Me an' Pearlie are in this with you to the very end.''

Chapter Twenty-One

As the sun rose above eastern slopes of the Rockies, Sundance walked among his sleeping men, kicking them out of their bedrolls with the toe of his boot. Hungover gunfighters and outlaws moaned and groaned, holding their aching heads and complaining about the early hour.

The smell of frying fatback and coffee finally roused the unhappy gang. They crawled out of their bedrolls, shivering and shaking in the early morning chill as they gathered around a fire gulping coffee, waiting for Sundance to give them their orders.

He sat on a boulder, his hands wrapped around a steaming tin cup, elbows on knees. His gaze flicked over the rag-tag group of misfits and murderers he brought with him while he thought about their forthcoming battle with Smoke Jensen. He realized most of his men would be useless—they were too dumb or too slow to be a danger to a mountain man. Their only benefit to Sundance would be to draw attention to Smoke's location by drawing his fire.

Sundance knew the gang stood no chance at all if they stayed together. Thirty men on horseback would be noticed before they could get in range, and would make a tempting target for ambushes and long-range rifle fire from cliffs and overhangs. He didn't like the idea of breaking up his followers, but there wasn't any other way to proceed in this country. Its thick forests, steep and narrow trails and passes were ideal for bottling up a large group, or catching them in a crossfire if Smoke managed to bring help with him. Sundance had few options, thus he made the only decision he could.

"Boys, I'm going to divide us up into groups of four to six riders. Each group will have a leader. We'll arrange meeting places and signals, in the event anyone catches sight of Jensen or his trail. I'll also give each of you a password so we won't be shootin' each other in the dark, if it comes to that."

George Stalking Horse thumbed his hat back. "Boss, General Custer divided his troops and you remember what happened to him."

Sundance smirked. "You fool! Custer got his ass kicked 'cause he was facing several thousand Injuns with nothin' but a bunch of green soldiers, and most of 'em had never been in an Injun fight before." He waved his arm at thick pines and steep slopes around them. "George, just how do you expect thirty of us to cross these mountains and manage to sneak up on a man said to be one of the best mountain men in the territory?"

George lowered his head, mumbling under his breath, while Sundance snorted in derision. "Anyone else gonna try an' tell me how to run this outfit?"

When he got no answer, he continued. "Bull, I want you and Toothpick and El Gato to pick some men to ride with. You'll be the leaders, so pick boys you think you can work with who'll obey orders."

Lightning Jack narrowed his eyes and flexed his huge arms until the muscles bulged beneath his shirt. "What about me, Sundance?"

"I want you to ride with me. I need someone I can trust to watch my back. Besides, you're the meanest son of a bitch on the mountain and I want you between me and Smoke Jensen."

As chosen leaders began to pick their riders, it was only a few moments before Bull and Toothpick squared off in an argument over who would ride with them. Toothpick had the point of his knife at Bull's throat even as Bull stuck his sawed-off shotgun in the other's stomach and jacked back the hammers.

"Goddammit, hold on there!" Sundance yelled, quickly stepping between two angry men. He shook his head. "If you can't pick your bunches then I'll do it for you." He surveyed the band of milling outlaws. "El Gato, you and Chiva and those three men ride together." He pointed to three Mexican *pistoleros*.

"Toothpick, you take George Stalking Horse and those three cowboys over there," he said, pointing to three of the Southerners.

"Perro Muerte, you take Curly Bill and those four men." He picked two Anglos and two Mexicans to join them.

"One-Eye Jordan, you and Blackjack Walker grab those men by that tree over yonder." A Mexican and two Texas gunmen looked up from saddling their mounts and nodded agreement.

"Bull, you take Moses Washburn and the four men standing next to that rock and make your plans."

He looked at his followers as they began to split into small groups. "I'm taking Lightning Jack, Jeremiah Gray Wolf, and the two remaining cowboys with me." He put his hands on his hips, his face stern and eyes narrowed. "I'm only gonna say this once. Either you take orders from your ramrods, or you die. By their hands, or mine, it won't make much difference, 'cause you'll be in hell before you know you're dead."

He stepped off to one side. "I want the men in charge over here and we'll decide who goes where, and what our signals will be if anybody runs across Jensen."

Sundance squatted next to the fire and refilled his cup. El Gato, Toothpick, Suarez, Jordan, and Bull gathered around him, warming their hands over the flames, stamping their feet to get blood flowing.

As Sundance looked up, sipping his coffee, snow-swollen clouds overhead emptied and flakes began to fall. Within a few minutes visibility was cut to less than ten feet and the temperature seemed to drop twenty degrees.

"Okay men, here's our situation. We got a lot of mountain to cover, and not a hell of a lot of time to do it if'n we want to kill Jensen and get down to the flat-lands 'fore full winter." He paused to roll a cigarette and drain his cup. "El Gato, you and Chiva and your *vaqueros* head up the mountain on the main trail. Take your time and watch out for ambushes. Fire three shots if you see anybody or need some help."

He pointed down their backtrail. "One-Eye, you and Blackjack start down the trail behind us. After you make sure Jensen ain't back there, ride north and go straight up the slope through the trees. It'll be rough goin', but at least you won't have to worry about being bushwhacked.

"Toothpick, you and George Stalking Horse and your men head northeast toward the peak. See if that breed can manage to cut Jensen's tracks or pick up a trail on him. And don't try to take him alone if you find him. Give the signal and we'll all come ridin' hard as we can. I don't want that bastard gettin' away.

"Suarez, you and Curly Bill go upslope to the northwest and look for tracks or campfire smoke. Sing out if you see anything. Bull and Moses, take your men and head straight up the mountain. Spread out and cover as much territory as you can. Lightning Jack and Jeremiah Gray Wolf and I are goin' to roam, cuttin' back and forth across all of your backtrails. With any luck at all, we'll bracket that son of a bitch and catch him between us, and he'll be dead meat if he shows himself."

Sundance drew his Colt and flipped open the loading gate, checking his loads. "Oh, and by the way, tell your men that the shooter who puts the first lead pill in Jensen's hide will get a bonus of five thousand dollars, paid when I see his body."

Smoke raised his head where he lay hidden in weeds and brush near the outlaws' encampment. He had heard every word of Sundance's plan and now he knew the positions and numbers of each bunch of men searching for him. Old hoss, he thought, you're in for a few surprises before you see my dead carcass.

The outlaws mounted up and began to leave, talking quietly among themselves about their assignments and the five thousand dollar reward for Smoke's death.

Bull and Moses Washburn's group was the last to leave camp, four men trailing their leaders through tall pines, riding single file.

Moving silently through falling snow, his moccasins making no sound in the shallow drifts, Smoke pulled his knife from its scabbard and sprinted after the men. The last man in line leaned to the side to adjust his stirrup, and grunted in surprise when a tall figure wearing buckskins suddenly appeared at his side.

Smoke's teeth flashed in a savage grin. "Howdy, neighbor," he whispered. He grabbed the startled gunman by his shirtfront and growled, "Tell me, is this worth five thousand dollars?" In a lightning-quick move, Smoke's knife slashed through the gunslick's neck, severing both carotid arteries and cutting off his strangled yell. Smoke pushed the dying man over his saddle horn and slapped his horse's rump with the flat of his hand, causing it to bolt forward.

Smoke wiped his blade on his trouser leg and walked back through drifting snow, where he had left his rifle and mount.

Jack Robertson was surprised and almost jumped out of his saddle when Micah Jacob's horse galloped by him as he wound his way through thick stands of ponderosa pines. Robertson was trying to keep the riders in front of him in sight, squinting into driving snow flurries, as they followed Bull up a steep slope.

He glanced to one side as Jacob's mount brushed against his legs and could see the man leaning forward over his saddle horn as if he were too drunk to sit up. "Goddammit, Micah," he cried, "take it easy. You're gonna git us kilt ridin' like that in these here trees."

Jacob didn't appear to hear the shouted warning, and his

bronc continued to lope ahead, blundering into the next horse in line.

Robertson spurred his mount and pulled up next to Jacob's, grabbing the frightened animal's reins and pulling it to a halt.

Jacob's horse crow-hopped a couple of times, causing its rider to slowly topple sideways out of the saddle, landing with a loud thump in shallow snow.

Robertson stepped out of his saddle, calling ahead, "Hey, Bull, you and Moses wait up a minute! Micah's hurt back here!"

He grabbed both horses' reins in one hand, calming the animals a moment, then walked to where Jacob lay face-down on the ground. "You stupid son of a bitch," he said, grabbing Jacob by the shoulder, rolling him over onto his back. "What's the matter with . . ."

Vomit rose in his throat and he almost threw up as the dead gunslick's head rolled back, exposing a neck slashed open to his spine, blood and gore splattered over the front of his shirt.

"Goddamn! Shit . . . shit!" He raised his head and put his hands around his mouth and screamed, "Bull, git over here quick! Micah's been kilt!"

Bull and the others appeared out of the driving snow like ghosts, further scaring the terrified cowboy. "What the hell's goin' on here?" Bull asked, as he swung his leg over his cantle and dropped to the ground.

Robertson's voice rose in pitch as he stammered, "Micah's gone and gotten his throat cut! That bastard Jensen's done kilt him deader'n hell!"

Bull squatted next to the corpse, looking at the gruesome wound. After a moment, he glanced up at Robertson. "How'd this happen? He was right behind you . . ."

Robertson wagged his head, eyes wide as he looked around wildly. "I don't know, Bull. I didn't hear nothin'. I was just followin' along, an' then his horse came runnin' by with Micah dead in the saddle."

Bull's eyes narrowed. "He didn't call out or yell or nothin'?"

Robertson clenched his jaws to keep his teeth from chattering. "I told you, I didn't hear nothin'." He drew his pistol and whirled around when a clump of snow fell from a pine branch behind him with a soft plop. The Colt was shaking in his hand as he waved it around, aiming at nothing. "We're fightin' a ghost, boys, and we're all gonna end up like Micah if'n we don't git the hell outta here."

Bull quickly stepped over, grabbed Robertson by the shoulder, and spun him around. He slapped the hysterical man once across his face with an open palm, knocking his hat off and sending him sprawling on his back in the snow.

Bull stood over him, looking down in disgust. "Shut up, you sniveling coward!" He put his hands on his hips and swiveled his head slowly, examining his surroundings.

Moses Washburn sat on his mount, his palms on his saddle horn. "Jack's right, Bull." Moses pointed to the body on the ground. "This ain't no ordinary cowboy we're dealin' with here. Jensen's a hairy ole mountain grizzly, an' we're gonna take some heavy losses trackin' him here in his own country."

Bull scowled at the man. "You figgerin' on quitin' us too, Washburn?"

Moses's shoulders heaved in a deep sigh. "Nope. I took Sundance's money, so I'll stay." He pulled a shotgun from his saddle boot and eared back the hammers, resting it across his knee. His eyes flicked back and forth, trying to see through falling snow. "I'll stay," he repeated quietly, "but that don't mean I like it."

Bull stepped into a stirrup and swung a leg over his saddle, loosening thongs on his sawed-off shotguns. "All this means is, Jensen's drawn first blood. I still plan on collectin' that five thousand dollar reward fer killin' him."

Robertson swung into his saddle and looked over his shoulder at Jacob's body, stiffening in the frigid air. His dead, glazed eyes were slowly being covered with white flakes, and the gaping cavity in his neck was half-filled with pink-tinged snow. He shook his head sadly, "Bet that don't sound like near enough to Micah."

Chapter Twenty-Two

Cal was pouring himself a cup of coffee when he looked up through the falling snow and saw Smoke squatting by their small campfire, hands extended to get some warmth. He hadn't heard him approach, not a single sound.

He shook his head and wondered if maybe someday he'd be able to move through snow so quietly. "Want some coffee, Smoke?"

"Yeah. An' some breakfast if Pearlie left any."

Cal grinned. "There's a couple of sinkers and a hunk of fatback that Pearlie ain't had time to wolf down yet."

Pearlie looked at them over a plate of grub he was eating, hunched over, holding it against his chest to keep it from being covered by snow. "Only 'cause I didn't have no more room on this tin. Lucky you got here 'fore I went back for a second helpin', Smoke."

Cal grunted as he handed Smoke a steaming cup. "More like a third or fourth helpin', you mean." He shook his head. "Smoke, if'n this fracas lasts more'n a couple of days, we're gonna have to send to Big Rock fer more supplies. Pearlie goes through food like a grizzly bear fattenin' up fer the winter."

Pearlie gazed at them with an innocent look. "That's only

natural. A body needs more food up here in this awful cold."
He shivered and hunched his shoulders in the buffalo hide coat
he was wearing. "Hell, if'n I don't eat, I'm liable to freeze
plumb solid." Ice rimmed his moustache and turned his sparse
beard white.

Smoke filled his plate and began to eat. "Don't gripe about
the snow and cold, men. It's gonna help even up the odds if
it keeps up. It's sure to bother those flat-landers a lot more
than it does us, an' it'll cover our tracks and muffle any sounds
we make when we sneak up on 'em." He nodded toward their
horses standing nearby. "Did you cover your mounts' hooves
with burlap like I told you?"

"Yes sir," Cal answered. "We're ready to ride soon as you
give the word."

While he ate, Smoke smoothed a patch of snow with his
hand, then took a twig and began to draw a crude map of the
mountain in it. He made two small marks with the stick. "This
here is where we are," he said, pointing to the one near the
top of the mountain, "and this is where Sundance had his
camp."

Pearlie and Cal ambled over to watch him draw. Smoke
made six fine lines on the sketch, curving off from the camp
location at angles to one other.

"Sundance divided his men up into groups of five or six
men and sent them off in different directions."

Cal frowned. "Why'd he do that?"

Smoke shrugged. "It's not a bad plan, for a know-nothin'
outlaw. He hopes to cover a lot of territory in a short time. He
knows winter's coming and if his gang gets caught up in these
slopes during a blizzard they won't stand a chance of getting
us."

Pearlie made a cigarette and smoked as he studied the map.
" 'Pears to me it'll also make it a lot tougher on us to move
around without one of those groups cuttin' our trail or seein'
our sign, 'specially if'n this snow stays on the ground fer any
length of time."

Smoke nodded. "You're right, Pearlie. It's mighty tough to
cover your tracks in fresh snow. Sundance was shrewd enough

to spread his men out in different sections, so any tracks they come up on will have to be ours.''

Cal frowned. ''Jimminy, Smoke. If that's so, then how are we gonna manage to sneak around and Injun-up on them gunnies like you planned?''

Smoke grinned. ''Don't you worry 'bout that, son. Tracks are like women. They can seem to say one thing, and mean exactly the opposite.''

''Huh?''

Pearlie smiled, nodding his head. ''I understand, Smoke. You mean the man bein' followed is in control. He can lead the ones following him anywhere he wants to.''

''That's the idea, Pearlie. It's a situation made to order for setting up ambushes and traps. Our other advantage is that Sundance doesn't know about you and Cal—he thinks I'm up here without any help.''

Smoke bent over his map. ''Now, here's where I want you and Cal to go, and what I want you to do when you get there . . .''

For the next hour, the three men planned their campaign of terror against the Sundance Morgan gang. When Smoke was satisfied his allies understood, he got up and stretched cramped muscles. ''Okay men, now I want you to crawl into those blankets and get some shut-eye. We can't do anything until dark, then we're gonna be busy most of the night, and I want you fresh and ready to go at sunset.''

Cal looked around, a worried expression on his face. ''What if one of those bunches chances upon our camp?''

''Don't worry about that. Those galoots will be lucky to make it more'n two or three miles in this storm. Let them wear themselves and their mounts out fighting drifts and wind and cold.'' Smoke grinned fiercely in the gloom of the storm. ''That just means they'll be sleeping heavier when we come calling on 'em later.''

As the day wore on the sun rose higher in the sky, but it couldn't penetrate snow clouds and the temperature stayed just above freezing. Flurries of wind-driven snow coated the outlaws' faces and entered their horses' nostrils, making their search a living hell. Several of the groups stopped their trek up the mountain and hobbled their mounts in the shelter of pines and made fires to try to keep hands and fingers from freezing.

El Gato rode hunched over in his saddle, fighting his way along the main trail up the mountain. His men, strung out behind him, were barely visible through the white cloud that surrounded them. Julio Valdez spurred his mount and pulled up next to El Gato.

His moustache and beard were coated with a thick layer of ice and snow, his face was wind-burned a bright red, and blood was trickling from chapped, cracked lips that had split open.

"Jefe, momentito!" he yelled through the wind.

El Gato peered out from under his hat brim as he reined his horse to a halt. *"Sí.* What is it, Julio?"

"We must stop, *Jefe.* This storm, she is killing us." He held up his hands, gloves covered with ice. "I no can feel my hands."

El Gato twisted in his saddle to look to the rear. His other men were waiting, hands stuffed under their armpits, shoulders hunched against wind chill. He nodded, "Okay. Is time for food, and horses need rest." He pulled his bronc around and began to walk it toward a small clearing a few yards off the trail, Valdez grinning as he rode alongside him.

El Gato's mount stumbled over something buried in the snow, and a large pine branch suddenly whipped toward the pair of gunmen. The rushing tree limb took them both full in the chest, knocking El Gato backwards off his horse to land flat on his back in a snow drift, his left arm bent at an odd angle.

El Gato moaned and pulled himself up on his right elbow. He looked up to see Valdez sitting on his mount, leaning against the branch, head thrown back, screaming in agony. The other riders rode up and jumped out of their saddles. One helped El Gato to his feet, another walked over to Valdez, then turned away and vomited in the snow, gagging and choking and mumbling, *"Madre de Dios,"* over and over.

El Gato frowned, "What is matter?" He grabbed Valdez's shoulder and pulled him around. A two-foot long sharpened stake was buried in his stomach, just below his ribcage. It was attached to the branch with strands of rawhide, and had speared Valdez hard enough that several inches of the stake were protruding from his back.

El Gato shouted, "Goddamn!" He turned to his men. "Cut him down. Now!"

Juan Gonzalez, Valdez's partner, said, "But *Jefe,* if we pull stake out, Julio die."

El Gato stared at the man for a moment, then reached into his coat and withdrew a long, black cigar. He stuck it in his mouth, struck a lucifer on his saddle horn, and lit it. He stared at Valdez as smoke trailed from his nostrils. "Juan," he said as he put his arm around the *bandido's* shoulders, "what you want to do? Leave him there 'til priest comes to give last rites?"

Gonzalez shrugged. El Gato scowled around his cigar and inclined his head toward Valdez. "Cut him down." He grabbed his saddlebags off his horse. "Make fire, *muchachos,* I am very hungry."

Chiva held Valdez's shoulders while Gonzalez jerked the branch back, pulling the stake free. Valdez screamed again, scarlet jets of blood pumping between his fingers as he grasped his stomach, trying to staunch the flow. The gunhawk choked, gasped, and fell from his horse face-down in the snow, dying as he hit the ground.

Gonzalez knelt beside his dead friend, laying a hand on his shoulder. After a moment, he sighed and reached into a pocket of Valdez's vest and pulled out a gold pocket watch. He studied it briefly, then stuck it in his own pocket and stood, brushing snow off his pants legs.

Chiva frowned and spat on the ground. "You gonna take his boots, too?"

Gonzalez glanced at the dead man's shoes. "No. His feet is too small."

El Gato dumped an armload of wood on a fire his men had

started and said over his shoulder, "Take his *pistolas* and ammunition and put in my saddlebags."

Chiva asked, "You want us to bury him?"

"No. Drag him into bushes away from camp and leave him." El Gato pulled a coffee pot and burlap sack of supplies from his saddlebags and began to prepare food. "We make camp here and wait for this storm to pass. We begin looking again tomorrow."

El Gato built a roaring fire and everyone ate their fill of beans, tortillas, and jerked meat. After they ate, they sat in front of the fire, warming their hands and passing a bottle of tequila around until it was empty.

As the sky became darker and men settled down in bedrolls, Chiva asked, "El Gato, you want guards sent out *esta noche?*"

El Gato raised his blankets to his chin and pulled his *sombrero* low over his face. "No. No one can move in this storm in darkness. Get some sleep and we start fresh in morning."

Chiva grunted, staring out into the dark veil of blowing snow and wind. He shivered and moved his bedroll closer to the fire. As a final precaution, he drew his Colt and placed it on his chest under his blankets.

Smoke waited patiently for the outlaws' fire to die down, lying twenty yards from the sleeping men. Thick, fur-lined gloves kept his hands warm, and he shifted positions frequently to keep his legs and back from growing stiff in the frigid air. After two hours, when he could hear El Gato and his men snoring loudly, he started to move.

He crept silently among the horses, running his hands over their necks and backs to soothe them and keep them quiet. He cut their tether ropes and led them, one by one, away from the camp to the trail. Once there, he gently slapped their rumps, causing them to trot down the mountain. Before he sent the last horse off, he lifted Valdez's lifeless body and laid it over the animal's back, tying his hands and feet together under the gelding's belly.

As the horse and its dead rider moved away, Smoke grinned,

his teeth flashing in the darkness. Now it was time to really put fear of the unknown into his adversaries.

Smoke walked softly into camp, sliding his feet so he would make no sound as he broke through crusty, frozen snow drifts. Slipping his knife from its holster, he squatted between Gonzalez and the other Mexican. He placed his left hand over one *bandido's* mouth and quickly slit his throat, holding tight while the dying man quivered and shook with death throes. When the body lay still, Smoke turned to Gonzalez and repeated the procedure.

As Gonzalez choked on his own blood, he spasmed and kicked out with his legs. One of his boots hit a coffee pot next to the fire, sending it spinning and tumbling and clanking against a nearby tree.

Chiva was startled awake by the sound and sat up, fumbling with his blanket to get his gun out and aim it at the ghostly figure squatting next to Gonzalez. Smoke saw the motion from the corner of his eye and looked over his shoulder as Chiva's Colt appeared from his blanket, pointing at him. Employing lightning reflexes, Smoke leaned to the side and lashed out with his right leg. The toe of his boot caught Chiva on his temple, knocking him unconscious, sending him spinning to one side.

Before Smoke could straighten up, a heavy weight landed on his back, driving him down in the snow. A beefy forearm wrapped around his neck, bending his head back and squeezing his throat, cutting off his air.

With a tremendous effort, Smoke arched his back and reached over his shoulder to grab a handful of hair. As his vision began to darken, he heaved with all his might, throwing El Gato over his shoulder to land on his back in the fire.

Smoke gasped for air, drawing in huge lungfuls with a heaving chest. El Gato rolled off the fire and stood up, shaking his head. Smoke pulled his Colt and aimed it at the outlaw's chest.

El Gato spread his arms and grinned insolently. "You going to shoot unarmed man? That not sound like Smoke Jensen."

Smoke glanced at the Colt .44 he held in his hand, then back to El Gato. He grinned, teeth white against his mud-blackened face. "You're right, outlaw. Though I don't usually hesitate to shoot snakes or rabid dogs, killing a man who has no weapon does kinda go against my grain." He holstered his pistol. "How about I just beat you to death? That sound better to you?"

El Gato's teeth glinted in the firelight. "Oh yes, *gringo,* that make El Gato very happy." He flexed his arms and tightened his hands into fists, muscles bulging under his shirt. "I gonna kill you, *gringo,* then I will cut out your heart and carry it with me to show how you died."

Smoke shook his head. "All I see you doin' is shootin' off your mouth. Now, you gonna fight or are you gonna try an' talk me to death?"

With a roar, El Gato bounded over the fire and charged Smoke, his massive hands reaching for the mountain man's throat. Smoke leaned to one side and planted the toe of his boot in his solar plexus, his boot sinking almost out of sight in El Gato's gut.

The *bandido* bent over with a loud "whoosh" and grabbed his stomach. Smoke straightened and swung his fist in a wide arc, ending behind El Gato's ear with a sickening crunch, driving him to his knees. Smoke stepped back, rubbing his fist and wincing at the pain in his knuckles.

He was amazed when El Gato shook his head and struggled to his feet. The outlaw's chin was canted to the side, indicating his jaw was dislocated or broken. He looked at Smoke with hate in his eyes. "Gonna kill you, *gringo,*" he mumbled, spitting blood as he came at Smoke. More blood flowed from his ear, and his hands flexed with anticipation.

Smoke stood his ground, assuming a classical boxer's stance. El Gato swung his right hand at Smoke's head, but he ducked and hit El Gato twice under the chest with sharp left-right jabs, crushing his lower ribs. El Gato doubled over, gasping, hands on knees. Smoke danced back, fists up, in no hurry to finish the fight. He was thoroughly enjoying himself, and wanted to make El Gato suffer as much as possible.

Suddenly, without warning, El Gato dove forward, wrapping his arms around Smoke's back while burying his head against

Smoke's chest. He locked his hands against Smoke's spine and grunted as he squeezed with all his might.

Smoke groaned in pain, thinking his back was going to break under the pressure of El Gato's arms. After a moment, getting short of breath and unable to take in air, Smoke seized one of El Gato's ears in each hand and twisted with all of his might. El Gato shrieked as his left ear came off with a wet, ripping sound. The outlaw loosened his grip to feel his head, and Smoke took the opportunity to plant his knee squarely in El Gato's crotch, again doubling him, a high keening sound like a gut-shot pig coming from his lips. Smoke took a deep breath and swung his right hand up in an uppercut with all of his two hundred and twenty pounds behind it. El Gato's neck snapped back with a noise like a dry twig breaking and he did a backward dive, arms outstretched, landing spread-eagled in the fire again. This time he didn't move, but lay there, eyes staring at eternity as his flesh sizzled and burned.

Smoke worked his hand, making sure it wasn't broken, then stepped over to the spot where he left Chiva unconscious. The wiry Mexican was stirring, not fully awake yet. Smoke rolled him over onto his stomach and pulled his boots off. As Chiva began to struggle weakly, Smoke drew his knife and quickly slit the achilles tendons of both ankles.

Chiva screamed and rolled over, grabbing his legs, eyes wide with fright. "What you do? Why you cut me, Jensen?"

Smoke sleeved sweat off his forehead and sheathed his knife while he stood before the writhing man. "I'm a mite tired of killin' just now, so you're gettin' off lucky."

Chiva struggled to his feet, then fell awkwardly when he tried to walk, his ankles flopping loosely at the end of his legs. His severed tendons prevented him from being able to move at all.

Smoke said, "I'm taking your guns, so you can't signal your friends, but I'm gonna leave you some food so you won't starve to death."

Chiva stammered, "But, I no can walk. I will freeze!"

Smoke shrugged. "There's that possibility, I suppose." He

glared at Chiva through narrowed eyes. "If it happens, I suspect it won't be any great loss."

Chiva frowned, fear-sweat beading his forehead. "Why you not kill me?"

"Simple. Dead, you don't help me at all. Alive, it'll take at least one, maybe two of your friends to take care of you and keep you from dying. That's one or two who won't be gunnin' for me."

Smoke bent and picked up his hat off the ground. He smirked at Chiva as he prepared to leave. "I hope your friends don't think you're too much of a burden on them. Otherwise," he shrugged and settled his hat low on his head, "they're liable to kill you themselves and mess up my plans."

Chiva shook his fist at Smoke from where he lay on the ground, hate and pain clouding his eyes. *"Chinga tu madre, gringo!*

Smoke grinned as he disappeared in the night. "You keep warm now, you hear," he said.

Chapter Twenty-Three

Smoke planned to cover the north part of the trail himself and to slow down, or eliminate that bunch of paid assassins. He directed Cal and Pearlie farther down the mountain to harass and attack a second bunch headed up the mountain along a winding deer trail through tall timber.

By the time Cal and Pearlie made their way down the slopes to locate the gunmen's campfire, it was past ten o'clock at night and snow had stopped falling, dark skies beginning to clear.

Cal and Pearlie lay just outside the circle of light from the fire and listened to the outlaws as they prepared to turn in for the night.

One-Eye Jordan, his hand wrapped around a whiskey bottle and his speech slightly slurred, said, "Blackjack, I'll lay a side wager that I'm the one puts lead in Smoke Jensen first."

Blackjack Walker looked up from checking his Colt's loads, spun the cylinder, and answered, "You're on, One-Eye. I've got two double-eagle gold pieces that say I'll not only drill Jensen first, but that I'll be the one who kills him."

The Mexican and two Anglos who were watching from the

other side of the fire chuckled and shook their heads. They apparently did not think much of their leader's wager, or were simply tired and wanted them to quit jawing so they could turn in and get some rest.

Finally, when One-Eye finished his bottle and tossed it in the flames, the men quit talking and rolled up in their blankets under a dusting of light snow.

Pearlie and Cal waited until the gunnies were snoring loudly and then they stood, stretching muscles cramped from lying on the snow-covered ground. Being careful not to make too much noise, they circled the camp, noting the location and number of horses, the layout of surrounding terrain. They crept up on the group of sleeping gunhawks, moving slowly while counting bedrolls to make sure all of Sundance's men were accounted for.

Pearlie leaned over and cupped his hand around Cal's ear, whispering. "I count five bodies. That matches the number of horses."

Cal nodded, holding up five fingers to show he agreed. He took two sticks of dynamite from his pack and held them up so Pearlie could see, then he pointed to Pearlie and made a circular motion with his hand to indicate he wanted Pearlie to go around to the other side of camp and cover him.

Pearlie nodded and slipped a twelve gauge shotgun off his shoulder. He broke it open and made sure both chambers were loaded, then snapped it shut gently so as not to make a sound. He gave Cal a wink as he slipped quietly into the darkness.

Cal waited five minutes to give Pearlie time to get into position. Taking a deep breath, he drew his Navy Colt with his right hand and held the dynamite in his left. He slowly made his way among sleeping outlaws, being careful not to step on anything that might cause noise. When he was near the fire, he tossed both sticks of dynamite into the dying flames and quickly stepped out of camp. He ducked behind a thick ponderosa pine just as the dynamite exploded with an ear-splitting roar, blowing chunks of bark off the other side of the tree.

The screaming began before echoes from the explosion

stopped reverberating off the mountainside, while flaming pieces of wood spiraled through the darkness, hissing when they fell into drifts of snow.

Cal swung around his tree, both hands full of iron. One of the outlaws, his hair and shirt on fire, ran toward him. He was yelling and shooting his pistol wildly.

Cal fired both Colts, thumbing back hammers, pulling triggers so quickly the roaring gunshots seemed like a single blast. Pistols jumped and bucked in his hands, belching flame and smoke toward the running gunnie.

The bandit, shot in his chest and stomach, was thrown backward to land like a discarded rag doll on his back, smoke curling lazily from his flaming scalp.

One-Eye Jordan threw his smoldering blanket aside and stood, dazed and confused. His eyepatch had been blown off, along with most of the left side of his face. He staggered a few steps, then pulled his pistol and aimed it at Cal, moving slowly as if in slow motion.

Twin explosions erupted from Pearlie's scattergun, taking Jordan low in the back, splitting his torso with molten pieces of lead. His lifeless body flew across the clearing where it landed atop another outlaw who had been killed in the dynamite blast.

One of the Mexican *bandidos*, shrieking curses in Spanish, crawled away from the fire on hands and knees. Scrabbling like a wounded crab toward the shelter of darkness, he looked over his shoulder to find Pearlie staring at him across the sights of a Colt .44.

"Aiyee . . . no . . ." he yelled, holding his hands in front of him as if they could stop the inevitable bullets. Pearlie shot him, the hot lead passing through his hand and entering the bandit's left eye, exploding his skull and sending brains and blood spurting into the air.

Blackjack Walker, who was thrown twenty feet in the air into a deep snowdrift, struggled to his feet. As he drew his pistol, he saw Pearlie shoot his *compadre*. Pearlie was turned away from Walker and did not see the stunned outlaw creep slowly toward him, drawing a bead on his back with a hog-leg.

Cal glanced up, checking on bodies for signs of life. He saw Walker with his arm extended, about to shoot Pearlie in the back.

With no thought for his own safety, Cal yelled as he stood up, drawing his Navy Colt, triggering off a hasty shot.

Walker heard the shout and whirled, catching a bullet in his neck as he wheeled around. A death-spasm curled his trigger-finger and his pistol fired as he fell.

Cal felt like a mule had kicked him in the chest as he was thrown backward. He lay in the snow, gasping for breath, staring at stars. In shock, he felt little pain—that would come much later. He knew he was hit hard and wondered briefly if he was going to die. His right arm was numb and wouldn't move, and his vision began to dim, as if snow clouds were again covering the stars.

Suddenly, Pearlie's face appeared above him, tears streaming down his cheeks. "Hey pardner, you saved my life," he said with worry pinching his forehead.

Cal gasped, trying to breathe. He felt as if the mule that had kicked him was now sitting on his chest. "Pearlie," he said in a hoarse whisper rasping through parched lips, "how're you doin'?"

Pearlie pulled Cal's shirt open and examined a blood-splattered hole in the right side of his ribs. He choked back a sob, then he muttered, "I'm fine, cowboy. How about you? You havin' much pain?"

Cal winced when suddenly, his wound began to throb. "I feel like someone's tryin' to put a brand on my chest, an' it hurts like hell."

Pearlie rolled him to the side, looking for an exit wound. The bullet had struck his fourth rib, shattering it, and traveled around the chest just underneath the skin, causing a deep, bloody furrow, then exited from the side, just under Cal's right arm. The wound was oozing blood, but there was none of the spurting that would signify artery damage, and it looked as if the slug had not entered his chest cavity.

Cal groaned, coughed, and passed out. Pearlie tore his own shirt off and wrapped it around Cal, tying it as tightly as he could to staunch the flow of blood from the bullet hole. He sat back on his haunches, trying to think of something else he could do to help his friend. "Goddammit kid," he whispered, sweat beading his forehead, "it shoulda been me lyin' there instead of you."

The sound of a twig snapping not far away caught Pearlie's attention and he jerked his Colt, thumbing back the hammer.

"Hold on there, young'un," a voice called from the darkness, "it's jest me, ole Puma, come to see what all this commotion's about."

Pearlie released the hammer and holstered his gun with a sigh of relief. "Puma! Boy, am I glad to see you!"

Puma sauntered into the light, then he saw Cal lying wounded at Pearlie's feet. He squatted down, laying his Sharps Big Fifty rifle near his feet, and bent over the kid. He lifted Pearlie's improvised dressing and examined Cal's wound. Pursing his lips, he whistled softly. "Whew . . . this child's got him some hurt."

He pulled a large Bowie knife from his scabbard and held it out to Pearlie. "Here. Put this in that fire and get me some fatback and lard out'n my saddlebag."

When Pearlie just stared at him, Puma's voice turned harsh. "Hurry son, we don't have a lot of time if'n we want to save this'n."

Pearlie snatched the knife from Puma and hurried to carry out his request.

Puma took his bandanna and began wiping sweat from Cal's forehead, speaking to him in a low, soothing voice. "You just rest easy, young beaver, ole Puma's here now an' you're gonna be jest fine."

When Pearlie returned carrying a sack of fatback and a small tin of lard, Puma asked him if he had any whiskey.

"Some, in my saddlebags, but . . ."

"Git it, and don't dawdle now, you hear?"

After Pearlie handed Puma the whiskey, the old mountain man cradled Cal's head in his arms and slowly poured half the bottle down his throat, stopped to let him cough and gag, then gave him the rest of the liquor.

Without looking up, he said, "Git my blade outta the fire, it oughtta be 'bout ready by now."

Pearlie fished the knife out of the coals, its blade glowing red-hot and steaming in the chilly air. He carried it to Puma and gave it to him, dreading what was to come next.

"Pearlie, you sit on the young'un's legs and try an' keep him from moving too much. I'll sit on his left arm and hold down his right."

When they were in position, Puma pulled a two-inch cartridge from his pocket and placed it between Cal's teeth. "Bite down on this, boy, an' don't worry none if'n you have to yell every now'n then. There ain't nobody left alive to hear you."

Cal nodded, fear in his eyes, jaws clenched around the bullet.

Puma laid the glowing knife blade sideways on Cal's wound and dragged it along his skin, cauterizing the flesh. It hissed and steamed, and the smell of burning meat caused Pearlie to turn his head and empty his stomach in the snow.

Cal's face turned blotchy red and every muscle in his body tensed, but he made no sound while the knife did its work.

When he was through, Puma stuck his blade in the snow to cool it, sleeving sweat off his forehead. He looked down at Cal, who was breathing hard through his nose, bullet sticking out of his lips like an unlit cigarette. "Smoke was right, Cal," Puma whispered. "You're one hairy little son of a bitch. You were born with the bark on, all right."

Cal spit the bullet out and mumbled, "Do you think you could move, Pearlie? You're about to break my legs."

Pearlie laughed. "Sure, Cal. I wouldn't want to cause you no extra amount of pain."

Cal chuckled, then he winced and moaned. "Oh. It hurts so bad when I laugh."

While they were talking, Puma gently washed the wound with snow, then packed the furrow with crushed chewing tobacco."

"What's that for?" Pearlie asked.

"Tabaccy will heal just about anything," Puma answered,

as he dipped his fingers in the lard and spread a thin layer over the tobacco-covered wound.

Cal looked down at his chest, then up at Pearlie. "Would you build me a cigarette, Pearlie? I think I'd rather burn a twist of tobacco than wear it."

Puma sliced a hunk of fatback off a larger piece, laid it over Cal's chest, and tied it down with Pearlie's shirt. "There, that oughtta keep you from bleedin' to death 'til you git down to Big Rock an' the doctor."

Pearlie handed Cal a cigarette and lit it for him. "How are we gonna git him down to town, Puma? I don't think he can sit a horse."

Puma stood up and walked off into the darkness, fetching two geldings back, leading them into the light. He tied a dally-rope from one to the other and then turned to the two younger men. "We'll sit Cal in the saddle, and you'll ride double behind him, with your arms around him holdin' the reins. That way, if'n he faints or passes out, you can hold him in the saddle. 'Bout halfway down, change horses when this'n gets tired." He glanced up at the stars. "I figure you'll make it to town about daylight."

Pearlie said, "But what about Smoke? How'll he know what happened to us? He's expectin' us back at camp in the morning."

Puma smiled. "Don't you worry none about that. I'll tell him what you done and where you're gone to. Now git goin' if'n you want to make it in time fer breakfast."

The two men lifted Cal into the saddle, and Pearlie climbed on behind, his arms around the younger man. "Just a minute," Cal said, feeling his empty holster. "Where's my Navy?"

"Don't worry about it," Pearlie said, "I'll get you another one."

Cal shook his head. "No. That was Smoke's gun when he came up here with Preacher. It means somethin' special to me, an' I won't leave without it."

Puma dug in the snow where Cal had fallen until he found the pistol. He brushed it off and handed it to the teenager. "Here ya' go, beaver. You might want to check your loads 'fore you put it in your holster.'' He glanced back, surveying the outlaws' bodies lying around camp. ''Looks like you mighta used a few cartridges in the fracas earlier.''

Pearlie grinned as they rode off. ''That we did, Puma. That we did.''

corpse. It lay atop that of another man who'd been blown

Chapter Twenty-Four

Sundance stood in the middle of a small clearing, hands on his hips, surveying the carnage surrounding him. It was a little past dawn and he, Jeremiah Gray Wolf, Lightning Jack Warner, and two of his hired guns from the Mexican border came here when they heard an explosion and gunshots the previous night.

The two Texas cowboys riding with him were standing to one side, trying not to look at the mutilated bodies covered with a thin layer of snow, slowly rotting in early morning light despite low temperatures so high in the mountains. Their faces pale and drawn, both men appeared to be about to lose their breakfast over the grisly sight, bloody remains scattered everywhere, fire-blackened corpses sprawled in patches of pink snow.

"Gray Wolf," Sundance snarled, his voice thick with anger, "scout around camp to see if you can tell how many men did this."

"Okay, boss, but it's gonna be tough. The tracks're messed up and the snow's startin' to melt."

Sundance fixed him with a hard stare. "Don't give me any of your goddamn excuses, just do it!"

"Yes sir."

Lightning Jack squatted beside One-Eye Jordan's mutilated

corpse. It lay atop that of another man who'd been blown into several pieces by the force of a dynamite explosion. Jordan's body, cut virtually in half by double-barrel shotgun loads, was intermingled with various parts of other bodies.

Lightning Jack thumbed back his hat and stood up. "These boys died hard, Sundance, real hard."

Sundance made a face. "You know any easy way to die, Jack?"

Lightning Jack grunted. "Sure. Shot in the back when I'm ninety years old by a mad husband while I'm humpin' his twenty-year-old wife." His eyes narrowed as he looked around at other bodies lying in the snow. "But that don't appear too likely if we stay on this mountain huntin' Smoke Jensen."

Sundance glared at his companion. "You figuring on leavin', Jack?"

Jack shrugged. "No. This Jensen's startin' to piss me off. I plan to dust him through and through, then piss on his lifeless carcass."

Sundance gave a tight smile. "Good." He glanced at the two Texas gunmen, talking quietly off by themselves. "How 'bout you two?" he asked. "You boys havin' any second thoughts 'bout the job I hired you to do?"

Both men shuffled their boots in the snow, refusing to meet Sundance's gaze. "Uh, no boss. We're in fer the duration," one of the cowboys mumbled, although he didn't sound all that convinced. "It's just that ..." he hesitated, looking at his partner. "Well, this Jensen's done kilt some of the toughest men I ever rode with, an' it don't appear that any of them managed to get a shot into him while he was doin' it." He shrugged his shoulders, looking down at his feet. "Me and Josh here was just thinkin', maybe it'd be better if'n we went back down to the base of the mountain an' waited fer him to come outta these hills."

Sundance asked sarcastically, "An' just how long do you two think we'd have to wait?"

The other cowboy, Josh, said hopefully, "Not too long, boss. Winter's comin' an' he'll have to come down sometime fer supplies an' such. Nobody could live through a winter in these mountains without stockin' up on vittles and necessaries.''

Sundance shook his head in disgust. "You idiots. Jensen is a mountain man. Do you know what that means?"

When they failed to answer, he went on. "You could stick Jensen buck naked in the middle of a blizzard without a horse or a gun and he'd be sittin' by a fire, covered with furs, eatin' deer meat before you could get back down the mountain.''

Jeremiah Gray Wolf looked up, no longer studying tracks, and nodded. "He's right, boys. My people have a name for these old mountain men. They call them ghosts of the mountains, an' sing songs about them at tribal gatherings.''

Lightning Jack frowned down at him. "You sayin' we don't stand a chance agin' him, Gray Wolf?"

Gray Wolf straightened, looking around at the heavy, snow-clad forests surrounding them. "No, they can be killed only if your heart is strong and your medicine is powerful." He pointed to blood-stained snow near his feet. "They're flesh and blood, just like us, an' they bleed if you manage to put a slug in one, like this one here did.''

Sundance and Lightning Jack ambled over to where he stood, followed reluctantly by the pair of Texans. "What do you see?" Sundance asked.

Gray Wolf squatted, pointing to tracks and blood in the snow. "Looks like one of the attackers was hit hard, maybe even killed. He spilled a lot of blood before he was moved.''

Sundance's forehead wrinkled. "You say one of the attackers. That mean there was more'n one?"

Gray Wolf pursed his lips as he studied the tracks. "Yeah. At least two, maybe three. Look here," he bent down and pointed at hoof prints. "This bronc's a pony, an' he ain't wearing any shoes.''

"You mean an Injun is helpin' Jensen?" asked Lightning Jack, a puzzled expression on his face.

Gray Wolf shrugged. "Don't know. Could be an Indian, or could be another mountain man. Some of the ancient ones ride in the Indian way, on ponies without shoes.''

"Damn!" Sundance slapped his thigh with an open palm.

"I was afraid of that! Jensen's got himself some help." Before he could say anything else, a shout rang out while a rider galloped down the trail toward them, waving his arms in the air.

As the rider's horse slid to a stop in mushy, melting snow, Lightning Jack stepped to Sundance's side and spoke softly in his ear. "That there's Jack Robertson, boss. He was ridin' with Bull and Moses Washburn's group."

The sweating cowboy, chest heaving, jumped out of his saddle and ran over to Sundance. His eyes bugged wide at the sight of the devastation around him and the mutilated bodies lying like so much cord wood. "Jesus and Mary . . ." he whispered, sleeving sweat off his forehead.

Sundance glanced over his shoulder at the corpses, then back at Robertson. "You've seen dead men before. Now, what's so all-fired important for you to leave your bunch and come runnin' up here like your tail's on fire?"

Robertson shook his head, gulping to swallow bile rising in his throat at the sight of his comrades blown to hell. "Well, Bull sent me down here to tell you what's happened further up on the mountain."

An impatient Sundance frowned, "Okay, get on with it, what the hell's goin' on?"

"Micah Jacob had his throat cut an' he was ridin' no more'n ten feet behind me when it happened, an' I didn't see nor hear a damn thing!"

Sundance clenched his teeth. "So? Look around you, boy. We got a whole passel of men killed here, not just one rider." He spat disgustedly on the ground. "You mean Bull sent you down just to tell me that?"

"No sir, that's not all. We heard some gunfire last night over to the north trail, an' rode over there this mornin' after breakfast to see what was goin' on." He took a deep breath, looking at the other outlaws. "We found El Gato an' his three Mex's as dead as doornails."

Sundance cursed, "Goddammit! How'd they die?"

"One of the Mexicans had a stake through his gut, went all the way through him and stuck out the back. The other two had their throats cut while they was sleepin'. They was still in their bedrolls.''

"How about El Gato and Chiva?" asked Lightning Jack.

Robertson's face paled as he remembered what he had seen at their camp. "El Gato had been beaten to death. His ear was torn plumb off and his face looked like he'd been kicked by a bee-stung stallion. His ribs was caved in and his privates was squashed and mashed 'til you couldn't hardly tell what they was. His jaw was drove up into his brain and his neck was broken half in two, hardly holdin' his head on at all.''

The two Texans glanced at each other, eyebrows raised. One said softly, awe in his voice, "El Gato was one mean *hombre.*"

The other whispered, "It 'pears Jensen was a mite meaner."

"And Chiva?" reminded Lightning Jack impatiently.

Robertson shook his head. "Oh, he's alive all right, if'n you can call it that. The muscles in his ankles have been cut, and he cain't walk nor stand up. And . . .''

"Go on," urged Sundance.

"Well, it ain't my place to say so, but I think he's gone a little loco, scared crazy, you might say."

"Whatta ya' mean?"

"He just sits there, rockin' back and forth, kinda foamin' at the mouth, an' when he hears any kinda sound, he jumps like he's scared to death and starts to cry and wail in Spanish. If you ask me, I think Jensen done scared the hell outta that boy and he ain't never gonna be right in the head again.''

Sundance said, "Damn! I can't believe Chiva saw something that scared him that bad . . .''

Before he could say another word, a loud thump sounded from Robertson. Blood and tissue erupted from the front of his shirt and he was thrown backwards to land spread-eagled in the snow. A hole as big as a fist tunneled through his chest. Just as he hit the ground, the loud, booming sound of a Sharps Big Fifty echoed across the slopes.

The remaining men all dove to the ground in the watery mush and melting snow. As they looked around, their guns drawn and ready, Lightning Jack yelled, "There he is, up yonder!" pointing up the mountain.

In the distance, a small figure dressed in buckskins could be seen holding his rifle up, and the faint sound of an Indian yell filtered down through early morning mist. "Yi-yi-yi-ahhh!"

"Goddamn," said Sundance, "that shot must've been almost fifteen hundred yards."

Lightning Jack scrambled up on hands and knees until he was behind a thick ponderosa pine. "Yeah, an' I don't think it was a lucky hit, neither."

The other men rolled and crawled and ran wildly until they were also behind cover, shoulders hunched against the next shot, hoping it would be one of the others and not them.

Sundance muttered, "Damn!" as he took a deep breath. He jumped to his feet and ran to his horse, pulling his Henry rifle out of its saddle boot and positioning himself behind his mount. He jacked a round into the chamber, aimed over the saddle, and began to fire.

The mountain man could be heard laughing as bullets dug up earth and mud less than a third of the way upslope. Puma Buck put his Sharps to his shoulder and fired, the .50 caliber bullet hitting Sundance's horse in its shoulder. The force of the slug knocked the horse sideways, killing it instantly, throwing it on top of Sundance, who began to scream for help from his followers.

No one moved. Lightning Jack peered cautiously around his tree. "Maybe Bull or one of the others will hear the shots and come to help us."

Jeremiah Gray Wolf muttered under his breath without raising his head behind a fallen log. "Not if he's got any sense at all, he won't!"

One of the Texans, rattled by Sundance's cries for help, called out, "Hey, Lightning Jack, you think maybe we ought a clear on out an' head back down the mountain?"

Jack shook his head. "Ain't no use, boys. Jensen's bound to have our backtrail covered." He paused, sweat pouring off his face despite the chill of the early morning air. "No . . . the only way off this mountain is over Jensen's dead body."

The Texan glanced at his partner, eyes wide. "Or stretched out face-down across a saddle!"

* * *

Smoke raised his head above a bush where he was hiding and peered through binoculars down the slope toward a group of men working their way up a trail toward him. They were headed north-east, toward the peak, and if he didn't stop them now, they would soon discover his fortress.

George Stalking Horse was leading, leaning over his saddle horn, studying the ground for any sign of tracks. He was followed by the Southerners, spread out three abreast, their rifles resting on saddle horns, eyes flickering back and forth for any sign of danger. Toothpick brought up the rear, the butt of his Greener ten gauge resting on his thigh.

Through his glasses, Smoke could see they were almost even with one of his traps. He worked the lever on his Henry repeating rifle, shucked a shell into the chamber, and brought it to his shoulder. The range was too far for an accurate shot, but close enough for what Smoke had in mind.

He elevated the barrel to forty-five degrees to give him maximum distance and squeezed the trigger gently. His big gun exploded and slammed back into his shoulder, spurting fire and smoke.

The .44 caliber slug plowed into a large boulder next to the trail, ringing loudly, sending sparks and rock-chips flying.

At the sound, the outlaws' horses shied to the left, toward the edge of a cliff, whinnying and crow-hopping in fear.

A man on the outside shouted as his mount's legs broke through the thin layer of sticks and leaves Smoke had placed over his dug-out area, and pitched sideways off the mountain ledge. Both the man's and horse's screams could be heard echoing off nearby ridges for several seconds as they fell, pinwheeling in free-fall. A loud crash from below silenced the horrible sounds.

One of the Southerners spurred his horse into a gallop, trying frantically to escape. The bronc's front leg sank into a hole, causing him to swallow his head and somersault forward. His rider sailed ahead, twisting and turning in midair. He landed on his head, the fall snapping his neck and breaking his back in two places, killing him instantly.

The remaining Southerner, enraged at his comrades' deaths, put the spurs to his mount and charged up the trail, firing his rifle from his waist as he rode, screaming a rebel yell at the top of his lungs.

Smoke stepped out from his bush, drew his Colt, and took an unhurried shot while bullets from the charging man's rifle pocked dirt and mud at his feet.

The slug from Smoke's Colt took the gunnie in the middle of his forehead, blowing blood, brains, and hair into the air. The lifeless body slumped forward, remaining in the saddle as the horse galloped past.

Toothpick looked down at his Greener, useless at this range, even if his near-sighted eyes could see far enough to aim it. George Stalking Horse asked softly, "Toothpick, what'll we do now? That scattergun ain't no use to us an' I don't carry nothing but a pistol."

Toothpick grinned, shaking his head. "Only one thing to try. Follow my lead, and kill the sonofabitch if you git the chance."

He stood, walking out onto the trail in plain sight. When he was away from cover he threw the shotgun to the side and called out, "Hey, Jensen. I'm unarmed. Come on down and let's have a parley."

Smoke shouted back, "Have your Indian friend come out and throw down his weapons and we'll talk."

George Stalking Horse stepped from the bushes at one side of the trail and tossed his pistol out in front of him.

The two outlaws watched with hooded eyes as Smoke rode down toward them, Colts in each hand. He stopped his horse a short distance away and holstered his guns. "Okay gents, what's on your minds?"

Toothpick said, "The way I heard it, you never did shoot an unarmed man, so I guess that makes us your prisoners."

Smoke gave a slow smile and shook his head. "No, I don't think so. You got two choices. Fight or die where you stand."

Toothpick held out his arms and looked around, grinning. "Fight? With what? I done throwed my shotgun away."

Smoke nodded at the knife in Toothpick's scabbard. "I hear you think you're pretty good with that blade. Want to give me a try?"

"Sure, mister. I ain't never found nobody I couldn't cut to ribbons."

Smoke stepped out of his saddle. He pointed to the Indian. "You, stand in the middle of the trail. If you make a move, I'll kill you."

George Stalking Horse gulped, "Yes sir."

Toothpick pulled his knife slowly out of his belt, kissed the blade, and held it low in front of him in a classic knife-fighter's stance.

Smoke drew his own knife and began to circle Toothpick, shifting the knife from hand to hand, his eyes boring into the outlaw's.

The two men closed, arms and hands moving faster than the eye could follow, swiping and slashing, blades twanging and sparking as they hit. After a moment Smoke stepped back, breathing hard, blood flowing from a three-inch gash on his forearm.

"How'd you like that, Mister Smoke Jensen? I'm gonna cut you up, you bastard."

Smoke slowly raised his arm to his mouth and licked the wound, blood trickling from his lips. "If your blade was as fast as your mouth, I'd be worried. As it is, I can see I'm gonna have to give you a lesson in manners."

Toothpick's forehead wrinkled. "What? What's that mean?"

Smoke bared his bloody teeth. "It means I'm gonna show you what it's like to be cut up, really cut up. Then I'm gonna scalp you and leave you alive to live with the shame of it for the rest of your days."

Toothpick's face screwed up in rage and he screamed as he ran at Smoke, knife slashing back and forth in front of him in a windmill motion.

Smoke parried the thrust with his left hand and flicked his right arm in a lightning fast back-and-forth movement as Toothpick rushed by. The outlaw stumbled and almost fell, then turned back to face the mountain man.

Toothpick's right wrist dangled limply, its tendons cut to the bone, his knife lying in the mud at his feet. He snarled and picked it up with his left hand and advanced on Smoke, but a bit more carefully this time.

Smoke took a quick step in and whipped his blade to and fro again, then danced lightly back. Toothpick's eyes were wide, both his cheeks flayed open, flaps hanging down exposing his teeth. He sleeved the blood off his face with his useless right arm, growling with hate. "You sonofabitch, I'm gonna—"

Before he could finish his thought, Smoke rushed in and swung his knife again, cutting the biceps tendon on Toothpick's left arm, leaving raw muscle edges dripping blood into the mud.

A low, mewing sound came from Toothpick's carved face. "I give up . . . you win." He let his knife fall to the ground.

Smoke shook his head and swung backhanded, catching Toothpick across his chin with the steel butt of his knife handle. Toothpick whirled around and fell face-down on the ground, semi-conscious, moaning and groaning in pain.

Smoke stepped over to him and knelt, putting his knee in the middle of Toothpick's back. He reached down, grabbed a handful of hair, and pulled the man's head back. He made a quick incision along the hairline on his forehead from ear to ear. With a loud grunt, Smoke jerked back with all his might, ripping hair and scalp off Toothpick's skull.

Toothpick screamed a bloodcurdling howl, his split cheeks flapping and blood spurting from his head, then he passed out.

Smoke held the dripping scalp in front of him as he approached a terrified George Stalking Horse. "Here," he flipped the bloody mess to the Indian who caught it without thinking, then he quickly dropped it to the ground, gagging.

Smoke smiled gently, asking, "Have you had enough, or do you want to finish this now?"

The man held his hands out in front of him and began to back away, saying, "No . . . no . . . please mister."

Smoke glanced down and noted that he wore his holster on his right hip. Without another word, Smoke drew his Colt and shot him through the right hand, blowing off his index and middle fingers at the first knuckle.

The outlaw yelled and grabbed his hand, holding it to his stomach while retching in the mud. After a moment, he looked up with tears streaming down his face. "Why'd you do that?"

"I want you out of this fight." He shrugged. "It was that, or kill you." Smoke pointed over his shoulder to an unconscious Toothpick. "Now, pick up your trash and get on down the mountain. If I can still see you in five minutes, I'll change my mind and kill you both." He hesitated, then added, "And, if I ever lay eyes on either of you again, no matter where we are, I will kill you without another thought."

Smoke walked to his horse, stepped into the saddle, and sat there until George Stalking Horse had revived Toothpick and they were both stumbling down the mountain as fast as they could move, leaking scarlet blood to mingle with the black mud on the trail.

"*Adios,* boys," Smoke said to their backs. "Be sure to tell your friend Sundance Morgan I said hello."

Chapter Twenty-Five

Bull and Moses Washburn drank coffee at their tiny campfire, leaving two remaining gunmen stationed on opposite sides of camp, standing guard.

Chiva, his ankles bandaged with blood-stained bandannas, sat rocking back and forth, mumbling "Jensen *es el diablo,*" over and over again. His fear-widened eyes took in every detail and he jumped, reaching for a gun when he heard the slightest noise in the surrounding forest.

Moses cut his eyes to Bull. "What're we gonna do, Bull? We can't just sit here all day waitin' fer Jensen to show up." He sighed and drained his cup. "We're sittin' ducks here."

Bull shrugged, his eyes staring into his coffee as if he might find some answers there.

Johnny Larson, the outlaw guarding one side of camp next to the trail cried, "Hey Bull! We got company comin'!"

Bull drew his sawed-off shotgun and got to his feet, followed by Washburn, who shucked a shell into his rifle. They hurried over to a spot where Larson stood, hidden behind a pine tree, aiming his rifle upslope.

Two men could be seen, lurching, stumbling down the middle of the path, their arms around each other's shoulders for support.

As they drew nearer, they were easy to identify as George Stalking Horse and Toothpick.

Bull cursed softly under his breath at the sight of both bloody men. "Goddamn, will ya' look at that?"

Toothpick's bare skull was covered with dark, crusted blood, shining blackly in the mid-morning sun. Scarlet liquid trailed from gashes in his flayed cheeks, running down his chin to soak his shirt all the way to his waist. His eyes were wide and he had a haunted look, as if he had danced with the devil and hadn't much enjoyed the experience.

George wore a bloody bandanna wrapped around his right hand, tucked tight against his stomach, and he hunched over in obvious pain.

Larson let the hammer down on his rifle and walked slowly to greet his comrades, motioning them back to camp.

As soon as they were settled in front of the fire, Toothpick whined, "Whiskey, give me whiskey."

Bull took a bottle out of his saddlebags and passed it to Toothpick, wincing over the gruesome sight of his scalped head and the flayed edges of his slashed cheeks dripping blood.

Toothpick grabbed the bottle, his only good hand trembling, and upended it, gulping, swallowing fiery liquid convulsively until the container was empty. He sucked air through broken stubs of teeth and gaping holes in his face, then pitched the bottle into the flames, choking and coughing up more blood.

Bull put his hand on Toothpick's shoulder, causing him to flinch and pull away. "What happened up there, Toothpick?" he asked gently in his high voice.

Toothpick shook his head and stared into the fire, unable to answer.

George Stalking Horse looked up through pain-slitted eyes. "Jensen ambushed us as we was ridin' up the trail. He kilt the others, then came after Toothpick an' me." He moaned, cradling his mutilated right hand. "Ya' got any more whiskey? Bastard shot two of my fingers off an' it's hurtin' like hell."

After Moses handed him another bottle and he gulped most of it down, George continued with his story. He told them about the deadly knife fight and how Jensen tortured Toothpick, inflicting terrible wounds before finally scalping him as he lay dazed on the ground.

"Jesus," whispered Moses as he listened to George's tale. "I never heard anything like that." He glanced at Chiva, then back to the men who'd tangled with Smoke. "The son of a bitch is worse than Apaches back home."

George Stalking Horse looked over his shoulder at Washburn, nodding his head. "Yeah, only I'd rather face ten Apaches than one Smoke Jensen. At least Apaches kill ya' 'fore they scalp ya'."

The sound of horses approaching caused the outlaws to grab their guns and jump to their feet. All except Chiva, who covered his head with his arms and lay on the ground, whispering, *"Este el diablo . . . aiyee . . . este el diablo!"*

"Hello, the camp! It's me, Sundance, so hold your fire!"

Bull and Moses holstered their weapons as Sundance and his men rode into the clearing. Coffee had been brewed and while beans and tortillas were passed around, the outlaws wolfed food down as if they hadn't eaten for days. As they ate, Sundance told them how he and his men had been fired on and forced to stay under cover for several hours by an old mountain man with a large bore rifle. He'd finally grown tired of making them cower behind trees and logs and disappeared into thick forest.

After they were sure he was gone, they got their horses and rode upslope, hoping to meet with remnants of Sundance's band.

Sundance looked around at the wounded, beaten men sitting with Bull and Washburn. "I guess the time for sneakin' around is over. I think we'll do better ridin' together. Maybe a large bunch of riders will have better luck against Jensen and his friends."

Bull frowned. "We sure as hell ain't done too good so far." He inclined his head toward Chiva, Toothpick, and George Stalking Horse. Lowering his voice, he told Sundance and Lightning Jack what had happened to the three of them, pausing now and then to emphasize a point.

Sundance nodded. "Yeah, Jensen's a mean bastard, all right.

But there's no way he can stand agin' all of us at once.'' He got to his feet and approached the wounded men. "You boys gonna be able to fight, or are ya' gonna lay here lickin' your wounds like whipped dogs?''

Chiva didn't answer or bother to look up. Toothpick and George glanced at each other, then lowered their heads.

"I'm done, boss," said George Stalking Horse. "Jensen shot off two fingers on my gun hand. I ain't got the stomach fer any more of this, an' I'm headin' back down the mountain soon as I finish this grub."

Sundance raised his eyebrows. "How 'bout you, Toothpick? You done, too?''

Toothpick shrugged without raising his eyes. The hot coffee had started his cheeks bleeding again, blood trickling over his chin in fat, red drops onto his shirt.

Without another word, Sundance drew his Colt and fired three times in rapid succession, putting a slug into each man's forehead. Their bodies were slammed into the ground to quiver and spasm in grotesque dances of death as they died.

Bull's and Washburn's eyes widened in horror, while Lightning Jack's teeth bared in a fierce grin of satisfaction.

Sundance whirled, his smoking Colt pointed at his other followers. "There ain't no room in my outfit for quitters or slackers. Either you ride with me, or you die by my hand right now! Any questions?''

As the echoes of his gunfire died, and gunsmoke slowly drifted away on a gentle mountain breeze, his men were silent. None dared speak out against him.

Sundance broke open the Colt's loading gate and punched out empty brass casings one by one. "Now, here's what we're gonna do . . .''

Smoke was dozing, conserving his energy for the fire-fight he knew was coming later. He had made a small camp and ground-reined his horse, then walked seventy-five yards into thick ponderosa pines. He lay down, covering himself with pine boughs and branches so as to be invisible, should any of the outlaws chance upon him.

He was resting there, half asleep, his Colt in his hand, when a soft voice whispered in his ear. ''Wake up, son, we gotta palaver.''

Smoke was startled into full wakefulness in an instant, his thumb automatically earing back the hammer of his pistol as he sat up. He was astonished that anyone could have approached him without him hearing it.

Puma Buck sat squatted on his haunches, baring stubby teeth in a wide grin. ''Don't look so damn surprised, Smoke, this ole beaver's been Injunin' up on critters with better hearin' than you longer than you been alive.''

Smoke shook his head, a rueful expression on his face. ''How'd you find me, Puma? I thought I was pretty well hid.''

''Same way a squirrel finds nuts fer the winter, child. 'Cause he knows where to look.'' He cut his eyes toward Smoke's camp nearby. ''Ya' got any *cafecito* over there? I be a mite parched.''

Smoke scrambled to his feet and led the mountain man to his fire, mostly embers now. He scattered dry twigs and pine needles over the coals, then added larger pieces of wood when flames began to lick at the tinder.

While Smoke was building the fire, Puma got canteens and Arbuckle's coffee out of his saddlebags and prepared the tin pot with an abundance of coffee and a sparse amount of water.

Smoke cut strips of meat and grabbed a handful of dried apples and a tin of peaches out of his bags. As they ate, Puma informed Smoke of Cal's wound, and told him how he had sent the younger men down to Big Rock to see Doc Spalding.

Smoke's brow furrowed with concern. ''Is Cal gonna be all right, Puma? Do you think he'll make it?''

Puma smacked his lips after draining his cup of the thick, black brew. His faded blue eyes softened as he glanced at Smoke, knowing he thought of Cal as his son. ''Don't you worry 'bout that'un, Smoke. That boy's got the heart of a mountain grizzly.'' Puma pulled a cartridge from his pocket and handed it to Smoke, showing him tooth marks in the brass casing. "He never made a sound when I scorched his wound."

Puma nodded, his eyes twinkling in the afternoon sun. "He's a natural born mountain man, an' he'll have some impressive scars to show an' tales to tell about his experiences in the high lonesome, fightin' *bandidos* with Smoke Jensen an' Puma Buck."

Smoke grinned. "That's good, 'cause Sally'd have my hide if I let anything happen to that boy."

Puma topped off their cups with more coffee. He took two stogies from his buckskin shirt and handed one to Smoke, then lit them both with a burning twig from the fire. After puffing his cigar to life, filling the air with thick blue smoke, he asked, "What's your plan, Smoke? Best I can figger it, you still got over a dozen hardcases on your trail."

Smoke thought about it a moment, drinking coffee and smoking while he considered his options. "I'm gonna end it tonight." He glanced at the cloudless sky. "There won't be any snow tonight, an' the moon's still almost full, so there'll be plenty of light to shoot by."

Puma nodded.

"I plan to hit and run, takin' a few of 'em from ambush, an' leading the rest up the slope, to a spot where I have a forting-up place ready. I'll make my stand there."

Puma pursed his lips, staring at the glowing end of his cigar. "Ya' want some help?"

Smoke put his hand on Puma's shoulder. "This is my fight, old friend. I don't want anyone else hurt on my account."

Puma started to argue, "But—"

"No, you've done more than enough already." Smoke hesitated, then added, "However, if you could cover my left flank with your Sharps, you could keep 'em from sending a party to circle around to my rear."

Puma chuckled deep in his throat. "They've had a small taste of my Sharps once. I guess another bite or two will keep 'em in line."

Smoke's face got serious. "Puma, there's one more thing. If something happens . . . if things don't go as I plan, I got two more favors to ask."

Puma's eyebrows raised.

"One, make sure Sundance Morgan doesn't leave the mountain alive."

"Done. An' the other?"

"Take me home to Sugarloaf, and tell Sally what happened."

Puma stuck out his hand. "You got my word on it, partner."

Smoke took his friend's hand. "Now, it's time to do some serious damage. There's some stinkweed on this mountain that needs pruning."

Chapter Twenty-Six

Smoke was loaded for bear. He had his two Colt .44 pistols, a knife in his scabbard, a tomahawk in his belt against the small of his back, a Henry repeating rifle in one saddle boot, and a heavy Greener ten gauge shotgun on a rawhide thong over his shoulder. He was ready to hunt, and to kill anything that got in his way.

He rode through thick ponderosa pines, making no sound that could be heard from more than a few feet away. By late afternoon he located the party of gunmen looking for him. Unused to traveling in the mountains, they were making so much noise they were easy to find.

Smoke stepped out of his saddle, leaving his horse ground-reined for a quick getaway should it be necessary, and slipped down a snowy slope toward a ribbon of trail the gang was following.

As the last man in line came abreast of his hiding place, Smoke took a running jump and leapt on the rider's horse behind him. Before the startled man could make a sound, Smoke slit his throat with his knife. Smoke pulled the dying man's gun from its holster and a knife hidden beneath his mackinaw as he slumped over his horse's withers.

He pushed the dead body out of the saddle and threw the knife at the next rider in line. The blade buried itself in the gunman's back, causing him to arch forward, screaming in pain.

Smoke thumbed back the Colt's hammer and began to fire. Two more of Sundance's hired killers were mortally wounded before any had time to clear leather.

Smoke whirled the dead man's horse in a tight circle and galloped into the brush, leaning over the saddle to avoid low-hanging branches and limbs.

Sundance's gang jerked their reins and tried to turn around to give chase, but the trail was narrow and all they managed to do was get in each other's way. Two men were knocked from their mounts, one sustaining a broken arm in the process.

Only minutes after the attack began, Smoke had disappeared and the gunhawks counted four dead and one injured, while not a shot had been fired at the mountain man.

Sundance was furious as he rode among his followers. "God-dammit! You worthless bastards didn't fire a single round!" He leaned to the side and spat on one of the bodies lying in the dirt. "Hell, I thought I was ridin' with some tough gun-slicks." He shook his head in disgust. "I might as well have hired schoolmarms, for all the help you galoots have been."

"Fuck it!" yelled Curly Bill Cartwright. "I'm gonna kill that son of a bitch!" He filled his hand with iron and spurred his horse into the brush after Smoke.

Three other men pulled guns and started to follow Cartwright.

"Hold on there," yelled Sundance. "That's just what Jensen wants us to do." He waved the gang toward him. "Circle up and get ready in case he comes back. We'll stay here and see what happens. Maybe Cartwright'll get lucky."

Lightning Jack chuckled. "I doubt that, boss. He's goin' into Jensen's territory now, an' I'll bet a double-eagle he don't come out."

A loud double explosion came from the forest, startling the outlaws' mounts, causing one of the Mexicans to begin shooting wildly toward the noise while shouting curses in Spanish.

The gang waited expectantly, every gun trained on the spot

where Smoke and Cartwright entered a stand of dense trees. After a few moments the sound of a horse moving through brush could be heard.

The men cocked pistols and rifles as a horse walked out of the trees onto the trail. In its saddle was the decapitated body of Curly Bill Cartwright. His head and upper shoulders had been blown off by a double load of ten gauge buckshot. A tree branch had been stuck down the back of his shirt and his feet were tied together under the animal's belly to keep him upright in his saddle.

Lightning Jack spoke quietly. "You think maybe Jensen's sending us a message, boss?"

Sundance said, "Damn! I want to kill that bastard so bad I can taste it!"

Perro Muerte walked his horse over to Sundance. "What now, *jefe?* We go into trees, or stay on trail?"

Sundance said, "Stay on the trail. If we can locate his camp, we can keep him from gettin' to his supplies and ammunition. Sooner or later he'll run low, and then we can take him." He pointed to Jeremiah Gray Wolf, "Take the point, Gray Wolf, and see if'n you can find some tracks or a sign showing which way his camp might be."

Moses Washburn spoke in a low voice to Bull, "I don't like this, Bull. I don't like it one bit."

Bull shook his head. "Me either, partner, me either."

Jeremiah Gray Wolf leaned over his saddle and began to walk his pony up the trail, followed twenty yards back by the rest of the group.

After a quarter of a mile, he held up his hand and called over his shoulder, "I've found some tracks. Let's go."

The Indian straightened in his saddle and spurred his mount into a trot, disappearing around a bend in the trail. The others drew weapons and followed him from a distance.

Sundance rounded the bend and stopped short when he saw Gray Wolf's pony standing riderless by the side of the trail, grazing on the short grass partially hidden by melting snow. "Crap," he whispered under his breath. He hadn't heard a sound, not even a call for help.

When the rest of his men rode up to him, Sundance slowly urged his horse forward, scanning trees and brush on either side for a sign of Gray Wolf.

From behind him, Sundance heard a sharp intake of breath, and the words *"Madre de Dios,"* spoken in a hoarse whisper. He turned to see Perro Muerte crossing himself and staring up at a nearby tree.

He followed Perro Muerte's gaze, and found Jeremiah Gray Wolf hanging from a limb, a rope around his neck, his legs still kicking, quivering in death throes. The Indian's bowels had let loose and the stench was overpowering.

Sundance held his bandanna across his nose and rode over to examine the area under the body. Horse tracks showed that Smoke had probably roped the man while hiding in the tree, then dropped to his horse, pulling Gray Wolf out of his saddle by a rope he'd looped over the branch.

Bull said, "He never knew what hit him."

"Shut up!" yelled Sundance. "Come on, he can't be more'n a few hundred feet away. Let's go!"

The group cocked their weapons and started to follow Sundance up a steep slope past the tree with the body hanging from it. It was a steep grade, covered with loose gravel and small stones, and they were only about halfway up the incline when a gunshot from above caught their attention.

They looked up to see Smoke standing next to a large pile of boulders, grinning, holding something in one hand and a smoking cigar in the other. He cried, "Howdy, gents," and put his cigar against the object in his other hand. As a fuse began to sputter and sparkle, he dropped the bundle among the rocks and ducked out of sight.

"Holy shit, it's dynamite," yelled Moses Washburn, as he jerked his reins and tried to turn his horse around. The men all panicked and reined their horses to turn in different directions, running into each other, knocking men and animals to the ground.

The explosion was strangely muffled, yet the pile of boulders shifted. Slowly at first, then with gathering speed, huge rocks rolled and tumbled, racing down the slope, bounding as they descended toward the trapped riders milling about on the trail.

A huge dust cloud enveloped the area, covering screaming men and horses as rocks crushed bones and flattened bodies and ended life.

When dust had settled, the only men left alive were Sundance, Lightning Jack, Bull, and Perro Muerte. The slide had killed four Texas gunfighters and Moses Washburn, who could only be identified by his hand showing from beneath a huge boulder.

In the sudden quiet of dusk, the remaining men could hear the sounds of Jensen's horse in the distance galloping up the mountain.

"Moses," Bull said through gritted teeth, "I'm gonna kill him for you."

Sundance took a deep breath, looking around at all that was left of his band. "Okay, boys. He's headed straight up the mountain. There ain't much cover up there, an' there ain't nowhere to run to once he gits to the top."

He pulled his pistol and checked his loads. "Let's go git him!"

The moon had risen and in the cloudless sky made the area as bright as day. Smoke was hidden in his natural fortress leaning over the edge, peering below through his binoculars, waiting for Sundance and his men. It was time to end it, and he was ready.

There was movement below, and Smoke could see Bull and Perro Muerte crawling on hands and knees off to his right. They were going to try to inch up the slope, using small logs and rocks on that side for cover. Smoke grinned, remembering tricks Cal had devised for just that eventuality.

Smoke waited until they were halfway up the incline. Bull, panting heavily in the thin air, motioned for Perro Muerte to stop so he could catch his breath.

Smoke worked the lever on his Henry and sighted down the barrel. "Hey Bull!" he cried.

The big man squinted in semi-darkness, trying to see where

Jensen's voice was coming from, hoping to get off a lucky shot. "Yeah, whatta ya' want, Jensen? You wanna know how I'm gonna kill you?"

Smoke grinned. "No, I was just wondering if you'd noticed all those gourds and pumpkins down there."

Bull and Perro Muerte glanced around them and saw for the first time a number of small squash and pumpkins resting on the ground. Bull looked up the slope. "Yeah, what about it? You hungry?"

Smoke laughed out loud, his voice echoing off surrounding ridges. "Did you ever wonder, you ignorant bastard, how gourds could grow on bare rock?"

Bull's eyes widened in horror and he opened his mouth to scream as he realized the trap they had fallen into.

Smoke squeezed his trigger, firing into the pumpkin directly in front of them. Molten lead entered the gourd, igniting black powder. The object exploded, blasting hundreds of small stones hurtling outward. Bull's and Perro Muerte's bodies were riddled, shredded, blown to pieces. They died instantly.

Below, Sundance sleeved sweat off his forehead and turned to Lightning Jack. "Maybe we oughtta head down the mountain and come back later, with more men."

Lightning Jack looked at the gunfighter with disgust. "You coward. You got over thirty good men killed lookin' fer your vengeance. You ain't backin' out now."

Sundance dropped his hand to his Colt, but froze when a voice behind them said, "Hold it right there, gents."

Lightning Jack and Sundance turned to see a small, wiry man in buckskins pointing a shotgun at their heads. "Ease them irons outta those holsters and grab some sky."

As they dropped their pistols to the ground, Puma called out, "Hey Smoke. I got me a couple of polecats in my sights. What do you want me to do with 'em?"

"Bring 'em up here."

Puma pointed up the hill with his scattergun. "Git."

As the outlaws struggled uphill, the mountain man, more than twice their age, walked nimbly up the slope with never a misstep, nor was he breathing hard when they reached the top.

Smoke stood there, hands on hips, shaking his head at Puma. "It's easier to tree a grizzly than to keep you ornery oldtimers out of a good fight."

Puma nodded. "Yeah, I'd rather bed down with a skunk than miss a good fracas." He cut his eyes over at Smoke. "You want me to dust 'em now, or just stake 'em out over an anthill?"

Sundance's eyes widened. "You wouldn't do that . . . would you, you son of a bitch?"

Smoke pursed his lips, rubbing his chin. "Well, I'm feelin' real generous tonight. How about you boys picking your own way to die? Guns, knives, fists, or boots, it makes no difference to me."

Lightning Jack grinned, flexing his muscles while clenching his fists. "You man enough to take me on hand to hand?" He inclined his head toward Puma. "Winner goes free?"

Smoke removed belt and holsters and took a pair of padded black gloves out of his pants and began to pull them on. "Puma, if this loudmouth beats me, take his left ear as a souvenir and let him go."

Puma grunted and spat on the ground. "How 'bout I take his top-knot instead?"

"Wait a minute . . ." began Lightning Jack, until Puma jacked back the hammers on his shotgun, shutting his mouth for the moment.

Smoke stepped into the middle of a level area at the top of the plateau. He bowed slightly and said, "Let's dance!"

Lightning Jack worked his shoulders, loosening up. "Any rules?"

Smoke grinned, but his eyes held no warmth. "Yeah, the man left alive at the end is the winner."

"Just the way I like it. Say good-bye to your friend, mountain man."

The two men circled slowly, bobbing and weaving and throwing an occasional feint to test their opponent's reflexes. Lightning Jack suddenly rushed at Smoke, swinging roundhouse blows with both arms. Smoke ducked his chin into his chest, hunched his shoulders, and took two heavy blows on his arms. He grunted with pain, and thought, this man can hit like a mule! As Jack drew back to swing again, Smoke unloaded two short, sharp left jabs, both landing on Jack's nose, flattening it, snapping his head back hard enough so that Puma could hear his neck crack.

Jack shook his head, flinging blood and snot in the air, a dazed look on his face. Smoke stood, spread-eagled, his fists in front of him, waiting patiently.

After a pause Jack sleeved blood off his lip and felt his flattened nose. He glared at Smoke, hate in his eyes. Growling like an animal, he advance toward the mountain man, pumping his arms while swinging his fists.

Smoke stepped lightly to one side and swung a left cross against Jack's chin, stopping him in his tracks. Smoke followed with a straight right to the middle of his chest, knocking him backward, rocking him back on his heels. Another left jab to the forehead to straighten him up, and then a mighty uppercut to his solar plexus, just under his sternum, lifted him up on his toes before he fell to one knee. Jack remained there a few moments, catching his breath.

He looked up at Smoke, blood pouring from his ruined nose. He grinned wickedly, then snatched a slender knife from his boot and rushed at Smoke with the blade extended.

Smoke took the blade in the outer part of his left shoulder, bent to his right, and swung with all his might. His fist hit Jack in the throat, crushing his larynx with a sharp crunching sound. The knife slipped from Jack's numb fingers and he fell to his knees, grabbing his neck with both hands. A loud whistling wheeze came from his mouth as he tried to pull air in through his broken trachea, and his eyes widened, bugging out like a frightened frog. His skin turned dusky blue, then black as he ran out of air. His eyes glazed over and he died, falling on his face in the dirt.

Smoke took the knife handle in his right hand, closed his eyes and set his jaw, and yanked it free with a jerk. He staggered at the pain, then straightened, a steely glint in his eyes as blood seeped from the wound to stain his shirt.

Puma started toward him, but Smoke waved him away. "Not

yet, Puma. We got one more snake to stomp 'fore we're through.''

Sundance stuttered, "But, I'm not much good with my fists. I ain't no prize fighter.''

"You fancy yourself a gunfighter?''

"Yeah, and I'm a hell of a lot better'n I was last time you bushwhacked me, Jensen. I been practicing for years.''

Smoke, his left arm hanging limp at his side, bent down and picked up his belt and holsters. "Buckle this on for me, would you Puma?''

Puma placed the guns around Smoke's waist and snapped the buckle shut, then tied the righthand holster down low on his thigh. Smoke slipped the hammer thongs off both guns using his right hand, stepping over to the center of the plateau. "Give the low-life his pistol, Puma, then watch your back. Sundance is famous for shooting people from the north when they're facing south.''

Sundance put his hand on the handle of his Colt. "You're gonna die for that, Jensen.''

The two men squared off, thirty yards apart, hands hanging loose, fingers flexing in anticipation. "You called this play, Sundance. Now it's time for you to pay the band. Fill your damn hand!''

Sundance snarled and grabbed for his pistol, crouching and turning slightly sideways to give Smoke less of a target. Smoke waited a second, giving the gunfighter time to get his gun halfway out of his holster. In a move that was so fast Puma blinked and missed it, Smoke cleared leather and fired. His bullet took Sundance in the right wrist, snapping it, flinging his Colt into the dirt.

Sundance howled, cradling his right hand with his left, hunched over, tears running down his cheeks. "Okay, you bastard. You win,'' he sobbed.

Smoke shook his head. "No, I don't think so. You've got another gun and another hand. Use 'em.''

Sundance looked up in astonishment. "My left hand against your right? That ain't fair!''

Smoke shook his head, twirled his righthand Colt once, and

then he settled it in his holster. "I'll cross-draw my left gun, if that's more to your liking."

Sundance's lips curled in a tight smile. The cross-draw wasn't a speed draw. No one could beat him with a cross-draw, even lefthanded, he thought. "Okay. It's your call, Jensen."

He stood up, threw his shoulders back, and went for his iron.

Smoke's right hand flashed across his belly, drawing and firing again before Sundance could fist his weapon. This time, Smoke's slug took the outlaw in his left shoulder, shattering it while spinning him around to land face-down on the ground.

Smoke looked at Puma. "Bring me a rope from that bag over yonder."

He took the rope from Puma, formed a large loop, and passed it over Sundance's arms to tie it around his chest. He dragged the sobbing, sniffling gunman across the plateau to the edge of the cliff on the east side of the clearing.

"Help me lower him down onto that ledge down there, Puma."

"What . . . what are you doing? No . . . no . . . please . . ."

The two mountain men lowered the crying outlaw twenty feet down the side of the sheer cliff, letting him down gently on a three-foot ledge that stuck out over a drop of two hundred feet.

Smoke leaned over the edge and called down, "I'm gonna do something for you that you never did for your victims, Sundance. I'm gonna give you a choice about the way you want to die. You can lay there on that ledge and slowly starve to death, or you can jump and fall two hundred feet so you'll die quickly. It's all up to you."

"Wait, you can't do this to me. It ain't right . . ."

Smoke and Puma slowly walked away, ignoring cries from the coward below. Neither one much cared how he chose to die, just so long as he died, and that was a certainty.

William W. Johnstone
The *Mountain Man* Series